HE'S GOING DOWN

KELLY SISKIND

ORIGINALLY PUBLISHED AS LEGS 2017

This book is a work of fiction. Names, characters, places, and incidents are the product of the author's imagination or are used fictitiously. Any resemblance to actual events, locales, or persons, living or dead, is coincidental.

First edition: published under the title Legs September 2017

Second edition: CD Books November 2019

The author is not responsible for websites (or their content) that are not owned by the author.

ISBN 978-1-988937-01-4 (ebook edition)

ISBN 978-1-988937-08-3 (print on demand edition)

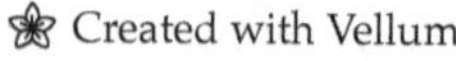 Created with Vellum

PRAISE FOR KELLY SISKIND'S ONE WILD WISH SERIES

"Addictive and refreshing." ~ Rebecca Yarros, #1 *New York Times* bestselling author on He's Going Down

"I devoured this book." ~ *USA Today* bestselling author Brighton Walsh on He's Going Down

"It was impossible not to lose my heart (and occasionally my breath) from this sexy, smart, wholly consuming story." ~ Bookgasms Book Blog on He's Going Down

"Siskind knows how to write characters that have off-the-charts chemistry." ~ RT Book Reviews on Off-Limits Crush

"Funny, charming, and hot as hell." ~ author Beth Anne Miller on Off-Limits Crush

"Sexy, funny, and at times heart-wrenching. I loved every moment!" ~ author Rachel Lacey

"An emotional rollercoaster, with sexy highs and what-will-happen-next lows. The perfect mix of romance, friendship, self-discovery and mystery." ~ *USA Today* bestselling author Stefanie London on 36 Hour Date

ALSO BY KELLY SISKIND

One Wild Wish Series:

He's Going Down

Off-Limits Crush

36 Hour Date

Over the Top Series:

The Snowflake Effect

One Degree of Perfect

Slammed into Focus

Showmen Series:

New Orleans Rush

Don't Go Stealing My Heart

The Beat Match

The Knockout Rule

The Bower Boys series:

Fall in love with the Bower brothers! A decade after being forced into Witness Protection, they're finally allowed to return home and fight for the women they lost.

Visit Kelly's website and join her newsletter for great giveaways and never miss an update!

www.kellysiskind.com

CHAPTER 1

RACHEL

DRINKING wine was my form of Russian roulette. My first glass usually led to smiles and silly ramblings as I joked with friends. Glass two had the potential to set off laughing fits, the kind that produced tears and sore abs as onlookers gawked. Glass three could lead to dancing in public. *Not* a pretty sight. But glass four was the real risk.

Glass four often transformed me into Reckless Rachel.

Tonight I was on glass three, but my usual giddiness was absent. Ainsley, Gwen, and I sat perched around our high-top table, music swelling through the club. Vesper's usual business-casual crowd mingled in clusters, all lit by large hanging globes. The type of light that turned a two into a ten after a few drinks.

"I need those shoes." Ainsley zeroed in on a brunette's mile-high pink heels. The stilettos wouldn't mesh with my wash-and-wear wardrobe, but Ainsley's closet could double as a Fashion Week boutique, complete with indexed shoe collection. The tagline on her Personal Shopper card read *Style Whisperer*.

"If you tackle her," I said, trying to get into our people watching, "you're on your own."

Ainsley sighed longingly, her blue eyes locked on the coveted heels. "Some friend you are."

"I can take her down for you." Gwen flexed her defined biceps. My non-existent muscles had major arm envy. "But you'll owe me, and I take payment in jeans."

Gwen's CrossFit ninja moves could get the job done, but the stilettoed woman nuzzled into a man's side. He was blond. Handsome. And too built for Gwen to tackle.

Cute men abounded tonight, but the few who caught my eye were already chatting women up—men in button-down shirts with sleeves rolled to their elbows, dress pants tailored to slim hips, hair trimmed short enough to accentuate a strong jaw. The type who'd sail on the weekends and probably loved to play golf and drink good wine, and who had successful careers.

Unlike yours truly.

"Enough with that face, Rachel." Gwen licked the salt from her margarita rim and took a sip.

I loosened my jaw. "What's wrong with my face?"

"It's depressing." Ainsley's husky voice battled with the hipster R&B tunes. "This is our night, and that sad puppy-dog look is far from festive. You're not allowed to be sad on April twelfth."

She was right, of course. April twelfth meant wine and loud music and jokes with Ainsley and Gwen. If I'd ditched them as contemplated, they would have kidnapped me, rolled me in honey and feathers, and left me in the San Francisco Zoo with a sign reading *Yellow-bellied Traitor*. The least I could do was force a smile.

"We should buy her another drink," Gwen said. Ainsley nodded vigorously.

Both my friends bobbed to the music, but all I could muster was a foot twitch. "Four drinks are dangerous for me."

"Dangerously *awesome*." Gwen had a doctorate in peer pressure.

Last time she coaxed me into a fourth glass of wine, Reckless

Rachel was unleashed. The video of me shouting "I have a penis" while waving a dildo *in public* would haunt me forever. But she could be onto something. Tonight was my birthday. *Our* birthdays. Not only were we celebrating another trip around the sun, but it was the sixth anniversary of the night we all met.

That memorable evening, I'd been dancing—nowhere near the dance floor—eyes closed, my arms doing some sort of Vogue-on-acid thing. Someone had toasted me, hollering, "Happy birthday!" at the top of his lungs, then Gwen was in my face with a smile that screamed trouble, shouting, "It's my birthday, too!" Before we knew it, Ainsley was hugging us both, her "Mine, too!" slurred for all to hear. We woke up, officially twenty-one, all three of us in Gwen's apartment with mussed hair, foul breath, booze leaching from our pores, permanent friendships forged over a greasy breakfast.

I needed to revisit that happy.

The funky bass thumped in my chest. "I'll take that drink, but I still have half a glass to finish." Since my giggly self had yet to appear, I prayed Reckless Rachel was on hiatus, too.

Ainsley finished her appletini. "You have to catch up with us anyway. I'll get the next round, and maybe find someone to buy it for me."

Considering she had more curves than Kate Upton, that shouldn't be a challenge.

Ainsley hopped off her stool and nodded at my drink. "Another Pinot Grigio?"

I swirled my glass. "No. Pinot Noir. Only if it's from Sonoma. If not, I'll go with Cabernet Sauvignon, but nothing from Argentina. Preferably from Western Australia. Margaret River, maybe? But whatever."

"But whatever?" She batted her thick eyelashes. "I'll buy you something red."

If I were at home, I'd choose a bottle from my wine fridge, not a loser in the bunch. Wine reviews were read and compared and entered into my spreadsheet before I gave up valuable real estate for a new bottle, all mine, all beautiful, all wondering which would get to breathe next.

Instead I'd be drinking something *red*.

She pushed up her boobs, her white minidress displaying ample cleavage, and sashayed toward the bar.

Gwen scooted closer. "Since I haven't heard about any blind dates involving men with more hair in their ears than on their heads, I'm guessing your dating pool dried up?"

"For now," I said. "Next time a family member sets me up, I'm planning to remove my contacts. Better to bang into walls than be faced with unruly ear hair."

Gwen massaged her shoulder, likely sore from some insane workout. "I'm taking a dating sabbatical myself."

"To focus on work?"

"Because I'm an asshole magnet."

After talk of ear hairs, my mind conjured furry assholes bumping down the street pursuing Gwen. I stifled my laugh. "Wouldn't it be easier if we dug chicks?"

"Tell me about it." She tilted her head, scrunching her nose in concentration. The look she assumed when dissecting my crappy dates and job woes. Gwen the problem solver. "But I don't know. I could totally make out with you and maybe get in on some boob action, but all the business downtown"—she motioned to my crossed legs—"freaks me out."

I cackled, an unattractive sound that had me second guessing another drink. "I'm bad enough with men. If a woman were between my legs, I'd freeze up."

"Define bad enough."

Water circled the base of my glass. I dipped my finger in it and spelled the word *frigid*. "I just get so in my head, stressing about...I don't know what. I can't come from oral."

Her mouth dropped open. "Like ever?"

I mentally catalogued my oral history: Daniel Bend's tongue spelling out the alphabet *nowhere near my clit*. Allen Goldstein motorboating his stubbled face so roughly I got a rash. My last boyfriend, Maxwell Bush-Wetter (his name was a total sham), who mistook my lady parts for an ice cream cone. "From sex, yes. Just not, you know."

"*You know*? Is that your code for eating pussy?"

I ducked, and she shook her head.

"You need to get over yourself. The first step to owning your sexuality is by using words like pussy. Your mother can't hear you. Her head will not explode."

As if on cue, my cell phone rang. Without looking at it, I knew it was *her*. Even my mother's ring had a tone. Urgent. Unrelenting. *Shrill*. Unable to handle a longwinded conversation about a distant relative diagnosed with The Cancer or The Gout, I dug through my purse to silence it, barely able to find the thing among her throng of paranoid gifts.

Bear bell: One never knew when a grizzly would charge down Market Street.

Swiss Army Knife: The need to drink wine or, say, *skin a deer*, easily solved.

Cortisone cream: Her cure-all.

I found my phone and hit mute. It wasn't like we hadn't spoken twice that morning, and she'd no doubt bring up my crappy job again, something I needed to suppress for a few hours. I sipped my wine, glad the call had at least cut Gwen and my conversation short.

Unfortunately, the next thing Gwen said was, "How did I not know about your oral issue?"

She was nothing if not persistent. Although us girls gossiped endlessly, the nitty gritty of my sex life wasn't usually up for discussion. "It never came up?"

"Our definition of friendship differs, and we need to fix this handicap of yours."

An unlikely fix. But my gaze slid back to that blond man and the woman pressed against him, to her hand resting on his very fine backside. It had been too long since I'd seen a man naked. Too long since my hands had roamed freely over a man's physique. I'd given up on the elusive oral "O," but I was all in for the rest—the slide of skin against skin, the belly swoop at the first kiss. Hopefully the next guy who took me out would be cute and fun enough to get us to second base.

That thought had me grinning.

The music pumped louder, a decibel higher than deafening, like someone hit the wrong switch. Ainsley returned with our drinks and placed my glass of *red* next to my half-full glass of Pinot Grigio. Guess I'd be double-fisting it.

"What are you two smiling about?" Ainsley may have shouted, but we still squinted, as though that would allow us to hear her better.

Unsure what was wrong with the sound system, I yelled back, "Getting head!"

Reckless Rachel territory.

She leaned closer and shouted, "Sorry, what?"

I inhaled deeply and, remembering Gwen's sexuality comment, I screamed as loudly as possible, "Eating pussy!"

But the music had shut off. Abruptly. At once.

All nearby heads cranked my way.

Gwen tipped over, grabbing her belly as she nearly laughed out a lung. Ainsley followed suit. My cheeks and neck flamed, my freckles likely glowing.

The music returned just as quickly, most people picking their conversations back up, all except one man who did *not* belong in this swanky club filled with hair gel and primped women. With his threadbare jeans and a buckle that could double as a boxing championship belt, he'd have been more at home in a back-country bar. Add his boots, that looked like they'd marched to China and back, the shaggy black hair, five-day scruff, and the ink peeking out of his cuffed sleeves, and he was maybe more biker than backcountry.

The girls were chatting again, and I tried to listen, catching the odd word from Gwen about her job at the adoption agency or Ainsley gushing about some new purse, but my attention kept drifting back to that man. That dude. That *bad boy*.

His gaze didn't shift from mine. Not cocky, exactly, but confident. One elbow on the bar, he leaned on it as though he owned the place. My attention shouldn't have been snagged on him, but he was gorgeous, smoldering the way he was, intensity in the sharp lines of his face.

"That guy is staring at you like you're dinner."

I swung my attention back to Ainsley. "Because Gwen told me to own my sexuality, and everyone and their mother heard me scream *eating pussy*." Words I apparently couldn't keep contained.

"I wish we had that on video," Gwen said. "I'd play it at your wedding. And anniversaries. And funeral."

I flicked her arm. "Glad to know who my friends are."

She rubbed her bicep. "Whatever. You'd do the same."

"Probably."

"Seriously," Ainsley said, still focused on Bad Boy. "That guy hasn't even blinked, and he's crazy hot. He has that whole lone wolf thing going on."

Gwen propped her chin on her hand. "He could be on *Sons of Anarchy*. I bet he knows how to *ride*. A Harley," she added with a wink.

Jesus. Like I needed to add that visual to all the rough and tumble he had going on. But I did. With relish. It had been ten long months since I'd had sex, and any sex I'd experienced had always been nice. *Fine*. The word that encapsulated my life. I'd never experienced the type of sex I read about in romance novels, with the arched back and lust-filled moans and dirty words whispered against sweaty skin. I'd bet my Chateau Montelena Chardonnay that Bad Boy knew how to make a good girl like me fall to her knees and fall apart around him.

I sipped my Pinot Grigio. Gulped may have been more like it, my buzz *buzz-buzz-buzzing* through my veins.

That's when Bad Boy kicked off the bar, all that grit and swagger aimed right for me.

"Oh my God." This from Ainsley.

"Holy shit." Gwen's acute observation.

What the hell? Embarrassment still burned my neck, but something hotter burned lower.

Bad Boy neared our table, his cheekbones and strong nose a study in male magnetism. A beer bottle swung from his hand, a few rings on his fingers glinting, the thick leather cuff around his wrist impossibly manly. His eyes were zeroed in on me. Because I'd screamed *pussy* in a crowded room.

The girls gawked as he stopped at my side. He placed a presumptuous hand on my back, on the area left bare by my top's dipping fabric. "I'd like to buy you a drink."

There was no question in his tone. No "can I?" or "would you mind?" Not that I could focus on much with his hand gliding over my skin, the tips of his fingers curling around the back of my ribs. This man definitely knew how to *ride*.

And I promptly said, "No."

"Pretty sure your eyes said yes. They practically called me over here."

Hello, overconfident. "You should pay attention to my mouth, then."

"That I am."

Excuse me? Never had a man been so forward, so unapologetic in his advances. My fingers floated to my neck, my skin burning hot. "The answer is still no."

He didn't remove his hand, just studied me, his lips so full and tempting. So close to mine. A chain dipped below the top button of his shirt, the worn material shifting over what looked like a hard body. I gulped more wine, the dregs of glass three disappearing fast.

Gwen kicked my ankle. "What she meant to say was 'My place or yours?'"

"I said what I meant." I returned her kick and tried not to

stare at the dark curls tumbling over Bad Boy's forehead, the glistening of his plump bottom lip as he swiped his tongue over it. I was in skinny jeans, my halter top conservative except for the dip at the back, but under his scrutiny I felt naked—and it felt dangerously good.

He removed his hand from my back, nonchalance in the tilt of his head. "That's a shame."

With that, he turned, disappearing into the crowd, taking my rush of heat with him. I attempted to dampen the quickening of my heart, my back and ribs still tingling from his touch.

Gwen glowered at me. "What is wrong with you?"

"With *me*?"

"That"—she gestured in the direction Bad Boy had disappeared—"was bound to be a Hall of Fame Fuck, and you turned him down."

Ainsley followed with a dreamy sigh. "I'd let him tie me up with that belt of his."

"Come on," I said. "You both know I'm not cut out for one-night stands. Forget the fact that I'm too much of a prude to enjoy that type of thing, the only reason he came over was because I shouted *eating pussy*. He's probably a freak."

"A wild and kinky freak." Gwen craned her neck, searching for him. "Too bad I'm on an asshole break."

Gwen's strapless top flaunted her physique, kept toned through CrossFit, free-climbing, and surfing—anything to feel an adrenaline rush. Dangerous men also spiked her heartrate, the type who made false promises only to ditch a girl when it mattered. I knew the sort all too well.

Gabe had left his mark on me.

"What's done is done," I said, swirling my wineglass. "We're out to celebrate our birthdays, and it's almost midnight. We should make a wish. A big one this year. Something important. Something life changing."

Something to shove my train onto a different track.

We shared glances. Ainsley twirled a lock of her golden hair around her finger, Gwen tapped her thumb, and I spun my wineglass in endless circles. My biggest stress in life since college, and every wasted diploma following, had been work. My job. My lack of purpose. Each day, before I left my apartment, I'd read the quote framed in my hall:

"Aim for the moon. If you miss, you may hit a star." ~ W. Clement Stone

Problem was, I didn't know the shape of my moon. It certainly didn't look like my current loan officer gig, complete with cold calls and angry hang-ups. It didn't look like the life coaching job I *maybe* lost for telling a guy his toupée was on the endangered species list. My stint as a Reiki therapist had been short-lived, too. It lasted until one client suggested I do Reiki on his cock.

Instead of aiming for the moon, I'd been bouncing around the solar system, and I'd hit nothing but refuse.

That made my wish easy. A grand ambition to find a rewarding job and start over, *again*, but this time I'd do it right. I'd suffer through my current boss's thinly veiled sexual harassment as he searched for the meaning of life in the valley between my breasts. Once I found something exciting, then, and only then, would I hand in my pink slip. Year twenty-seven would be my Oscar bid. My Super Bowl win. I'd even settle for a Teen Choice Award for Best Lip Wax.

I shoved my watch in the girls' faces. "You have one minute until midnight. I've got my wish, but no sharing or it won't come true. Ready?"

Ainsley sat taller, fortitude in the press of her lips. "This will be our year. And I agree about making it a big one. Like a resolution-type wish. Something we can work toward."

Gwen picked at her nails. "We could even bet. Make each other do something horrible if we fail."

"I'm not doing some psycho CrossFit marathon, like dragging a tire behind me while scaling a building." Ainsley looked horrified.

Gwen snickered. "You're right. Betting *is* kinda dumb. I'll settle on a pinky swear."

Gwen's pinky swear was akin to a blood oath. Guess I wasn't the only one with a desperate wish on the line. "You mean business."

Her eyes clouded briefly. "I do. Which means we can't bail on our resolutions. We need to accomplish them by next year. We should even write them down, read them together at our twenty-eighth birthday."

We agreed, and Gwen fished a notepad and pen from her purse. She passed us each a torn-out sheet. When my turn came, I wrote my resolution in all caps, no mistaking my intended goal: *I WILL FIND A REWARDING JOB.* Giddy, I folded my paper and handed it to Gwen, who stored our aspirations in a zippered purse pocket.

Wearing matching looks of determination, we all linked our pinky fingers.

"On the count of three," Ainsley said, "we make our wish."

"No sharing," I reminded them. "And no peeking at what we wrote," I told Gwen.

We traded excited glances as Ainsley counted us down, landing on her final *three* with a flourish. I made my wish, the prospect of quitting and finding a fulfilling career spurring my heart nearly as fast as it had thrummed at Bad Boy's touch. *Nearly.*

Then we were plunged into darkness.

The lights went out. As did the music, *again.* Shouts and gasps sounded for two frantic seconds. Our pinkies clenched harder, anchoring us to one another in the darkness. Just as quickly, everything sparked back to life.

The lively crowd became more boisterous, but we'd fallen silent. The air seemed to vibrate. My shoulders shivered, the hairs on the back of my neck at attention. Nervous energy was mirrored on my friends' faces.

"Jesus." Ainsley shattered the tension. "That was horror-movie creepy, but it was worth the price of admission."

Gwen released our fingers and studied her hands. "They must be having some serious technical difficulties tonight."

"Right. Technical difficulties." But my erratic pulse didn't slow. Something was screwy with the electrical system, all right. Still, the lights shutting off just as we'd made our wishes had felt eerie. Magical even. A ridiculous notion. Magic was for children and movies and fantasy novels.

Shaking off the tingles dancing up my arms, I moved aside my empty wineglass—*glass three*—and reached for "the red."

Glass four disappeared quickly, too. We linked arms and traipsed outside on a happy high. I was on the talkative side of tipsy, Reckless Rachel hovering below the surface. We crossed the quiet street, the spring air cool enough to bring the bars and streetlights into focus. My promising future had me leaning my head back to gulp in the possibilities. Gwen waved down a cab, and I hummed to myself, practically floating.

This birthday felt different, our wishes holding more weight. I wouldn't treat it lightly. When the timing was right, I'd quit my job and follow my (yet to be determined) dreams, and my life would be more than fine. It would be *exciting* and *rewarding* and *fun*. It would be zestful! A zesterific life! Completely zestastic!

A drunk giggle tripped off my tongue, but the sound died on a heavy sigh. Bad Boy was across the street, leaving the bar, that swagger of his ever present. I watched him like I would a spider crawling near my leg—fear, intrigue, and fascination intermingling. He pushed into a blue door a few buildings down. The sign above the bar read *The Blue Door*.

The sight of him had me wishing I'd accepted his drink offer. A sketchy thought. I'd been tempted by a rebel once, an experience I'd rather not repeat. I stared at that door anyway, desire curling through my blood stream. If my wish suddenly *was* a magical thing, I'd spin it on its head. I'd wish I could handle one wild night with Bad Boy. Not get shy. Not lock up when naked in front of a stranger, as though having sex for the first time. I'd let him ride me—no, *I'd* ride *him*—until the sun kissed the sky.

"We've made a decision."

I turned to Ainsley, unaware they'd been talking. "What?"

"We're getting in a cab," she said, her voice even raspier after yelling in Vesper, "and you're following your tongue into The Blue Door."

"No way." Was I that transparent? As lonely as I'd been, as many bad dates as I'd endured, I hadn't realized how unfulfilled my body was until I'd watched couples flirt in the bar, a guest at a show. Until Bad Boy had touched me.

"Yes way." Ainsley tucked my hair behind my ear. "Rachel, this is your birthday. *Our* birthday. You've been kind of down lately, and we think you need to let loose. Have fun. Not everything in your life has to fit into your spreadsheets. He's not the type of guy you date or take home to meet Mom. I know you want that, but sometimes you have to turn things upside down to find your feet."

"You did see how hot he was, right?" Gwen added. "Don't tell me you weren't picturing all the ink he had under that shirt. Go out and have fun." She hit me with her trouble grin—one corner of her mouth kicked up, her eyes narrowed yet twinkling. The grin she'd unleashed the night of the Dildo Incident.

Reckless Rachel stirred to life.

But who was she kidding? *Me* have fun with the guy who heard me scream pussy? The kinky freak? "What if he has body parts in his freezer?"

Gwen raised her phone. "I'm friends with the bartender at The Blue Door, and I've already texted him. Turns out he knows the Lone Wolf and says he's a decent guy, family owns a winery or something. But if he turns out to be a creeper, all you have to do is tell Cameron. He'll make sure you find a cab." Again with her trouble grin.

The same grin that now tugged at my lips.

Nothing about walking into a bar to stalk a stranger was smart, but I was amped up, my *fine* life and *fine* job itching at me until the urge to scream or dance or proposition a bad, *bad* boy had my blood thrumming. A cool breeze whispered across my back, echoing the sensation of Bad Boy's fingers, but nowhere near as sweet.

"Go," Ainsley said as she patted my ass.

"Hall of Fame Fuck," Gwen reminded me.

Heart in my throat, my string of painful dates and lonely nights coaxing me on (as well as four glasses of wine), I let Reckless Rachel out to play.

CHAPTER 2

JIMMY

I SHOULD NEVER HAVE WALKED into Vesper. I'm not sure what idiocy drove me there. Curiosity, maybe. Wondering if I'd feel like an outcast, or if the clinking of glasses and flashing of perfect teeth would prompt nostalgia. I didn't miss it, exactly, but the familiarity scraped at me. Two years ago, my styled hair and designer shirts would have fit in with the Rolex-wearing crowd. But that was an eternity and a different guy ago.

The Blue Door was more my speed—unpretentious people, guitar licks strumming from the speakers, hushed conversations at cramped tables, and, most important, a killer wine list.

I fell onto a stool at the empty bar and pushed my hand through my hair. I nodded to Cameron. "Any good Russian River Pinots?"

He spun around like usual, no hesitation in his reach. He pulled the Lynmar Pinot Noir down from his wall of bottles and held the label toward me. "Black raspberry on the nose, floral notes, smooth tannins."

He nailed all of that, even if he hadn't mentioned the hints of cardamom, but he should have known better than to offer me a 2011 Pinot. "Are you new?" I said, and he chuckled. "I'm not after anything from that mess of a drenched season. Try again."

Instead of telling me off, he smirked. A smirk that widened as he put me on hold to check his phone. His gaze jumped to the door, then back to me, his grin widening as he texted someone. "Something tells me I have just the thing for you tonight." He glanced over my shoulder again, and I frowned at the still-closed door.

"Hit me with it," I said, unsure what he kept staring at.

Cameron, with his inked sleeves, didn't look the part of the wine geek. Not that I did anymore, either. But I'd warmed that barstool enough to test his wine knowledge, and he rarely disappointed. He went right for the 2013 Foursight. That killer season had produced fruit-intense grapes, and Foursight was a boutique winery, everything made in small batches. My weakness.

At my nod, he grabbed a glass from the rack above his head. The deep ruby liquid swirled up the sides as he poured.

I stuck my nose in the crystal and inhaled scents of ripe berries and damp earth, hints of rhubarb teasing me. *Fucking sensual.* "Why didn't you start with this?"

My first sip was perfection.

"I like screwing with you. Most people pretend to know their wine. It's nice serving someone who isn't full of shit."

"I know a thing or two." Or a thousand and two. My blood practically pumped with the divine nectar, my ancestors having grown grapes when all of Greece revered the gods.

Two years ago, when my life imploded, I avoided anything and everything to do with wine. I tossed my collection and drank beer and hung out in dive bars, hair growing longer, tattoo collection building. Buying the Harley I'd had a hard-on for since twelfth grade eased the sting, but nothing erased my anger. Still, I couldn't stay away. Not from wine. Not from the lure of a Pinot as pure and ripe as the Foursight. Plus, staying away meant my family won, when they all deserved to be gloriously, ceremoniously fucked over.

Cameron grabbed a glass from the washer behind him and shined it from stem to rim, before hanging it on the overhead rack. The same end-of-night routine I did when closing up Rudy's Tavern.

His attention kept flitting to the door, but he said, "You should enter that sommelier contest. Odds are it'll be filled with wannabes and egos."

I swished a sip around my mouth and swallowed. "What contest?"

He dropped his cloth, grabbed a flyer farther down the bar, and slapped it on the wood next to me. "Sommelier of the Century. Some lame attempt for the Adriano brothers to dig themselves out of the hole they've sunk in. Their restaurants have been tanking, and they're trying to attract attention. Press."

"Sounds like bullshit."

"Maybe, but the opportunity is no joke. Head sommelier position is up for grabs, for all three restaurants, and it's open to anyone who's ever uncorked a bottle. With that kind of prize and no background needed, it'll be a circus. But entertaining."

Probably would be a laugh, but if Cameron knew my background, he'd never have suggested it. My résumé was a wet dream for most restauranteurs, no sommelier position out of my reach. My lats bunched as memories scratched under my skin, the thoughts more unpleasant than sipping a corked Merlot.

I stretched my neck, and my mind wandered to the club and that proper girl and her dirty mouth. A nice diversion for my acerbic thoughts.

She'd sat at her table, back straight, shoulders locked in perfect posture, hands folded on her lap. It had me wanting to unlace her fingers, dip my head down, and lick her until she pulled my mouth against her wet heat, her crossed legs trembling for hours. She was even better close up, a spray of freckles covering her sun-kissed skin.

So California. So innocent. A princess with a dirty mouth.

Who'd turned me down.

While Cameron continued with his nightly clean, I blinked the disappointment away and read the flyer on the bar. The Adriano brothers were San Francisco celebrities, but their restaurants had slipped from hot spots to backup plans. The contest was smart marketing, a way to shine a light on their venture while involving the city. What caught my eye, though, and halted my throat mid-sip of wine, was the bullet point at the bottom:

After two months of tasting sessions and elimination rounds, the best two contestants will work the restaurant on June 28th, serving top wine writers and reviewers to determine the winner.

Top wine writers. In one place. On one night.

An idea caught, a taste of justice a hell of a lot sweeter than the Pinot Noir finally traveling down my throat. A chance to right a wrong that should never have happened. It would mean being a finalist in that farce of a contest, but like Cameron said, the circus would attract more wannabes than wine devotees, and I could taste the best under the table. I'd just have to use a different last name.

As I sipped my wine, my tension less acute, a feminine voice said, "Is that drink still on offer?"

After the flyer and the potential it held, I grinned. The first true smile I'd unleashed in months. I slid my gaze to the dirty princess and took in her fidgety hands.

Her deep brown eyes flitted over the room, landing repeatedly on the door. Ready to escape? I was revved up, her reappearance in my field of vision too perfect to back off. I'd enjoyed women the past couple of years, would lose myself in their soft skin and heady moans, but the release was always short-lived.

With my mind still processing my plan, the night now felt more like a celebration than escape. Who better to toast with than the contradiction before me?

"Drink's on offer. Under one condition."

She hesitated, working her fingers over one another, still glancing at the exit. Then she clenched her hands, dropped her arms to her sides, and met my eyes. "What condition?"

I leaned toward her, so close I could see each freckle dotting the ridges of her lips. "I hear you say pussy again."

Her eyes snapped wide, her posture even straighter than before. "Sorry. I should go. This was a bad idea."

As she turned, I grabbed her elbow. "I'm joking." *Sort of.* "It was worth saying that to see the look on your face. Promise, I don't bite." Unless she asked me to.

At least the comment drew her attention to my mouth. I gestured toward Cameron. "We even have a chaperone. One drink. And I might need an explanation for your outburst earlier."

She shifted on her heels and swung her attention to Cameron. Something passed between them, as though they knew each other. When he nodded, a slight tilt of his head, she seemed to relax. "Okay. One drink."

The night was looking up. She settled onto the stool beside me, her spine still ramrod straight. She tucked her elbows to her sides.

"What's your poison?" I asked.

"Apparently dangerous men I don't know, but I'll have a glass of the Lynmar Pinot."

I could do dangerous. "If I'm your poison after two minutes, imagine how you'll feel in a few hours." That earned me a long swallow from her. "She'll have the Foursight," I added to Cameron. It was sweet how confident she was ordering that wine, but her lips would taste so much better after a sip from my glass.

She shot me a look, her freckles sharp against her reddening cheeks. "Pretty sure I can order for myself, and I'd like the Lynmar."

"You don't want the Lynmar. 2011 was a shit year. Trust me." No need to bore her about the early rains that season and the lack of fruit. Better to get her a glass and steer the conversation back to pussy. Hers, specifically.

"Actually I do want the Lynmar."

Cameron moved to grab the bottle, but I held up my hand. He halted.

To her, I said, "I've been sipping the Foursight since I got here. You telling me you don't want a taste?"

Her attention dropped to my lips again, and she grazed her teeth over hers. Fire sparked in her brown eyes. "I may want a taste of that wine. Later. For now I want the Lynmar."

"It's inferior."

"It's splendid."

"The season was crap."

"The season was hard, not crap."

"The Foursight is a sure thing," I said. She must have seen the heat in my gaze.

"I like the underdog," she countered, a sultry note to her voice. "Finding a diamond in the rough. The vines that survived 2011 were stronger, and a few vintages shone. Like the Lynmar. Hints of spice. Creamy mouthfeel." A quiet hum passed her lips.

Okay. The girl knew her wine, and my attraction to her spiked. With the haunts I'd been frequenting, and my bartending gig at Rudy's Tavern, I hadn't been around a woman like her in ages. No visible ink, her outfit more conservative than racy. Her straight brown hair would look sexy as hell tangled in my fist. "You sure you don't want to skip to the mouthfeel part?"

She smiled freely, the first hint of her letting loose. "I'm still not sure how bitter the aftertaste will be."

My answering grin was just as carefree. "I know how to make it sweet, Sunshine."

She barely reacted, but her nostrils flared. "Then get me a glass of the Lynmar."

"You'll regret it."

"I'm already regretting walking in here."

I chuckled, unsure the last time flirting had been this much fun. "How about a bet?"

"I don't bet with strangers."

"But you have drinks with them?"

She paused. "What sort of bet?"

Between her rejection at Vesper and her stiff posture now, sitting beside me was probably pushing her beyond her limits. Limits I wanted to test. The women I'd messed around with weren't tough to reel in. We were always after the same thing: a fun night between the sheets. The girl at my side was tipsy, but not so drunk she didn't know what she was after. Something told me if I could unlace her, it would be lightyears beyond fun.

"You do a blind tasting of the Foursight and the Lynmar," I said. "If you *can't* tell them apart, then I buy you a glass of my choosing, and I get to taste it on your lips. At my place."

"That escalated fast." So did her breathing.

"Did you want this to go slow?"

Instead of turning me down, she said, "If I win…if I guess each wine, what do I get?"

"You tell me."

"A winery?"

I barked out a laugh, but there was nothing funny about her joke. Two years ago, I'd have been able to ante up. "Might be out of my budget. Anything else?"

She looked at me through lowered lashes. "My place."

Now we were getting somewhere.

I leaned in nice and slow, her ragged breaths shallowing as I neared her ear. "Sounds like we have a deal."

At my instruction, Cameron poured two glasses out of sight while we sat in silence, but my mystery date's eyes spoke volumes. Her attention lingered on my forearms, traveling over the ink. When I curved my arm around the back of her chair, her gaze swept to my chest, to the chain dipping below my shirt. Its weight felt heavier than usual, or maybe it was her rapt attention.

She hooked her crossed legs tighter, and all I wanted was to slip my hand between her thighs, over the thick denim, and feel the heat radiating from her.

Instead I toyed with the ends of her straight hair. I rolled them between my fingers. She nearly purred, and lust pooled in my groin. What would she sound like on the edge of her orgasm?

When Cameron set down the glasses, she straightened and tried to shake my hand from her hair. I didn't budge, and she didn't push. She swirled the glasses, raising each to her nose in turn. A straight nose with a slight slope in the center, those same freckles dotting the ridge. Each inhale sent her upper back into my palm, and when she tipped the first glass for a sip, I slipped my fingers below her hair and cupped her neck.

The wine never met her lips.

"That's cheating," she said, a quiver tumbling over her shoulders.

I dragged my thumb down the side of her neck, along the delicate vein that pulsed below the surface. "My hand is nowhere near the wine or your mouth. How exactly am I cheating?"

"You play dirty."

"If this night goes according to plan, you'll find out just how dirty."

Her wineglass shook, but she didn't shrug me off. Without further delay, she sipped both wines, swishing the liquid around her mouth. She closed her eyes as she swallowed. My hand stayed on her neck, and I had to restrain myself from pressing my lips to the dip at her collarbone, to feel the speed of her pulse.

She tapped her left glass. "The Lynmar. Cherry cola and cranberry on the front end with a hint of smoke and fig on the finish. Silky texture." She ran a slender finger over the stem of the right glass. "The Foursight is also stunning, but any wine-maker worth their salt can make something beautiful out of the

2013 harvest. The Lynmar proves skill and perseverance bring success."

Passion bled through her words, as though she were talking about more than vintages, and her conviction stirred something in my chest. It had been a lifetime since I'd really talked wine with someone, shared my passion. Although I couldn't stay away from viticulture, I didn't twist the knife in my gut by attending tastings or trading notes with enthusiasts. The back-and-forth I shared with Cameron was as close to discussions as I'd get.

"It's a valid point, but there's no arguing with excellence. 2013 bred excellence. Being the best of a shitty year doesn't make for the kind of wine that brings your taste buds to their knees." I turned to Cameron. "Is she right?"

"She is. The lady knows her wine."

Like I needed to find her more attractive. "Looks like you win. Shall we get a cab?"

Her shoulders hitched back toward her ears, the pulse below my finger revving, and an adorable, nervous laugh bubbled out of her. She grabbed the flyer at my side and scanned it, a reminder I should tuck it in my pocket before leaving.

She toyed with the corner of the page. "Just so you know, I never do this sort of thing."

That had me frowning. She'd walked into the bar looking for me, or something I could offer her. A craving I felt in spades, but I'd only go there if she was all in. "I need an elaboration."

"The one-night-stand thing. I don't do them. I mean, I've had casual sex, but it's never happened on the first date. Or the second. Not that this is a date. Obviously. But the only reason I'm here is because my friends peer pressured me, and there was a fourth glass of wine, and Cameron messaged one of them that you don't have children locked in your basement."

Mental note to thank Cameron, and damn if her honesty wasn't refreshing as hell. Candor that had her pulling away, the promise of unravelling her inhibitions slipping through my fingers. I'm not sure why I walked into Vesper earlier. I'd avoided women like her the past two years, for good reason. But her innocence, potential dirty mouth, and how she savored her wine had me tied in knots.

"Are you attracted to me?" I asked.

She angled her knees my way, a blush creeping up her freckled chest. "Yes."

"That's half the battle. The other half is this." I placed my free hand on her knee, gentle pressure, the antithesis of the fire building under my skin. "I don't remember the last time I've wanted to rip a woman's clothing off her so badly. If you let me, I'll have you relaxed with one touch."

Her shoulders trembled. "Because you do this often?"

"The one-night thing?" She nodded, and I held her gaze. I didn't lie to women; I knew how devastating lies could be. She either got on board with the little I had to offer, or I'd let her walk away. "I've done this, yes. If I have an itch, I scratch it. But it's not a weekly occurrence. By the looks of things, I'd wager you're itchy as hell." One of my hands was still on her neck, the other on her knee, a connection I hated to relinquish. I dragged my thumb under the edge of her jaw. "Bet I could ease the burn for you."

Her eyelids fluttered, her long lashes almost blond toward their tips. "How about a rule?"

"I'm game."

"No names. No strings. One night, and that's it. If I know I'll never see you again, I might be able to relax and enjoy myself. And even though I won your little game, I'd prefer your place. More wine will help, too."

I'd normally have talked and joked less with a woman before taking her home, but I would have learned her name. Basic conversation. No fun bets and intriguing wine discussions.

I could live without names, though, and no strings was the only way I rolled. "Done. I still need to know why you shouted 'eating pussy' at Vesper."

She shook her head at the ceiling. "My friend and I were bitching about guys and how much easier it would be if we were lesbians. Then we started talking about the logistics of it, but the music was loud and we were shouting when it shut off, hence the incident."

Again she had me wanting to know more, ask more. "What was the result of this conversation? Are you curious? Interested in experimenting with women?"

"You sure are nosy for a one-night stand."

"It's not every day a woman shouts 'pussy' in a club."

"Alcohol and I have a love-hate relationship." She paused, attention fixed on her fingers until she smirked. "I said that if I were with a woman, I'd probably freeze up."

"Because?" I was taunting her, testing how far I could push her boundaries.

She sipped her wine, her nose lingering in the glass. The rim was barely out of her lips when she said, "Change of topic, please."

Those boundaries wouldn't bend easily, but I enjoyed a challenge. I leaned in close and dragged my nose along her cheek, breathing deep along the way. She smelled like the ocean—mint and jasmine mingling with her arousal. "Whatever you want, Sunshine."

CHAPTER 3

RACHEL

I ATTEMPTED to peel my eyes open, but my lids were dry and gritty. The movement sent bursts of pain through my body. Everything ached—my head, my back, my calves all throbbed in unison. Maybe I'd been hit by a Mack Truck, or bulldozed by a derailing train. Possibly dropped from an airplane to test if girls dumb enough to follow strange men into bars could withstand the plummet to Earth.

The light streaming through the window made me wince, another sharp stab slicing through my temples. I fought the urge to melt back into the mattress and blinked. Or tried, at least. My eyelids were glued to my contacts.

A few thousand blinks later, I rolled my tongue around my gums. My mouth was thick and stale, like I'd eaten one of Ainsley's vegan desserts.

As I took in my surroundings—the unfamiliar ceiling, the too-soft mattress, the closet with more clothing on the floor than on the hangers, *the large body beside me*—the dryness in my mouth amplified, sourness following. I clamped a hand over my lips to prevent the violent reaction churning in my gut from decorating the floor.

Some heavy swallowing and a few breaths through my nose later, the feeling subsided, but not the horror. I was as stark as naked got, and from the looks of the tattooed back beside me, so was my bedmate. Too embarrassed to glance Bad Boy's way, I assessed my aches and pains, and the tenderness between my thighs. Sex had definitely happened.

In this bed. With me. And that man.

Hopefully that man.

For all I knew, there could have been other players involved.

Lying as still as possible, I racked my brain, desperate to remember details of the evening. I squinted hard enough to increase my headache, but only snippets came back.

Me spilling wine? *Us* on the floor?

I was pretty sure laughing happened, too, but no images of his body hovering over mine resurfaced, or of him pushing into me, or me riding him, or us ripping off each other's clothes. I had no idea where his apartment even was.

At least the night of the Dildo Incident, I didn't black out. The recollection was hazy, but I remembered traipsing down the street with Ainsley and Gwen and dragging them into a sex shop. We cackled at the toys, and some sections of time were blurry, but the part with me running out the door, waving a massive dildo, screaming, "I have a penis," was kind of hard to forget.

For the life of me, I couldn't remember the details of my night with Bad Boy.

I didn't know his name. That part was clear, along with my one-night-stand rules that had led us here. So was sitting in the bar, him all know-it-all about his wines, pushing me to drink what he deemed acceptable. As was the masculine energy radiating off him as he'd promised to relax me with one touch. A touch lost in translation courtesy of Reckless Rachel.

How many drinks did we have? Did I have an orgasm afterward? Multiple?

God, I hoped we used condoms.

Gingerly, so as not to wake the guy who *may* have been a Hall of Fame Fuck, I slipped out from the covers and stood. I nearly fell back down. Pain. Lots of pain tightening around my scalp, and tenderness on my tailbone. More pain than my twenty-first birthday and the ten million tequila shots. My tongue felt swollen. I teetered, and the room swayed. When I remembered my naked body, I got over my nausea and hauled ass into the bathroom.

Where I promptly saw four condoms in the trash.

Four.

A rush of pride swelled at the sight. *I totally rocked Bad Boy's sex world.* But those condoms hadn't necessarily come from us. Not all, at least. He'd seemed honest in the bar, admitting he'd taken a number of women to bed. That bed. The bed I'd slept on. Naked. I shivered, suddenly itchy all over. Remembered games of catching cooties as a kid had me wrinkling my nose. *That* I could remember.

But not fucking Bad Boy *four times.*

I splashed water on my face, but it did little to dull my headache or sober me up. I was still drunk as a skunk. Where did that saying even come from? Was it because my breath stunk? Because I could clear a room with one word?

I grabbed Bad Boy's toothpaste and used my finger to scrub my tongue and teeth and gums, all the while eyeing his meager toiletries: razor (which clearly hadn't been used in a while), shaving cream (ditto), and a toothbrush. My sink with its plethora of moisturizers and eye creams had *girl* written all over it.

I sucked back as much water as possible and grabbed a towel from his hook. The blue cotton was clean and plush. It smelled like leather and clove and a hint of musk. I might never recall what went down between Bad Boy and me, but my regret over the situation ebbed. At least I'd done something fun. Something out of character.

Something to start my twenty-seventh year with a *bang*.

Unfortunately, my attraction to him brought with it painful memories, too. Of my time with Gabe, which led to my father's last words, forever saved on my phone.

I shook my head. This was just one night. One wild fling. Nothing more. Except an uncomfortable feeling welled up, and something hazy niggled at me. One of those blurry memories, linked to the birthday wish maybe—my resolution to find a fulfilling career—but the source of my dread remained obscured.

Clutching the towel around my chest, I shrugged off my worry and eased open the bathroom door. I tiptoed into the bedroom. My clothes were strewn over the hardwood floor, as though we'd been harried and frantic to remove them, and the sheets were a mess. God, I wished I remembered what had happened. My gaze cut to Bad Boy, one last peek before leaving and never seeing him again. This time I *looked*.

He'd shifted since I'd gotten up. The covers hovered around his knees, the ends of his black hair curled at the base of his neck. His back and ass were displayed for prime viewing, and *what a view*. Ink swept over the grooves and creases of his toned physique, some images reminiscent of the Greek art I'd studied during my *I'm going to be a curator!* phase. He was lean but fit, the boxing gloves hanging from his wooden dresser likely the source of his build. With one arm tucked below his pillow and the other thrown in front of his face, the ridges of his ribs and hips stood out, so delicious I barely refrained from crawling on the bed and running my fingers over every dip and curve.

My attention moved to his ass, and the red marks on his left butt cheek—four marks, long and thin, that could have come from my nails. Wow. My fingers tingled as though *they* remembered gripping that toned flesh to force him deeper. The tenderness between my thighs tingled, too, but the longer I stared, the more the lust gathering in my core curdled, and that dread returned. Heavier this time. Foreboding so thick my nausea resurfaced as a lost memory teased me.

His ass. Something happened with his ass. No. Not his ass. His *butt crack*? Jesus, what the hell had happened? The memory advanced and receded, out of my grasp. I blinked and refocused, no longer scoping his chiseled form. All I could see was his butt, knowing deep, deep down that something bad went down.

Something very bad.

Then it clicked, the rush so forceful all air left my lungs.

Not his ass. *My* ass. Oh, God. Still clutching the towel around my chest, I scooped up my clothes and purse and ran from his room, falling to my knees the second I was out. I dumped the contents of my purse on the floor, and snatched up my phone, all the while whispering, "God, no. *Nonononononono*. Please, *no*."

But there was no undoing what I'd done.

I pulled up my sent emails, and there it was, what might as well have been a neon billboard that said "You Are So Screwed." I'd emailed my sexual-harassing boss a photo of my butt crack with the subject line: Shove your crappy job where the sun don't shine.

Holy mother of God.

Stupid alcohol and that stupid resolution *to quit my job*. Even worse was that Bad Boy must have taken the photo, because *my* two hands, each holding up a middle finger on either side of my *butt crack* (seriously?), couldn't have snapped the selfie to end all selfies.

Unfreakingbelievable.

Never again would I drink a glass of wine. Not a drop. Never let Reckless Rachel out to play. Bad Boy should never have happened. I should never have made that wish.

What the hell am I going to do?

I stared ahead, not seeing a thing. Shock leached my energy. Hunching lower and lower, I spun the possibilities, anything to undo what I'd done. Set fire to our office building? Divert attention from my idiocy by instigating World War Three? Enter the Witness Protection Program?

It was Saturday, and my boss never worked on weekends. In fact, he'd mentioned having issues with his server, something about incoming messages disappearing…which meant he wouldn't have seen my ass yet. He might not see it at all. The room swayed, a slow undulation—the wine still swimming through my veins—but my spirits rose.

All was not lost, *yet*.

Still queasy, I lay on my back and shoved my feet into my jeans, wiggling to get them done up. Once dressed, I folded Bad Boy's towel and hung it over the end of his leather couch, taking in my surroundings for the first time. His bedroom may have been on the messy side, but the open kitchen/living room was simple and neat. But not homey. His white walls were harsh, not a photograph visible; only a couch, coffee table, and TV filled the space. There wasn't even a dinner table or chairs.

The starkness was *sad*.

I'd made it clear this was a no-strings affair, but it was odd leaving him in bed, sleeping, this lonely apartment all he'd wake up to. No thank you note. No kiss goodbye. After he'd snapped that shot of my ass, and whatever had transpired between us, I'd never be able to meet his eyes anyway. Better to forget this ever happened.

As soon as I made it to the street, I pulled out my phone and called Gwen. Ainsley often worked on weekends, shopping for her clients. Plus Gwen's "I know the bartender" was partly responsible for this fiasco.

Three rings later, she picked up. "Please tell me he was an epic lay."

"I would, if I could remember what happened."

"How much did you drink?"

"A buttload." Which was an actual measurement of wine. A butt or barrel of wine held precisely one hundred and twenty-six gallons. Apparently when one drank a *buttload* they sent shots of their *butt* into cyberspace.

I cringed.

"Did you go shopping for dildos again?"

I was in no mood for her teasing. "Hilarious, but no. It was a thousand times worse than the dildo." People jostled me as I scoped the street and realized I was only a few blocks from my place. Funny how I could live so close to a man as hot as Bad Boy and never have run into him. "I did a bad thing, and I'm on the verge of a nervous breakdown. I need you to talk me off the ledge."

I spilled my shame as I walked home, prompting Gwen to laugh for a solid three minutes. "That," she panted between breaths, "goes down as one of your more epic drunk sprees. I still don't understand how you could have forgotten the entire sexcapade, unless he wasn't good. Then it's for the best. But what a waste of a one-night stand."

"That's the least of my problems." It was like she hadn't even heard the part about my *butt crack* sent to *my boss*. At least focusing on that horror allowed me to ignore Bad Boy's participation in my fall from grace. Mortification to the nth degree.

I stopped in front of my apartment, the sidewalk bending under my still-inebriated gaze. "What if my boss gets the email? What will I do?"

"Move to Siberia."

I giggled, even though there was nothing amusing about this situation. The giggle grew, an uncontrollable laugh quaking my body, culminating in an unattractive snort. My world was about to come crashing down, and I had to squeeze my knees together to stop from piddling on the street.

"You really are still drunk, aren't you?" Gwen's amusement didn't help.

I *was* still drunk. And anxious, the latter responsible for my mad cackle—aka my nervous laugh that was a cross between a wheezing emphysema patient and a two-year-old giggling at a fart joke. Gwen and Ainsley loved to get me going, if only to witness The Cackle in action.

"Yes," I said, my laughter under control, my anxiety unfortunately not. "Definitely still drunk. And freaked out."

"Okay," she said, adopting her *I'm serious* voice, "I get that. But can we discuss this whole job thing a sec?"

"Maybe…" I pressed my back against my apartment's brick exterior. It was either that or slide to the sidewalk. I readied myself for a dose of Gwen Truth.

Gwen was an expert at reading people. She worked at an adoption agency and spent her days interviewing candidates, making sure babies landed in the right homes. She also called me on my bullshit. When I'd convinced myself becoming a tattoo artist was my calling—I'd always been able to draw, and no diploma was needed—she'd dragged me into a parlor, ranting that I couldn't tattoo others without knowing how it felt.

We no longer spoke of the incident.

She cleared her throat. "Fact is, you hate being a loan officer. You hate it more than when you had to perform reiki on the creep with the perma hard-on, and probably more than that Thai massage gig. I don't even know how you touched those hairy guys. Granted, going out with this epic sendoff isn't ideal, but it will force you to find something better. You need to make a change."

A change I'd wished for last night. Maybe this was another form of Russian roulette, with my job instead of drinking to unleash Reckless Rachel. My boss may get my email. He may not. If he did, I'd be forced to realize my wish, which was more like a New Year's resolution. It would compel me to face my future head on, ready or not. But having a paycheck while researching careers would be preferable.

The bruise on my tailbone pulsed. I winced as the throbbing along my temples renewed. "I planned on quitting eventually, just not flashing my boss in the process, and not without a plan. Every time I've been fired or I've quit, I haven't had anything lined up. I think that's why I've rushed into jobs. The pressure, maybe? The need to make rent forced me into bad situations."

"I know, love. I'm sorry you mooned your boss."

Words I never thought I'd hear.

I almost asked her about the power outage that had followed our wishes, if she'd felt a change in the air, too. It could have been the drinks or my desire to believe something bigger would help change my life, but I could have sworn a wisp of magic had danced up my arms. Better not to admit that out loud. Especially since that type of thinking was probably responsible for my drunken lapse in judgment.

Gwen suggested I inhale Advil and water before we hung up. An excellent idea. When this hangover wore off, I'd feel better. I'd play *job* roulette and hope for the best. If that butt shot disappeared in cyberspace, I'd put the incident behind me. I'd move on from this catastrophic night. Considering I had no memory of the sex-fest with Bad Boy, and I'd never see him again, forgetting it would be a cinch.

But my phone pinged when I opened my apartment door. A message from my boss greeted me: *I wouldn't use me as a reference.*

CHAPTER 4

RACHEL

MONDAY MORNING ARRIVED to the tune of UB40's "Red Red Wine," the soundtrack to my downfall. Ignoring the subliminal message trilling from my alarm, I spent the morning reorganizing. My wardrobe consisted of blocks of order—nine-piece ensembles that could carry me from day to night to day again with the switch of an accessory. After I arranged each outfit by season, I polished the glasses on my open shelves and set them in perfect lines. Then I made my bed, tucking my lilac sheets snug enough to please a sergeant.

My goal: If I kept my visible life in order, the underlying mess may go unnoticed.

With those tasks completed, I scrolled the internet for possible jobs: Professional butter sculptor? Dog behaviorist? Pornography historian? Maybe I'd start a national walk-a-thon, all proceeds donated to Unemployed Girls with Bad Judgment.

Every few minutes, I'd dirty-look my wine fridge. *Nope. Never drinking again.* But the bottles prompted me to search winemaking careers. The notion of selecting grapes, overseeing the crushing and fermentation process, of bringing joy to people through each glass, was tempting. Wine also reminded me of my father, nights uncorking bottles the most vivid memories I had. The more I learned about wine, the closer I felt to him. Sometimes I'd pour a glass of a delicious new discovery by his gravestone.

My throat burned, a familiar sadness engulfing me. He'd missed another birthday. Another year of family dinners and baseball games. Some things never got easier.

Including the prospect of returning to school.

Two to three years of full-time studies, followed by an apprenticeship, when most of my endeavors had lasted but a few months, didn't make sense. Piling school loans on top of my rent and bills wasn't feasible, either. Not when I was determined to support myself. Frustrated with my fruitless searching, I plunked my forehead on my desk.

My cell rang.

The sight of my mother's name dampened my mood further. If I answered her, I'd have to admit I'd gotten fired *again*. Or had I quit? I didn't even know the truth of it. But delaying the inevitable seemed like more headache than it was worth. And I'd ignored her call last night…

Steeling my nerves, I pressed Talk. "Hey, Ma."

"I might be late for lunch today. If you get to Andros first, get us a table outside."

Crap. *Lunch.* I squeezed my eyes shut. So overwrought, I'd forgotten my mother wanted to treat me to a belated birthday outing. "Not sure I can make it."

Or deal with her crazy.

"Nonsense. We planned this weeks ago. I'll see you later."

She hung up. I stared at nothing and cursed my life.

An hour later, I waited at Andros, dressed in my gray skirt, heels, and white blouse, as though I'd come from the job I no longer had. My mother breezed in, oblivious to my deception.

She slung her massive purse over the back of her chair with a sigh. Her blond hair was sprayed into a solid block, her painted-on eyebrows and pink lipstick likely to melt in the heat. "I wouldn't have been late, but the cleaning lady came today. Last time she made my bed, she put the pillows backward, so I had to show her *again* how I like it. I swear, I should just do it myself."

Lydia Kates majored in melodrama. "Why don't you?"

She raised *one* eyebrow, a skill I could never master. "You know how busy I am with the Healing Hearts luncheon. I'm not Superwoman. I've had to spend time with Alyssa, too. Things have been tough for her at home."

I could mention five to ten hours of volunteering a week shouldn't limit her from making beds and mopping the floor, but I'd pushed her to get involved. Helping raise money for the heart disease that took my father's life had been her first step to regaining hers, and she'd met women like Alyssa through the foundation. Other women who'd suffered loss. I'd never belittle the effort.

"And did I tell you," she went on, "that your aunt Sarah's sister-in-law, Dahlia, just got diagnosed with liver cancer? Not even fifty, and The Cancer? If life were fair, those reality stars with their skimpy clothes and sex videos would get The Cancer, not poor Dahlia."

I winced as others glanced our way, judgment in their pinched faces. My mother only had one volume—loud nasal—and on a scale from one to Mel Gibson, the woman's inappropriateness hovered at Charlie Sheen. "I wouldn't go wishing cancer on people, Ma."

"Anyway," she said, talking over me, "I've just been a wreck and need to drop off some soup this week, so I'll make extra. You're looking thin, Rachel. Have you been cooking? I bet you're eating nothing but takeout."

The waiter arrived in time to save me the agony of listening to her concerns—*your arms are too thin, your skin looks pale, are you sleeping all right*? She'd tutted around my brother and me growing up, but this anxiety, this worry someone would get sick or hurt or worse, had developed since we lost my dad. I always let her fuss. Unless she took a page from Ainsley and commented on my boring clothes. I'd take "plain Jane" any day over wearing my mother's fuchsia blazer, complete with shoulder pads and a brooch the size of my face.

Our waiter smiled, clueless to his approaching doom. "Ready to order?"

He proceeded to write a novel on his order pad, ensuring my mother got her dressing on the side, roasted red peppers instead of red onion, green olives instead of black, no salt or feta, and an addition of chicken—poached, not seared—in her salad.

I smiled and said, "The regular Greek is fine for me."

"Modifications are not a problem." He gave me a wink. "I aim to please."

Normally his blatant flirting would be cute. His strong nose and sharp cheekbones made him easy on the eyes, but attraction eluded me. I couldn't help thinking of the tattooed back and sexy behind I'd left naked in bed two mornings ago. My mind may have been a blank where that night was concerned, but it was as though my body had perfect recall, my pulse revving for another glimpse of him. I shook the unpleasant thought away and ordered a glass of Riesling.

My no drinking motto lasted a whole two days.

My mother took the moment to latch onto the other thing I'd have preferred to avoid like the plague. "Have you spoken with your boss about a raise? You've put in three months, and no one works harder than my girl. If he doesn't give you a raise soon, you'll have to demand one."

Time for the lies. "Three months isn't that long, Ma."

"Nonsense. Three months is long enough for him to know you're a star."

"I think you're biased."

"It's God's honest truth, Rachel. Any competent boss would see it."

"That's not how the business works."

"Of course it is. You just need to stand up for what you deserve. Prove you're not a wallflower."

Pretty sure I'd proven that with my butt shot. "Enough, Ma. I'm not demanding a raise." But her faith in me warmed my heart.

She lifted her chin, squinting in her all-seeing way, and that warmth seeped out. The woman knew something was up. The time I'd told her I was staying at Lexi Wallcott's, my eyelid had twitched so incessantly my mother followed me to the house party and dragged me out by my ear.

My lying skills were up there with my ability to moonwalk.

I unfolded my napkin and smoothed it on my lap. I rearranged my cutlery next, avoiding my mother's gaze. The flirty waiter brought me my wine, and I took a lengthy sip. I didn't stop to smell the bouquet or swirl my glass, didn't pick apart the nuances. But as the liquid slid down my throat, an image flashed, sharp and short: *Bad Boy's body against mine as he licked wine from my lips.* Heat spiked between my thighs, the sensation potent and lingering. I could almost taste him, almost feel his fingers digging into my hips.

"Did you get fired?"

I plunked my glass down so hard, liquid sprayed my face. My mother didn't miss a darn thing. I dabbed my nose with my napkin, planning my reply, but part of me wanted to savor that fleeting glimpse of my one-night stand. Flustered, I excused myself to the bathroom.

Where I washed my hands three times.

I could keep up my ruse, attempting to lie about my job, but there was no point. I'd played job roulette, and I lost. And maybe this was my destiny. Maybe my wish, the blackout, and Reckless Rachel had all happened for a reason. Inexplicable twists of fate occurred all the time. Just like my father's final voice message.

Our last physical conversation had been a fight over Gabe, an encounter I hated to relive. But Dad had left me a message afterward. The day he passed away, he called to apologize. To say he loved me, only wanted what was best for me. Two hours later, he fell on his treadmill, his heart too weak to keep him with us. He'd treated my brother to a surprise lunch that day, had sent my mother flowers. He'd almost said his goodbyes as though he knew his time was up.

Maybe my actions were subconscious, too. The blackout at the club could have been more than coincidence. It could have bewitched our wishes, a higher power guiding our lives. The embarrassing stunt that had led me here could have been a mortifying type of fate.

Fate that became clearer when my eyes locked on a poster.

The same flyer I'd seen at the bar with Bad Boy was taped to the wall—the sommelier contest to earn a position at three San Francisco restaurants. Vibrating with nerves and the urge to touch Bad Boy that night, I'd busied my hands by plucking at the corner of the page, reading and re-reading the advertisement. I read it again now, more intently.

Working in a restaurant wasn't ideal—my waitressing gigs in school had involved many forgotten orders and bad tips—but my current predicament shrunk my options. I had no job, no prospects, and being a sommelier wasn't like being a server. Talking wine with customers could be fun. Exciting even.

A seed of possibility planted itself behind my breastbone and grew. There was no going back from here. Only forward.

I also had a resolution to fill by next April.

I returned to my seat and clasped my hands on the table. "I wasn't fired," I told my mother. "I quit."

Which was in fact true.

Her hand shot to her heart. "You were doing so well. Finally working toward something. I'm sure if you explain it was a lapse in judgment, your boss will rehire you."

"Ma…"

"Tell him you haven't been well. Take a week off if needed."

"Ma…"

"Promise it won't happen again. A reasonable man will understand."

"*Ma*, I'm not groveling for my job. I quit because I hate being a loan officer."

More truth offered.

She sagged, her shoulder pads curving forward. "I'm sorry. I just hate seeing you so unsettled. I only want the best for you."

A heartfelt admission that echoed my father's last words.

I wrapped my hand around her clenched fist. Her wedding ring nestled between my fingers. "I appreciate your concern, but I quit because…I have something lined up. Something I'll actually enjoy." I sipped my Riesling, notes of honeysuckle and wet stone lingering on my tongue, the memory of Bad Boy lingering, too.

My mother tilted her head and studied me. "If you have a job lined up, why lie about it?"

"It's something new. I wanted to get settled before mentioning it." There was no point discussing the sommelier contest unless I won. Admitting I'd failed at something else would only add fuel to her overprotective fire, and the lie tangled with enough fact to be passable.

She nodded, appeased. "If this doesn't work out, I'm calling in a favor with Uncle Charlie. You're twenty-seven, Rachel. It's time to plant some roots. Mitchell works his tail off at his firm. It's not fun, but he knows what he needs to do to succeed. You'll have time for the fun stuff later."

I *may* have earned enough diplomas to start a forgery business, but my younger brother's law degree and stellar job poked holes in my confidence, his every leap forward a floodlight on my stalled career.

Thankfully our food arrived before she could go on about Mitchell's success or Uncle Charlie's funeral home. I'd been avoiding that particular connection for the whole of my adult life. Working around death, dressing lifeless bodies and watching people sob, was not happening. Still, the disappointment in my mother's eyes hit home. I'd worked hard to keep her spirits up since we'd lost Dad. The first two years had been hell for her. For me, too. But she'd been a shell of her former self. Five years later, her happiness remained priority one.

"Fine," I said, eager to appease her and switch topics. "If this new venture doesn't pan out, we'll talk to Uncle Charlie."

Since that wasn't an option, the sommelier gig had to work.

CHAPTER 5

JIMMY

T HE FIRST DAY of the sommelier contest arrived without fanfare. Considering I'd waited two years to hatch the perfect plan and would finally deal with my family, I'd expected a bit more ceremony. A James Bond soundtrack, maybe.

But calm was fine. All I needed was the outcome.

The restaurant hadn't changed since it had opened four years ago. Egos inflated, the Adriano brothers had spared no expense and followed up their first two restaurants, Aroma and Blend, with Crush. Rave reviews piled up, and the wait list grew, all three hot spots offering killer wines and cool vibes. Crush still had a small tree growing in the center of the room, decorated with tiny white lights. The world class wines lining the back wall were as impressive as ever, the sleek wooden tables and white chairs cool and stylish.

The two major differences since I'd last visited were that, these days, a typical evening at Crush saw more empty chairs than full.

And I wasn't here with Sophia.

I swallowed the bitterness and scanned the space. Three quarters of the sixty-two seats were taken, each place set with five glasses, a sheet of paper, and a pen. I nabbed a chair at an empty foursome to keep my distance. Not that I needed to make the effort. The other contestants were business-casual junkies, from the slick of their hair to the shine of their shoes. My torn jeans, biker boots, and faded "Dare Me" T-shirt were preppy repellents, which suited me fine.

I doubted a person here could discern a 2004 Screaming Eagle Cabernet Sauvignon from a 2005. Probably wouldn't be able to afford their three grand price tags, either.

A bottle I'd opened the other night without a thought.

Although I'd cleared wine from my life, there were a few purchases too precious to disown, the Screaming Eagle among them, and I'd popped a cork for my dirty princess. When she saw it (after rummaging through my cupboards—the nosy little thing), she'd gasped and draped herself over the bottle. I hadn't given two shits about impressing a girl in ages, but the urge to see her face after her first sip was too hard to resist. Wine, no matter the price, was meant to be enjoyed.

The second it had touched her tongue, her head lolled back, a glorious sigh following. A sight to behold. Watching her drink that wine had been as unforgettable as the first lick up her thigh. Normally my evenings with women weren't all-night affairs. We'd enjoy each other, chase our release, then say our goodbyes. They didn't leave me aching for more, but it had been two weeks since I'd fucked my dirty princess, and I'd replayed every taste and bite between us until I'd memorized the feel of her.

A habit I needed to kick.

The seats filled up, all but the few around me, men and women ages twenty to sixty fixing their suit jackets, crossing and uncrossing their legs. A nervous lot, the bunch of them. I couldn't deny the excitement twitching up my spine. Although I was on a mission, the thrill of tasting wine again was hard to ignore. A breath later, that excitement smacked me upside the head.

Pushing through the doors was the dirty princess herself, as though I'd conjured her.

She smoothed her gray pencil skirt, then adjusted the buttons of her white blouse. She touched her hair next, the straight strands pulled into a ponytail. She wore as little makeup as the night I'd met her, but she was as done up as the rest of this uptight crowd. Difference was, I'd seen this particular woman throw her head back in ecstasy. My blood heated, the snippets I'd relived the past two weeks as fresh as ever.

Her moaning as she sucked me into her mouth.

Me sinking so deep inside her, I lost my mind.

Us laughing hysterically as we snapped that shot of her ass.

I'd barely cracked a smile the past two years, but I'd never howled like that with a woman. Never had to walk around, clutching my stomach to find my breath. I also couldn't recall having sex four times in one night because I simply couldn't get enough.

It was easy to chalk the wild evening up to me finally finding a way to deal with my family. Liberation had me ready to jump out of my skin. There was something more, though. The innocence of her freckle-stained face, willowy body, and big doe eyes as she told me to *fuck her hard* had shot my lust into overdrive. Now here she was again.

The last person I wanted to see.

She continued to adjust her clothes and clutch her purse, anxiety radiating from her in waves. The urge to walk over and test if my touch could ease her in the light of day like it had that night lit through me, unwelcome in its force.

Her jumpy gaze landed on me and her mouth dropped open. Steady chatter hummed through the space, but I could've sworn she squeaked. She clamped her jaw shut and searched the room for a free seat. Her frantic gaze was forced back to me, and the only three vacant spots. Again she searched in vain, the rounding of her spine a clue she wasn't thrilled about her options. She looked out the way she came, squeezed her eyes, then squared her shoulders and marched toward me.

Part of me—the lower half—wanted to pin her to the wall with my thighs while I hitched that proper little skirt higher. The other part hoped she'd wandered into the wrong place. Not because our night together had been shitty, or the fact that she'd disappeared without a trace. No. The thing that had the tendons in my neck bunching was remembering how *good* it all was. Too good and too much fun, and I'd imagined rounds two and three and four ad nauseam. But rounds always ended in a knockout punch.

This girl was nothing but trouble.

She paused at the table, drew in a long breath, mumbled something as she exhaled, then glared at the seat beside me and the ones across. She chose beside, probably to face the room.

The only reason we'd hooked up two weeks ago was because there were no names and no strings. She'd admitted how hard it would be for her to relax, how awkward she'd feel afterward. The relaxing part I took care of with one brush of my lips. The awkward was still alive and kicking.

What went down between us couldn't happen again. Distractions over the next two months weren't an option, and repeat affairs led to feelings, and feelings led to promises, and promises were nothing but lies dressed up to seduce. Not an outcome I was keen to revisit. Still, I couldn't ignore her anxiety, as long as she wasn't here because of me.

I leaned toward her. "You're the last person I expected to see."

She squished her lithe body farther from mine. "Kind of coincidental, don't you think? Did you follow me?"

"I got here before you. If anyone is stalking, it's you tailing me."

Indignation colored her cheeks. "I didn't follow you. I saw a flyer and thought it looked interesting, but you obviously read it, too. If I'd known you'd be here"—aggravation laced her hushed tone—"I'd never have shown up."

Her harsh words had me fisting my hands, or maybe it was how tempting the line of her neck looked, that column of tanned skin shifting as she swallowed. But she was right: having a diversion wouldn't help my plan. "Then we're on the same page."

"Excuse me?"

"Since we're both here for the contest, we can pretend that night never happened."

Her face fell, but a beat later, she said, "Good," nothing but ice in her voice.

I followed with "Great."

She spat, "Fine."

So much for stamping out the awkward.

Waiters began moving through the space, small measures of white wine poured into each glass. A reporter sat at the bar, snapping photos and taking notes.

"Besides," she added, "we won't have to worry about seeing each other once you're eliminated."

Hot, and cocky to boot. "You're right, we won't. You'll be gone by week two and won't get to congratulate me on my win."

The same competitive streak that had sparked between us at The Blue Door resurfaced, along with a punch of lust heading south. That night, we'd played drinking games, sipping wine and listing the notes dancing on our tongues. Then, at my place, I'd tasted them on her. A dribble in the hollow of her throat. A splash between her breasts. A dab of Cabernet on her pussy.

I almost groaned at the memory, but rustling at the front of the room saved me.

Alonzo Adriano had just introduced himself, and I hadn't even noticed him enter. He may have been a head shorter than my six foot two, his cufflinks and navy suit camouflaging him in this room of wannabes, but I should have been focused.

The group was rapt, hanging on the man's every syllable, and here I was, fantasizing about a woman.

Alonzo gave a brief rundown about his two brothers and their restaurants, his dark eyes intent as he gestured to the wall of wine bottles, extolling the beauty of their collection, reverence in his voice. At least the man was passionate.

A final contestant hurried into the room, the man's blond hair parted so severely, the edge of his scalp shone. He tightened his tie, distaste on his face as he judged my tattoos, but he slid into the chair opposite my dirty princess. Moisture beaded on his large forehead.

We sat in silence as a sign-in sheet was passed around. When it reached me, I didn't hesitate. I printed JIMMY LEON, using my mother's maiden name. If I'd written Giannopoulos, it wouldn't be long before Alonzo sussed out that his Offshoot Winery bottles came from my family vineyard, and this whole ruse would be shot to shit.

The dirty princess rolled her pen through her fingers, her gaze lingering on the page before she wrote RACHEL KATES. The letters were as neat and tidy as her appearance, but there was a wild woman beneath the surface. One I'd had grinding against my hips. My mind drifted back to that night again, to our sweaty bodies and her passionate cries, and my cock stirred.

Jesus. Next session, I'd need to find a seat away from her.

As she passed the page across the table, the latecomer made sure they brushed fingers. An obvious move. He thrust his hand toward her. "I'm Rufus. Looks like we'll be spending the next two months together"—he eyed the sheet—"*Rachel*."

She sat straighter. "Looks like it."

Her hand slipped into his, and I barely refrained from slipping *my* arm around her shoulders. To claim her? To mark her as mine? The notion grated at me. A couple of women I'd been with frequented the dive bar where I worked. We'd have our night of fun, then I'd pour them drinks at Rudy's Tavern and we'd make small talk and go on like it had never happened.

Once and done. Here I was, jealous over some jerk with enough hair gel to lube a Slip 'N Slide.

His slicked blond head and three-piece suit were more her style anyway. Probably came with a lot less baggage, too.

Still, after their exchange, I couldn't resist leaning over and whispering in her ear. "You know, if you marry him, you won't be able to take his last name."

She shivered, then craned her neck to check the sheet as he got up to pass it to the next table. A laugh exploded from her, the same bark of a cackle she'd let loose at my place, like an asthma sufferer on laughing gas. Annoyed glances shot our way, but I chuckled.

"It is a *shitty* name," she whispered.

"Downright *crap*," I agreed.

Rufus *Colon* probably had a hell of a time in high school.

While the Colon chatted up the next table, the tension between Rachel and me ebbed. Keeping things friendly between us might be a better tactic than avoidance. Labelling her as off-limits would only jack up my desire. Plus, if we talked about our night together, it might stop occupying my headspace.

But when I said, "Did you send that picture to your boss? Is that why you're here?" she dropped her forehead to her hands. I winced. "Wrong thing to ask?"

Without moving her head, she said, "As far as I'm concerned, that photo never happened." She pushed to her feet and leaned into my space, her angry whisper puffing against my cheek. "Since I can't remember a single thing from that night, it's easy to believe, as long as you don't feel the pressing urge to bring it up. And yes, that photo is why I'm here. I lost my job because of it."

She dodged the tables, her heels punctuating each angry step toward the bathrooms, and I was left...uncomfortable. She didn't remember our night together? The sex on the floor? Or in my bed? Against the wall? I'd been reliving every glorious detail for weeks and she remembered *nothing*?

My necklace felt heavy, the cuff circling my wrist tight. I'd given that woman six orgasms and not one of them had left a mark. When I came up for air from between her legs that night, she'd grabbed my hair, pulled my face to hers and said, "You are a god. I don't know what you just did to me, but you better do it again."

So I did. With gusto.

And she didn't remember.

The knowledge chafed at me, worse than if she'd faked every *yes* and *more* and *don't stop*. She had no idea how good I'd made her feel. How hard she'd made me come.

I was pissed.

Alonzo collected the sign-in sheet and proceeded to place five bottles of white—Chardonnay, Riesling, Gewürztraminer, Sauvignon Blanc, and Pinot Grigio—in a line.

"Tonight," he said, "is an elimination round. A blind tasting to separate those who are serious about their wines from those who are here for the show. If you don't guess all five varietals correctly, you're out. No second chances. The rest of you will be invited back. Each Tuesday and Thursday for eight weeks, we'll test your skills: opening bottles, pouring wines, and table-service exercises. Each session will involve a blind tasting and an elimination. Those with the two lowest scores will be sent home each round. Are there any questions?"

As hands flew up, Rachel and the Colon slipped back into their seats. She sat perfectly composed. Too stiff to be natural. Although taking that photo had been funny as hell, and we'd had a blast taking it, she was obviously uncomfortable. I could understand her embarrassment. I hadn't done something that ridiculous since college.

"I won't mention it again," I said.

She stared dead ahead. "You just did."

"No, I didn't."

"And *again*."

"Are you high? I didn't say a thing."

A few people shushed us, a dirty look shot from the Colon, and she lowered her voice. "Actually, everything you're *not* saying revolves around the one thing that's banned from discussion. As far as I know, it was the worst sex of my life, and I'm here to listen to Mr. Adriano, *not you.*"

Worst sex? *Of her life?*

She may have been defensive about that photo, but she didn't remember how she'd dared me to flash the entire street beforehand, or the kisses I'd trailed up her calves afterward, our laughter dissolving into breathy moans, all playfulness forgotten.

She didn't remember a damn thing.

We sat beside each other, invisible bricks stacking between us. All I could do was review every detail from our night, and she was oblivious.

By the time the questions died down, all five glasses in front of us had been poured. The Colon sweated profusely. Rachel fidgeted beside me. I should have been calm; the tasting was a joke. Even my brother, with his underdeveloped palate, could discern a Riesling from a Chardonnay. It was child's play. Except I was riled up, the only cures a long ride on my bike or a round with a punching bag.

I forced my focus on the wines. I knew each one by aroma alone.

Riesling: green apple, lime zest, a hint of petrol.

Sauvignon Blanc: asparagus, gooseberries, fresh cut grass.

The others were just as easy.

Rachel shifted and her skirt rode up, exposing her legs. Long legs. Sexy legs. Legs that had gripped my hips like iron.

When my grandfather first explained that the alcohol drips that clung to a wineglass were known as the wine's legs, I'd giggled. When I got older, I understood how sexy that sweep of liquid was, tantalizing and teasing. Exactly like the distracting legs beside me.

I jammed a hand through my hair and diverted my attention

to the posers around the room. Many were fumbling with their glasses, scratching out and rewriting their answers. It was laughable. Rachel paused on the Gewürztraminer, likely confusing it with the Riesling. If she got it wrong, we'd part ways and I'd never see her again. I'd get her out of my head once and for all. Eliminate any distractions. But the idea of her never knowing the feel of me inside her, when I could barely look at my bed without stroking myself, wasn't right.

When she wrote the correct answer, my relief shocked me in its intensity.

We were asked to swap pages, then Alonzo described each wine. The Colon, predictably, messed up the whole page. He scowled, and said, "*Shit.*" Rachel and I shared a laugh.

People stood, the room a mix of cocky smirks and dejected faces, at least half not invited back next week. Rachel exhaled, pleased with her success.

I wouldn't see her for five days, and if the past eleven were any indication, she'd occupy too many of my quiet minutes. She, on the other hand, probably wouldn't give me a second thought. Unaware what I was playing at, I wrapped an arm behind her chair, my breath close enough to skim her ear.

"Six," I said.

"What?" There was no hiding the tremor in her voice.

"Six. That's how many orgasms I gave you, Sunshine."

Her brown eyes widened then fell heavy. "There were only four condoms in the trash."

"You counted?"

"I *noticed*. And my name isn't Sunshine."

My first glimpse of her tonight was a reminder to keep my distance, her ability to unbalance me dangerous. But the contradiction of her wildness concealed below her measured appearance was too tempting. If she couldn't remember what had gone down between us, I'd have to remind her. "Sure it is, Sunshine. Unless you prefer Ray. And since we never formally introduced ourselves, I'm Jimmy, and I don't need my cock to give a woman an orgasm."

Her breasts strained against her top, the fabric quivering with each inhale. My naughty ray of sunshine. I lingered for a beat, long enough to run my nose up her ear.

Then I took off, unsure what the hell I'd just started.

CHAPTER 6

RACHEL

I was in serious trouble. I'd debated not returning for the second round of the contest, anything to avoid Jimmy and his *six orgasms*. Yet here I was, pacing in front of Crush, walking toward and away from the door at a dizzying pace.

When I saw him last week, the same vertigo had struck—the urge to turn and speed walk away—but I'd stood my ground. I wouldn't let one man, and one silly night, keep me from fulfilling my destiny, and this contest was *destined*. The more I played it over, the more convinced I'd become: the blackout and the shift in the air after making our wishes was the supernatural at work. A magical twist of fate. My father, probably tired of watching me flounder in career hell, must have arranged it.

Which meant I had to prove myself worthy, finally shed my stench of failure and stick to a rewarding career. My mother would help me financially if asked, but my father had paid his own way through college to become an electrical engineer and had worked hard to support us. I yearned to be strong, like him.

Self-sufficient, like him. Maybe I'd even meet a nice guy in the class.

If Jimmy and his six orgasms didn't interfere.

Which meant I needed reinforcements. Gwen could read me like nobody's business and always called my bluffs, but Ainsley was my go-to for advice on how to ditch men.

She answered after three rings. "Men are assholes."

"You and Gwen share that sentiment." I wasn't far behind. One particular asshole, who for sure lied about a certain number of orgasms, was likely awaiting my arrival.

"My client had me order this, like, over-the-top gift for his wife. Insane diamond necklace. Then he had me buy flowers for his mistress. Watching men like him cheat on their wives is enough to change the Pope's views on marriage." Ainsley didn't mention her ex, Brandon, and how he'd have fit into that boys' club, but her disdain embittered each word.

"Disgusting assholes," I agreed.

"It pays the bills. But forget my drama, what's up?"

I hugged my waist and focused on the motorcycle parked on the street. Smooth leather. Black trim. I'd always wanted to ride one, not on the back like I had with Gabe. Just me and the air in my face, so I could feel all that power buzzing up my arms. My mother, however, would swallow her tongue—which is also what would happen if she saw the man messing with my head. "I need boy advice."

"Another date with a Mr. Potato Head lookalike?"

"No, thank God. Remember the guy from our birthday? The one with the tattoos?"

"Are you kidding? I still have dreams about him, of the sexy variety."

"Yeah, well, turns out he's in the sommelier contest, and he's taunting me with memories of our night together. He's probably full of it, but I'm not sure how to handle things."

"You don't want to handle *him*?"

If it were only that easy. When he'd acknowledged the Butt

Crack Incident, humiliation had burned through me. Crawling into a hole (stocked with wine), never to be seen again, would have been preferable to sitting next to the man who'd witnessed that stunt. Except he *had* gone out of his way to change the topic and joke about the Colon's name, easing my awkwardness.

He was also hot as sin. A lethal combination. "I have to see this guy every week, maybe for a couple of months. Just tell me how to turn him down so I don't make it weird."

She barely took a breath. "Tell him you have a boyfriend. That you broke up briefly, hence the hookup, but you got back together. If he takes it well, thank him for understanding. If he doesn't, tell him the shitty sex made you realize how much you missed your man."

And that's why I called Ainsley. "You are a dating guru."

"It's a gift," she said, and we hung up.

Pumped, I tugged down my blouse—black instead of white, my gray skirt a cinch to mix and match. (The beauty of the nine-piece ensemble!) A roll of my shoulders later, I marched into Crush, head high, determination propelling me forward. With half the group eliminated, the day's tasting was in the cellar below. Wafts of wet stone hit me, followed by dark fruit and that earthy scent that clung to wine cellars. It smelled of nights organizing bottles with my dad.

Two long harvest tables filled the center of the stone room, three glass walls of wine surrounding them.

And Jimmy.

He sat in a far corner, on his own, one ankle hooked over his knee, the tilt of his shoulders the picture of effortless cool. The tattoos, those worn boots, that scruff just long enough to tickle, not scratch—the man oozed *dude.*

A dude who was intent upon me.

I clutched my purse against my hip, his potent gaze unrelenting. I reviewed Ainsley's advice. *Boyfriend. Bad sex. Shut the man down.* All I could do was return his stare, my knees weakening by the second. Did his full lips taste as delicious as they looked?

Had he growled when my nails bit into his ass? No memories replied. But he did.

Bad Boy held up six fingers.

Unbelievable.

I swiveled away, the humidity in the room descending between my breasts. Unlike Ainsley, I wasn't gifted with ample cleavage and burlesque curves. I was long-limbed and thin, no definition to my arms. Jimmy's rapt attention put the sexy in my step. I moved to the glass wall, my back to him, a sway to my hips that hadn't been there before. Like I was a thing to be admired. Like I could grip a stripper pole and blow the roof off a club.

A man had never made me feel so desirable with nothing but his eyes. But I was a relationship girl, and Jimmy was a bad, *bad* boy. I'd been down that road before.

He was also competition.

To quell the heat in my blood, I focused on the wall of bottles in front of me. The breadth of the collection was astounding, new and old world wines, each worth more than my savings. They even had a few bottles from Tamber Bey. I'd gnaw off my right arm to taste a drop of that Cabernet.

There were also a number of bottles I didn't recognize, enough that my confidence waned. At the first tasting, my nerves hadn't bested me. Discerning the whites poured was easy enough, and the hopefuls vying for the position were so varied my limited experience hadn't been a hindrance.

The stakes had changed.

In one quick move, Alonzo had eliminated over half the group, leaving only those with a nose for wine and the drive to win. I wasn't sure where I fell on the spectrum.

Sensing the room filling up, I turned to find a seat. Jimmy's attention had shifted from me to the wall of wines at the back, his steely eyes broody. Or maybe sad. I may not have remembered our night together, but the bleakness of his apartment was hard to forget. His forlorn expression now was difficult to ignore, too. The few seats around him were empty, the other contestants keeping their distance, scornful looks tossed his way. As though his tattoos were contagious.

At sixteen, I'd seen a Jane Goodall documentary and declared myself a future primatologist. I'd spend hours at the zoo, staring at the chimpanzee enclosure, taking important notes: *Murphy smacked Daisy's head.* When I realized actual documentation involved rain forests and bugs the size of Texas, I aborted the plan, but not before befriending one chimpanzee. Sir Lancelot would spend his days hunched in a corner, his back turned to the world. My best friend, Elise, had just moved away, and the group we'd eaten lunch with decided my hair wasn't stylish enough or my shoes weren't hip enough. They left me to fend for myself. Sixteen-year-old super villains.

Sir Lancelot had understood me. I'd tell him about my crush on Ross Zuckerman, and he'd pick at his fur. The day he held out a branch toward me, I cried.

Jimmy might have oozed dude and sexual confidence, but there was no denying the loneliness beneath his tough exterior, and Ainsley's advice drifted toward the shadows. I could have sat in the empty chair near me, put an end to whatever game Jimmy and his *six orgasms* were playing, but watching life through a one-way mirror wasn't fun for anyone.

Before I could overthink my decision, I rounded the tables and sat next to him.

He crowded my space, his elbow brushing mine. "Couldn't stay away, could you?"

"I wanted a front row seat for your elimination."

He edged closer. "Hope you don't cry when you're cut, Sunshine. I don't deal well with criers."

Maybe I should have pondered my seat choice longer. But his use of that silly nickname amused me, our banter more fun than irritating. "I don't deal well with cocky men who talk to mask their incompetence."

"If you remembered our night, you'd know my cockiness is justified."

"If it were that good, I wouldn't have blocked it out." He was toying with me, using my memory lapse to get under my skin. So why was I smiling? Biting back my grin, I removed two pens from my purse and set them perpendicular to the table's edge.

"Too much of a good thing can kick you into shock," he said.

"Too much ego suffocates brain function."

He leaned into my side. "It wasn't my brain that fucked you."

Whoa. My witty reply dried up, all moisture heading south. Since our last meeting, zoning out had become habit. The memory of his nose in my hair after the tasting, his lips by my ear, the word *cock* whispered for only me to hear, had played on repeat. Each time, my irritation rose—frustration that I couldn't remember details of the night in question.

And Bad Boy knew it.

Time for a topic change. "The Nose looks like stiff competition."

I nodded toward a contestant, but Jimmy's focus lingered on my face. He had deep blue eyes with hints of steel. Intense eyes. I liked the attention, enjoyed our flirtatious joking and our proximity, how his body heat mingled with mine. I liked it all too much.

Taking my cue, he searched out the Nose. I'd spotted him at the first round and his intimidation factor was still high. His navy vest and tie had country club written all over them, his gaunt cheeks and sharp chin debonair. His nose was the most worrisome. A nose that large and straight had the power to unlock scents from any glass.

Jimmy whistled. "That is one mighty schnoz."

"*The Wizard of Schnoz*," I said and cringed. My father and I had played this game, swapping words in movie titles, both of us cracking up. Men didn't often get my silly sense of humor.

Instead of raising an eyebrow, Jimmy played along. *"The Schnoz of Wrath."*

"Rebel without a Schnoz."

"The Naked Schnoz."

I snorted. *"The Schnozinator."*

He laughed then, a deep, rumbling sound that curled around me. My answering cackle wasn't as smooth. I clamped a hand over my mouth, and he gripped my thigh. "Don't hide that sound, Ray. Your laugh is a thing of beauty."

And the way he said it? Ainsley's husky voice made every giggle rich and sexy. Gwen's humor tended toward the sarcastic, but her laughter was musical. My outbursts were unattractive. Then Jimmy touched my thigh, told me to embrace it, and a hazy calm trickled below my skin, as though I'd enjoyed a glass of wine.

Unfortunately, once Jimmy gripped my thigh, the bastard didn't let go. His fingers tightened, and my blood rushed, a steady throb congregating below my skirt. This wasn't the light buzz after a sip of wine. This was a shot of tequila, a lick of salt, and a splash of lime.

Feverish, I gripped my seat.

Alonzo walked down the stairs, and all chatter in the room vanished. Jimmy's hand stayed put, tingles radiating from that point of contact. I was a hormonal mess.

Alonzo, with his goatee and gold rings, had an air of hustler about him, but he commanded the room, outlining the hour ahead. Few words registered. Jimmy's hand inched up my thigh, and I shifted forward. I shouldn't have shifted. I should have slapped his hand away and blurted my boyfriend story. My traitorous body did nothing. His focus was on our host, his fingers dipping between my thighs. Not touching me where it counted, but so, *so* close.

A sudden memory flashed.

Jimmy's weight on me. Deep thrusts. My legs gripping his waist.

A hard floor.

Teeth on skin.

Me screaming in pleasure.

Him whispering how beautiful I am.

Holy God. My tailbone (and other parts) throbbed, the lingering bruise confirming the flashback's authenticity.

But Jimmy pulled his hand away.

My thighs burned, followed by an urge to grab his hand and shove it up my skirt.

What was happening to me? I was a professional. A competitor in need of a freaking job. Not some sex-crazed woman after a quickie.

Warmth persisted from his touch and that memory. When he leaned in to say, "Number one happened against my bedroom door," that heat turned molten.

The man wasn't playing fair.

We each had a glass of water, and I gulped half of mine, catching Jimmy's smirk from the corner of my eye. Seriously unfair. That level of flirtation implied he was after a second round. Not altogether unappealing.

But if I let that happen, I couldn't pass out this time. I'd make sure I was wide awake for the entire show, which meant the aftermath would reach new heights of awkward. My no-strings, no-names rule would be toast. Twice a week we'd be in each other's faces, my current level of distraction amplified.

Bad idea.

I focused on the tasks at hand. A bottle of wine and corkscrew were placed in front of each contestant. Three judges made the rounds, marking our ability to open a bottle. The Nose cut his foil in one smooth move, the cork popping out in a clean stroke. Jimmy also made it look effortless, his wrists loose as he maneuvered the lever.

I fumbled.

I'd opened hundreds of bottles, usually with my dad's corkscrew, but I should have aced the test. Instead it took two swipes for the foil to come off, and I missed the center of the cork. Too many people were watching me—judging, wishing my failure. Performing under pressure was my kryptonite, a reason the jobs I'd burned through never involved crowds.

I fisted my hands on my lap, unsure what had made me think I could pull this off. Even if, by some miracle, I won, the position gained would be nothing but pressure and the spotlight, the event splashed across local papers, real sommeliers calling it a joke. How would I manage?

"Why doesn't Alonzo just do one day of tastings to choose the winner?" Dragging out this torture was unappealing, the possibility of my birthday wish never coming true making it all the worse.

"They need the publicity," Jimmy said. "They want to play it up. He'll only cut a couple people each session. Give the papers something to write about. And don't worry, a few on the far table messed up worse than you."

"*Worse* than me? Is that your way of making me feel better?"

He closed the distance between us again. His breath teased my cheek. "Number two was with you on the edge of my bed. I was kneeling on the floor with your legs over my shoulders. If you want me to make you feel better, all you have to do is ask."

Stop the presses. Bronze this moment. Bottle this bubble of time.

I brushed off last week's comment about him not needing his "cock" to please a woman. I knew my body, knew what it could and couldn't feel, and he was toying with me. But if he was truthful, if number two happened with him on his knees, that meant I came from oral. From him *eating my pussy* as Gwen would have said.

The impossible achieved.

I'd knocked one of my pens askew when opening the bottle, so I repositioned it. A small corner of order I could keep. "I don't believe you."

He squinted at me. "You're questioning my skill?"

"No. I'm sure you're plenty skilled, but that's never happened for me."

The contestants were chatting as our blind tasting was poured—a study of Pinot Noir in five glasses. My grape, thankfully. A chance to redeem myself. But instead of focusing on the wines I'd have to guess, I was sharing my sexual dysfunction with the man I should have been avoiding. And I wasn't even drunk.

"Are you shitting me?" he asked, incredulous. "You rode my face like it was your job."

That visual had me clenching *everywhere*. Could he be telling the truth? Had my body unraveled under his tongue? "I don't lie. Not well, at least. *You* clearly have no problem telling tales."

I tried not to glance his way, but he leaned forward, forcing the connection. His dark hair fell across his forehead. Hair I'd probably tugged in the throes of passion.

Glee shone in his eyes. "There's only one way to find out."

"Not happening." But I so wanted it to. To know once and for all if my frigidness in that position was my headspace, the man's inexperience, or a general lack of connection.

Since my father had passed away, and the whole Gabe fiasco, I'd always dated the "right" guys—boys with my mother's stamp of approval, similar upbringing making conversation easy and family dinners nice. The word *love* had been used, and I'd been happy, but passion had never played a role. Not even with Gabe. Touching his tattooed arms and wearing his leather jacket had made me feel wicked and wild, something I'd craved, but lust had never spurred my pulse.

My reaction to Bad Boy was lust with a side of longing and a dash of need.

"Your blush says you'd like to find out if I'm lying." He had no qualms calling me on the heat his presence stirred. Or goading me. "Don't fuck up the Pinot tasting. Flustering you is too much fun."

Such a jokester. "Pinot is my grape."

"I thought you were a Cabernet Sauvignon lover. You nearly fainted when I poured you the Screaming Eagle. Even plastered yourself against the bottle."

I flipped toward him and gripped his thigh. "Are you serious? You opened a Screaming Eagle? And I drank it?"

He chuckled, something different in his steely gaze. Not the sexy droop of his eyelids that had me wanting to nibble his neck, or the glazed sadness I'd seen. This was a sparkle, adoration behind the subtle glow. "You did. And unless you want the room to see how much you turn me on, I'd suggest releasing my leg."

We were sequestered, no one beside me or across the table to eavesdrop, but I snatched my hand back. "I can't believe I tasted a Screaming Eagle and don't remember. That's criminal."

"You loved it, if that helps." He lowered his voice, a quiet rumble just for me. "I think you liked it best when I poured a drop on your pussy before I ate you out."

What? *Whatwhatwhat?* It was all too much. Missing that wine, my possible orgasm with those full lips between my thighs. *That wine.* The knowledge of what I'd missed was worse than the Butt Crack Incident.

I turned toward him and hissed, "This conversation ends now. We're in a room with other people, and I need to focus. Keep the P-word to yourself."

He mumbled something about me having no issues shouting pussy in Vesper, and I cursed Reckless Rachel for the thousandth time.

I forced my attention to our tasting. Five glasses of Pinot Noir faced me, my pens neatly lined up. A paper with five numbers listed in rows awaited my answers. My phone buzzed, stopped, then buzzed again. For sure my mother. I ignored the noise, but Jimmy frowned at my purse, then he snatched one of my pens.

I gawked at him. "That's mine."

"You have two."

"In case one runs out of ink."

"You need to write down five names. What kind of crappy pens run out of ink after five names?"

I gritted my teeth. My phone buzzed again, him and that noise equally as grating. He also didn't return the pen. Not only did he not return it, but he placed his index finger at the base of my other one and tapped it out of position. I moved it back perpendicular. He tapped it again.

Motherfucker.

I dug my fingers into his side and pinched. "Next time I go for the nipple. Don't mess with me."

"Is that a promise or a threat?"

Probably both. My phone vibrated again, my mother never one to trust voicemail. (What if you're abducted and can't get to the phone? What if you've had a seizure?) Unable to add her to my stress, I reached in and silenced my cell. To afford participating in this contest, I'd taken a receptionist job at my gym. So unless I wanted to fold towels for a living, it was time to get my head in the game.

I plucked my remaining pen from the table, took a deep breath, and swirled the first glass. From nothing but a sniff and sip we had to name the region, extra points awarded for the winery and year.

My father had belonged to a wine club. Once I'd shown interest, he brought me along to tastings. Some were lateral, where we'd compare one wine across vintages. Others compared grape varieties. When I got them right, he'd hold up my sheet and boast about it to the room, then we'd talk wine the whole drive home. Hopefully those nights had left their mark.

The Nose already had his schnozinator in his glass, no doubt picking up every nuance. Jimmy was in no rush, swirling and sniffing. I steadied my hand, lifted my glass, and inhaled.

Black cherry. That was a given for most Pinots. I mentally reviewed the classes I'd taken, searching for the characteristics that defined each region. Dark plum for New Zealand, cranberry and earth for Oregon, and the subtle barnyard aroma from

France. I sipped and swirled and inhaled, narrowing the possibilities. Guessing the years would be harder, the wineries a shot in the dark. Good thing I'd pored over Crush's wine list the past week.

As I lifted my second glass again, Jimmy whispered, "Number three happened on my living room floor. After the butt shot."

My wine nearly sloshed on the table.

Us. Naked. On his floor. *After* the butt shot he wasn't supposed to mention. But I didn't even care. That must have been the memory that resurfaced, and I wanted to disappear in those sensations again—us rocking together, skin against skin.

If we'd been alone, no test or audience around, I'd have given up my charade. I'd have straddled him on that chair, ground against him and eased the ache building under my skirt. *Passion. Lust. Cravings.* Things I'd never experienced lit under my skin in a tantalizing cocktail. But we had an audience, and I had a test to ace.

The rest went relatively smoothly. Except for the moments Jimmy leaned over to list how orgasms four, five, and six had gone down—in his kitchen, the last two between his sheets. *God have mercy.* Wines four and five gave me trouble, but by the time my final answers were on the page, I was pleased.

The Nose folded his arms, smug as hell. Jimmy took his time.

He tapped *my* pen on the table, his bedroom eyes back on me, my skirt ready to combust. "You think you did well?" he asked.

I sat straighter, hiding my answers. "Do you doubt my ability?"

"I don't doubt you. The real question is, do you still doubt *me*? Do I need to prove I can make you scream my name with a lick of my tongue?"

Bad Boy didn't mince words, and I liked it—his dangerous air, his confidence. He had me rethinking my stance on one-night stands. Or *two-night* stands. My awkwardness with him had receded, jokes and flirtations in its place. He had me at ease. Yes, I wanted a relationship and he wouldn't be that man, but for the first time ever, I felt as though I could pull off a fling.

May as well strike while the iron was hot. "If you pass this session," I said, my determination building, "I might consider testing your claim. For scientific reasons."

His tongue stroked his bottom lip, leaving it wet and red and kissable. "Then I better get this last wine right."

He'd better.

Unlike me, who'd moved back and forth between my five wines, comparing and questioning and driving myself nuts, he'd sipped each in turn, leisurely. He was as contemplative with his final Pinot. The contrast of his strong hands, the chunky ring on his middle finger, and the leather cuff as he swirled his glass was strangely sensual. Those hands would look downright brutish on my freckled skin.

He observed the alcohol clinging to the crystal, assessing the legs that dripped downward. His focus was absolute. Then he brought the rim to his nose, inhaled…

And something changed.

His brows pulled tight, a deep crease sinking between them. The sip that followed sent a symphony of expressions across his face—jaw flexing, cheeks reddening, lips flattening into a grim line. His blue-gray eyes glazed. He plunked his glass down and pushed it aside, as though it were tainted, corked. Gone was the relaxed toss of his posture. Now he was all straight spine and crossed arms. His flirty glances ceased, too.

Nothing about wine five struck me as odd. It was a local California Pinot Noir, of that I was sure, but I couldn't peg the winery. Unsure what soured him, I didn't intrude. Aside from a hot night I barely recalled, and some flirting, we hardly knew each other. His scowl didn't invite questions, his sudden chill frosting my mood further.

Alonzo returned, but I barely listened as he explained the day's results would be emailed. Bitterness pulsed off Jimmy. He wouldn't glance my way and didn't make a joke when the Nose sneezed. I'd gone from unable to shake him to invisible. It shouldn't have hurt; he didn't owe me anything. But the emotional whiplash was jarring.

The second we were dismissed, he was up and out of his chair, his boots *thunking* toward the stairs, not a word to me. Like the flirting had never happened. Like he hadn't teased me all session with sensual promises, only to leave me wanting. I snatched my purse and pens and hurried after him. If nothing else, I wanted to grab his shirt and yank him around and ask what his problem was, but he was too quick. I made it outside as he straddled the motorcycle, *of course*, revved the engine, and tore off. Bad Boy with an attitude.

CHAPTER 7

JIMMY

I'M NOT sure when I became such a dick. Maybe when my family ripped the ground out from under my feet. It could have been when Sophia left me. All I knew was a sweet woman, who'd been honest about her sexual desires and awkwardness, had gotten caught in the crossfire. And it wasn't cool.

I'd clocked a lot of miles on my bike since our last session at Crush, pounded a punching bag within an inch of its life. My family's Pinot Noir still lingered on my tongue. It tasted of nights watching my grandfather bottle wine and days helping pick grapes. It tasted of deception.

One sip had sent me for a spin.

The other thing that had my knuckles raw from rounds of pummeling a speed ball was the hurt on Rachel's face when I blew her off. The woman who'd made me laugh, who matched my sarcasm blow for blow, didn't deserve to be toyed with. She didn't warrant my attitude. She was all long lines and soft skin, a little innocent and a lot of fun. All either of us wanted was another night, and I couldn't even manage that.

But I could muster an apology.

I got to our next session early and waited, knee bouncing, fists clenching, hoping to see her. If she'd been eliminated, I'd have no way to get in touch. I'd have to live with the tightness in my chest. With a second to spare, she waltzed in, and I relaxed. She sat on the far side of the room, stoic. She didn't spare me a glance. I deserved as much, and worse. All I could do was stare, guilt and frustration coiling.

We had to uncork Champagne, a tough feat for the uninitiated, and she struggled. If I were beside her, I'd have whispered some tricks. *Angle the bottle at forty-five degrees. Rotate the bottle, not the cork.* The blind tasting afterward was a sampling of Merlot, easy for me, but I watched her, apprehensive, worried she'd get cut. That I'd lose my chance to explain.

It was over too soon.

As Alonzo thanked us for coming, the man beside Rachel—his forehead as shiny as his dark hair—leaned into her side. He whispered to her and touched her elbow. He got as close as I had last week. She smiled at him, her nose crinkling in amusement.

Jealousy flashed behind my eyes. I wanted to capture that sunny smile. Bask in it. Hear her silly laugh, because it was *real*. As were her orgasms when I'd gone down on her. Knowing I'd been the only man to make her buck and moan with my tongue was a thrill. It made me want to pound my chest and growl, prove only I could reduce her to incoherent sounds.

The whole thing was a mess. I wanted her. For more than one night, maybe, but I'd already proven I wasn't ready for a girl like Rachel. Where did that leave us?

Alonzo scrubbed his goatee as he addressed the room, his blue suit more mobster than restauranteur. "Like last time, emails will be sent with results, and two of you will be cut. Next session will be Cabernet Sauvignon. Since our numbers are still high, four will be eliminated." He nodded. "Until next week."

My gaze cut to Rachel, who went white as a sheet. The night we'd hooked up, and I uncorked the Screaming Eagle, she'd lamented her challenge with Cabs, complaining that she'd always struggled tasting the grape. She wouldn't remember that confession, but there was no denying the worry in her pinched brow. Another four lost would take us down to twenty-two. She wasn't sure she'd last.

Which meant my time with her could be limited.

She was up and at the stairs as I reached for my jacket, but a tap on my shoulder stopped me from following her. "Have we met before?"

I turned and searched the woman's face. She had blond hair and narrow features, excessive makeup highlighting her blue eyes. Nothing about her was familiar. "Don't think so."

She studied me. "I just thought we'd met—at an event or something. I'm April. I pour wines for functions in Napa."

The odds of her remembering me from an Offshoot Winery tasting were slim. Back then my hair was clipped short, my face clean shaven. I had no tattoos, not a thread loose on my jeans. The prospect of being recognized wasn't pleasant. If Alonzo found out who I was, he'd plaster my name through the papers to up his publicity, and my plan would fall apart.

"Don't think we've met," I repeated. "I just moved to town. Must have a twin around."

Her pink lips turned down, but she didn't push.

I grabbed my jacket and spun for the exit, but my sights snagged on an Offshoot wine bottle. Our Cabernet, of course. Nothing but lies in sleek packaging.

My mind tripped back to the day my younger brother Dimitri and I caught our winemaker playing with our flagship Cabernet Sauvignon, blending in more than the twenty-five percent of other varietals allowed. We'd been on him to trim costs. His brilliant solution: pass off inferior—*cheaper*—grapes as Cabernet.

Dimitri had always been lazy, more corners cut than

followed, and he didn't bat an eye. I, on the other hand, was furious, could never have my name linked to such deceit. My father's reaction was to list wine's illustrious history, telling us of Pliny the Elder's claims that most wines were adulterated, falsehoods wrapped in scents of black cherry and spice.

Neither of them gave a damn.

I'd sure as shit cared, but I lost the winery before I could make things right.

Now it was time. I was stuck in a rut, that lie tethering me to my past, and this contest was my best shot. Placing an anonymous call wouldn't work. Laws weren't as strict in Napa Valley as they were in Europe, and Dimitri had too many wine critics in his pocket. With the top experts in the field present at the final round, I'd work the tables, plant seeds and watch the gossip spark. The fire would catch before Dimitri could control it. They'd be forced to recall all mislabeled wines, and their reputation would nose-dive. It was unavoidable.

It was also tragic.

The winery my grandfather and I had poured our lives into would crumble, his legacy forever tarnished. My gut hollowed at the thought.

Ignoring the queasiness, I made for the door, hoping to find Rachel and clear my head. Luck was on my side. She'd stopped a few blocks down to rummage through her purse. Probably for her cell. Last session it had vibrated incessantly until she'd shut it off. A guy calling her, maybe. Someone in her life who didn't spin hot and cold. That didn't seem like her style, to flirt with me and go home to someone else, but if my ex Sophia taught me anything, it was people weren't always who they seemed.

I glanced at my bike and debated leaving, not pursuing her pull. Not offering some weak explanation for my behavior. That would mean sitting through another session, waiting for a glance from Rachel. A twitch of her lips. Any reaction to me.

Fuck it all to hell.

She was on the move and turned into a grocery store. I jogged after her, unsure what I was after, unable to stop.

I found her in the produce section. A bag of cherries was in the basket on her arm. Her hips swayed in her black skirt, the folds of her white blouse whispering across her skin as she moved. She always wore conservative clothes, always black, white, or gray. I couldn't be sure who the real Rachel was—the woman with the witty humor, sexual appetite, and wild laugh, or the woman who wore prim outfits, straightened her pens, and couldn't come with any *other* man's head between her thighs. If I had to guess, I'd say she didn't know her true self, either.

Her back was to me as I approached, her attention fixed on an employee. "Do you have black currants?"

He scratched his pock-marked cheek. "Only dried, I think. Aisle three, with the bulk foods."

"And licorice? The real kind, black. Not the strawberry Twizzlers."

"Aisle two, with the candy. Should be there."

Cherries in her basket, currants and licorice—she either had some odd eating habits, or she was training her nose for the Cabernet Sauvignon tasting.

"You don't want licorice," I said.

Her shoulders jumped. She swiveled, surprise in her wide brown eyes. Her attention lingered on my leather jacket and dipped down the front of my T-shirt, landing on my belt buckle. Her eyes flicked up to my face, irritation replacing her desire. I saw it, though—the quickening of her breath, the parting of her lips. All wasn't lost.

"If I asked for licorice," she said, "then I want licorice."

"Not if you're using it to prepare for next class. For that, you need star anise and these." I grabbed a pint of blackberries and tossed them in her basket.

Her scowl was adorable. "What do you think you're doing?"

"Helping you."

The pink tinge on her chest rushed to her cheeks, indignation in her hitched shoulders. "I don't want your help, Jimmy. Since you need it spelled out, I don't want anything to do with you. I don't know what you're playing at, but this cat-and-mouse game doesn't do it for me." She grabbed the blackberries and shoved them at my chest. "Keep your hands out of my basket."

Except I wanted my hands *in* her basket, my fingers smudging her refined edges. I returned the blackberries to her bin and smirked.

She huffed. "You're incorrigible."

"I'm determined. I need to explain about last session."

She stepped to the side, hand on the berries to return them herself, and my heart stopped. No, not stopped. It lurched against my ribs, the muscle nothing but a giant bruise.

Sophia.

She was a few feet away—the woman who'd used me, chewed me up, and spat me out. The woman I hadn't seen in two fucking years. Her blond hair was shorter, no longer to her waist, but her lips still shone red, her ample curves emphasized in a tight red dress. The dress we'd bought together in Greece. That was also where I'd purchased the engagement ring she'd refused. I stumbled back, history and memories slamming into my chest.

What a goddamn week. First the blind Pinot Noir tasting, a sip of my family's wine secreted onto my tongue. Now Sophia.

Rachel appeared in front of me and placed her hand on the center my chest. My heart nearly leapt into her palm. "You okay?" she asked.

Our first round in the cellar, the same sympathy had softened her face. Right before she'd marched over and sat beside me. Her position now blocked Sophia from my view, and bitterness redirected my shock. "My ex is here, and I haven't seen her in a couple years."

Instead of removing her hand, she flattened her palm. "I'm guessing the relationship didn't end well?"

Understatement of the century. "If her turning down my proposal constitutes not well, then yes, I'd agree."

She glanced over her shoulder, still touching me. "The blond?"

I grunted, pulled between preserving Rachel's closeness and getting the hell out of Dodge. I chose immobility.

And maybe Sophia's appearance was a gift. A way to bury our past and, more important, a way to get Rachel alone. Convince her to hear me out. Plus, she could use my help. I placed my hand over hers, locking her palm against my chest. "I need a favor."

She flexed her fingers, and her nails bit through my shirt. "A favor because you spent an hour flirting with me, then blew me off?"

That hurt almost as much as seeing Sophia. "I want to explain that, and I'd like to show my ex, Sophia, I've moved on. If you play along, I'll come clean about my shitty behavior and help you with the Cab tasting."

She stiffened, frustration in the set of her jaw. Unsure if I'd made headway, I added, "Were you planning on tossing a green pepper in your basket? You can't study Cabernet Sauvignon without it."

Her gaze darted from the green pepper display to her basket, then back to my face. Her hand relaxed under mine. "You have a deal. But only because I need to nail that tasting."

"Of course," I said. Except she wanted to nail me, too. She'd admitted as much last session.

Not wanting to give her a moment to rethink, I placed her basket by our feet and wrapped my other arm around her waist, pulling her against me. "This okay?"

She pressed her breasts to my chest, a soft sigh puffing against my cheek. "Yeah, okay."

I was more than okay. I should have been a mess, the acid left in Sophia's wake still eating at me, but Rachel dulled the ache. She also revved my libido, my cock thickening at the contact.

Sophia was examining broccoli, filling her cart, working our way. I focused on Rachel, the freckles dotting her cheek, the silkiness of her blouse under my grip. I brushed my lips over her jaw. Then I stole a taste, just below her ear, savoring the feel of her. She all but melted.

The woman wanted to nail me, all right, and the feeling was mutual.

A thousand emotions should have been warring, Sophia's reappearance something I'd dreaded, but I could only focus on one: craving. Desire for Rachel. We were in a public place, kids hanging off grocery carts, men and women ticking through their shopping lists, but Rachel's hips were pressed to mine. Her hair tangled with the scruff on my cheek, need in her breathy sounds. My resentment toward Sophia was still palpable, but holding Rachel close dimmed my turmoil.

Unwilling to let the moment pass, I whispered, "Your place or mine."

Her hips pulled back. "Mine. But only for the tasting."

She was full of it, intent on denying our attraction. Not that I blamed her. After the stunt I pulled, I was lucky she hadn't kneed me in the balls. I opened my mouth to say as much, when Sophia passed my field of vision. It was now or never.

I gripped Rachel tighter, pulling her into my side. "Sophia?"

Sophia went rigid at my voice. She glanced at me, then away, then back again. Her mouth opened in shock. "Jimmy? Is that *you?*"

My transformation the past two years had been gradual. For me, at least. My hair growing longer, the first tattoo, the second, the nipple piercings—parts of myself I hadn't realized I'd denied. Growing up, all I'd ever wanted was my father's approval. I'd spend extra hours picking grapes, wave my report card in his face, date the right girls.

Until Sophia. I gave up everything for her, and she threw it in my face.

Here I was, a stronger version of myself in some ways. An

asshole, maybe, something I needed to fix, but my confidence had grown. I may not have looked the part of the former heir to one of Napa's most successful wineries, but I was finally me. I liked sex a little rough. I dug the burn of a tattoo gun digging into my skin, the sharp stab of a piercing needle. Sticking a tight turn on my Harley was a thrill. All these things I'd kept in the shadows were visible to the world, and Sophia barely recognized me.

"It's been a while," I said. "Thought you'd moved to New York."

Her mouth still hung open, until she shook her head. "Jesus, Jimmy. What happened to you?"

There. Right there. That was when the hurt and betrayal resurfaced. Like she thought losing her had pushed me into a downward spiral. It had, for a while. No use denying that. As had my family's actions. Until I stopped running on that hamster wheel. What she saw in front of her was the man I was supposed to be.

Dangerous? Maybe.

Pissed off at the world? Probably.

Someone who only relied on himself? Definitely.

Neither of us knew the other all that well in the end.

Rachel slid one hand into my back pocket, the other brushing my abs, just above my belt. "You must be Sophia. Jimmy's told me a lot about you, and honestly, I'm so thankful you were brave enough to do what Jimmy couldn't."

"Excuse me?" Sophia curled her lip, a tic of hers I'd always hated.

"The proposal? Turning him down when neither of you wanted to take that step? We're both grateful." Rachel tilted her head and gazed up at me, locking me in her orbit. Her eyes were often expressive, indignation or excitement played out in shades of brown. Right now all I could see was *love.* My heart was pounding again, a syncopated rhythm, unfamiliar in its urgency, and I nearly crushed my mouth to hers.

Damn, was she good.

"Well, glad to see you're happy." The distaste as Sophia sneered at my new style said otherwise. She held up her left hand. "I got married six months ago. Rocco and I moved back to the area."

Rocco put quite the *rock* on Sophia's finger, but the jealousy I expected wasn't there. No sting of longing. No urge to claim her, like when that guy had leaned into Rachel. Sophia had only ever wanted one thing from me, and when I'd lost that, she went digging for gold elsewhere. I was still pissed. Still wanted to scream and tell her she was nothing but a conniving bitch. That what she did had twisted my heart. But creating a scene wouldn't be cool with our audience, and Rachel's arms made the whole fiasco easier to bear.

"Congratulations," I offered instead. "Like Rachel said, thanks for what you did. Everything worked out for the best."

An insincere smile flitted across her face, then she moved on, a sway to her hips I used to love. Time healed some wounds.

Rachel pushed away from me, all looks of love gone. "Let's get shopping."

We grabbed spices, fruits, vegetables, and a few bottles of Cabernet Sauvignon, no physical contact between us, my mind spinning the whole while. Each time it returned to Sophia, I clamped my jaw and switched tracks. Without Rachel pressed against me, my spite resurfaced.

I never let myself think about Sophia. She'd used me, fucked me over, and I'd fallen for her crap. Suppressing my thoughts was survival, pure and simple.

Then there was Rachel. The adoration on her face before, although an act, buffed the hard edges I'd sharpened the past two years. I was happy on my own, had promised myself I'd never fall in love again. Leave no one to derail my life but me. Still, *that look*. I could live without my family, get along without the winery, but around her, my heart suddenly craved more.

CHAPTER 8

RACHEL

I MUST HAVE BEEN a glutton for punishment. The whole hour at Crush had been an Olympic effort to avoid Jimmy's persistent gaze. My attention would slide over, and I'd force it away. I'd catch sight of his hand dragging through his disheveled hair, and my mouth would water. I'd recall his descriptions of orgasms one through six, and I'd cross my legs. *Tightly.* As soon as our time had been up, I'd lurched out of my seat, only to be leading him into my apartment now.

The space had never felt so small.

Or smelled so good. The air around him was rich with scents of leather and musk, his hair tousled from his motorcycle helmet. His attention was everywhere. On the walls, lingering on the motivational sayings I'd hung, examining my tidy recycling bin, the books organized by color above my desk. Probably judging the pillow at the head of my bed embroidered with the quote, *"All our dreams can come true if we have the courage to pursue them." ~ Walt Disney.*

Even under his scrutiny, dealing with him in my place was preferable to returning to where my supposed orgasms occurred.

I unpacked our groceries—wine, fruits, vegetables, spices—my hands busy, my heartbeat erratic, my eyes unable to meet his. That's how it had been since our little acting scene.

I'd never been a drama geek. Standing on stage in front of people resulted in hot flashes, cold sweats, and more words forgotten than remembered. Even earlier, popping a champagne cork, something I'd done numerous times (Ainsley liked her mimosas), had me all thumbs. Because I'd had an audience. Not so with Sophia. For a spell, when Jimmy first spotted her, he'd turned ashen, devastation in the hollow below his eyes. A need to ease his pain had possessed me, and I deserved an Academy Award for my performance: Best Actress in an Awkward Grocery Store Scene.

Problem was, I was having trouble shaking the role.

He tossed his jacket on a stool and whistled at my wine fridge, appreciation in the extended note. "Nice collection."

"Thanks." I didn't glance up, didn't know what to do with the sight of him in my ordered apartment, all that danger and chaos tied into a delicious package. One I hungered to consume. I washed the fruit and put the blackberries in a bowl, the green pepper on a plate. I lined up the black peppercorns and star anise and chocolate, keeping occupied.

When I wiped the counter for a third time, he gripped my wrist. "Rachel."

God, his touch. I closed my eyes and exhaled.

"I'm sorry," he said. "Last time, at the end of the Pinot Noir tasting, I was a dick."

"You were." The apology diluted the tension between us, an acknowledgment I needed to hear. Still, I kept my focus on a small bruise on the green pepper. "Do I get an explanation?"

"When you look at me, you will."

So darn bossy.

He was on the opposite side of the island, his strong fingers circling my wrist, and I allowed myself a *glance*. A closer perusal of his ink. Tattoos began above his leather cuff, a swirling mass of ivy and swooping shapes in black and gray. The lines curled around a goblet on his forearm, a horned goat bleating on the inside of his bicep, a prowling panther clawing up from the outside of his elbow. Its head was hidden by the frayed edge of his gray T-shirt, the same one he'd worn the first day of the contest. It read *Dare Me*.

Boy, did I want to dare him. Beg him to leap over the counter and rip open my blouse. To prove he could undo me with nothing but his tongue. Dare him to make me scream.

Instead I said, "I'm looking."

His thumb moved to my pulse point, pressing gently. "That you are." He held us together like that, our eyes searching, his thumb eavesdropping on my restless heart.

Then he released me and slung his leg over the counter stool. "My family owns a winery in the valley, and my father decided to retire—travel and spend time with my mom—which meant passing the business to me and my younger brother, Dimitri." He scrubbed his hands down his unshaven cheeks. "Except my father and I had a falling out, and I was cut off. Everything went to Dimitri. I haven't spoken to my family in almost two years, haven't sipped a drop of our—*their* wine since then."

He spoke evenly, but the usual gravel in his voice roughened. The gray in his blue eyes darkened.

"Until the blind tasting?" I asked. "The fifth glass of Pinot Noir?"

"It was the first time I'd tasted the wine in two years."

I thought back to the exercise. *Offshoot Winery*. It was an impressive operation, large scale. If I had the chance to run a place like that, I'd plaster myself to the helm and never let go. The revelation also meant Gwen's intel the night the girls had coaxed me into The Blue Door was accurate. Her sales pitch had involved the bartender's approval—the fact that he'd vouched for Jimmy and said Bad Boy came from a good family who owned a winery *or something*. When flirting around our bet that night, I first asked Jimmy to wager a vineyard. He'd laughed off my joke, and I'd assumed Cameron's information was more "or something" than fact. Apparently I was wrong.

"That's why you shut down," I said, more pieces of Jimmy fitting into place. "I'm sorry. It must have been a shock."

"It was, and that makes two unwelcome surprises in a week, one of which you helped me face, so don't apologize. My only regret is how I treated you." He picked up my corkscrew and flipped it between his fingers.

"Inhaling your bike exhaust as you peeled off *was* unpleasant." As was the hurt that lingered.

The corkscrew froze mid-flip. He frowned. "I was an asshole and it won't happen again. I'd like to pick up where we left off."

Fifty percent bad boy, fifty percent smooth talker. "The part where I outperform you in the contest?"

A smirk eclipsed his scowl. He placed the corkscrew down, pushed to his feet, and prowled around the counter. My apartment was nothing but a uniform square. Kitchen, countertop, and stools in one corner, a king bed with my Ikea closet behind the headboard opposite; across were a couch, coffee table, and TV, my desk and book shelves finishing off the geometric shape. It was ordered. Precise. It was everything I tried to emulate, the details never quite in my grasp.

Jimmy threw it all askew.

Each *thunk* of his boots echoed in my belly. I gripped the edge of the sink, the cool stainless steel a contrast to the heat building below my ribs. He stopped at my back, a whisper of his body brushing mine. "I prefer the part where you wanted to perform a scientific study with my head between your legs."

His voice deepened, more gravel invading his tone, and my knuckles whitened on the counter. Need pulsed through me. I could have leaned back, just a millimeter, until the hard planes of his body pressed to mine, but I had a sneaking suspicion a simple touch wouldn't be enough.

Our one wild night wasn't my modus operandi. I was a relationship girl, mornings cuddling in bed and dinners out what I craved. Jimmy was trouble, and I was desperately attracted to him, in an unfamiliar way. Animalistic, almost. Every time he raked his hair—untidy waves that hung shaggy over his forehead, cresting the tips of his ears, brushing the base of his neck—I wanted to grip the dark strands and pull his head between my thighs, find out if he was all talk, once and for all. Or sit on his face. Either would work.

But playing girlfriend to make his ex jealous had changed things. As did learning about his past. A woman he loved enough to marry, gone. A family lost. His future career pulled from him. Ferment those ingredients together and you'd get vinegar, not wine. Something told me he was more fruit than acid, and one sip would lead to two, until tasting wouldn't be enough. I would end up wanting more. *Relationship* more. Nothing about him fit into my world.

"I'm not sure about that particular study," I said. "I've heard the side effects can be hazardous. Let's stick to our deal. I helped with Sophia, now you help with my tasting."

He hovered at my back, his hot breath caressing my hair. Then he stepped away. "Tasting it is."

We set up on my couch, and I stuffed a pillow between us, the lilac silk comical next to his roughness. But I needed space. He was here for one reason and one reason only: to help me pass our next test. Since I'd botched most of the service exercises, the tastings were my clincher. If I messed those up, I'd be back at my computer, searching for jobs, having to explain my umpteenth failure to my family. Thanks, but no thanks.

I sat with my back straight and legs crossed. Jimmy draped himself over my gray couch, his long legs sprawled apart. He tossed his arm behind me, resting his hand precariously close to my neck. It reminded me of The Blue Door, how he'd distracted me from my tasting. Come to think of it, maybe he was undermining me again. Using his manly wiles to mess with my game. "Is this a ploy?"

"Yes." He didn't miss a beat.

"Seriously?"

"Did you want me to lie?"

"But we have a deal."

"I'm holding up my end, Sunshine."

That nickname vacillated between sweet and claw-his-eyes-out, this particular rendition landing on vexing. "So you expect me to do a tasting with you when you've admitted you plan to feed me false information."

"I have planned no such thing."

"You just *said* it's a ploy."

"Because it is. To make you reconsider joining me for your scientific study." The Pot Stirrer ran a finger through my hair, the edge of his nail dragging behind my ear. Goose bumps erupted in its wake.

I smacked his hand away. "Fat chance." But one more second of his fingers stroking my hair could work in his favor. The bastard knew it. "Can you stop with the games for a moment and answer something for me?"

"Anything."

That was quite the window of opportunity. Instead of asking my intended question—why help me when we were competing against each other—I opted for one of more value. "What happened with Sophia? I barely know you, but she doesn't seem like your type."

Not that I did, either. Sophia reminded me of Ainsley, primped and polished to perfection, curves for miles. A hint of jealousy had burned at the sight of her, but I'd squashed that nonsense. Jimmy wasn't mine. But Sophia was one step from posing for *Vogue*, and I was a J. Crew catalogue in the making. Then there was Jimmy and his bad, *bad* self. None of it fit.

He pushed a hand up the back of his hair. "Sophia and I

dated for two years. I looked a lot different then, more like the cardboard cutouts in the contest."

No freaking way. "Was your hair short?"

"Yep."

"Did you have tattoos?"

"Nope." He popped the P at the end and winked.

The man was lethal. "I am intrigued."

"Let's just say it took some shitty things for me to figure out who I really was, and for me to figure out who *Sophia* was. When I lost the winery and my shiny future, she hitched a ride on someone else's train."

"Jesus." My heart squeezed, an urge to touch him and show my empathy surging, but his lips tightened into a stern line, like they had after he'd tasted his family's wine. I folded my hands on my lap instead, silence blanketing us. Seeing Sophia today must have been more painful than I'd realized.

Blowing out a breath, he leaned forward, elbows on his knees. His T-shirt rode up his back, and his black boxers peeked out. I wanted to peek *in*. Push his shirt up and pull his jeans down and grip the length of him, experience everything I'd lost to the haze of alcohol. Touch more, see more, *know* more. Ask what happened with his father and curl into his side, voices whispered as we shared our secrets.

My father would likely be unimpressed with this scenario.

I'd never erased his last voice message and would never forget our final fight. As hard as my father had worked to provide for us, my mother had worked *harder* to fit in with the country-club crowd. Tired of her incessant phone calls and insistence I date certain guys or wear "the right" clothes, I'd hitched a ride on Gabe's motorcycle, staking my independence. I was twenty-two and my mother still forbade me from bringing Gabe's tattooed, blued-haired self to a fundraiser.

My reply: "Then I'm not coming, either."

She didn't speak with me for weeks afterward, the whole thing culminating in a fight between my father and me.

I still played his follow-up voicemail from time to time. I'd let his apologetic words seep into my dark corners, filling me with memories and sadness…and happiness, too. *Men like Gabe don't stick around,* my father had said. *Boys like that are trouble. You are smart and talented and will be a success, and I don't want anything to stand in your way.* Then, *But I'm sorry* and *I love you* and *We'll chat soon.*

A chat that never happened, but Gabe had proven my father right. He dumped me via text shortly afterward, saying things were too complicated for him.

My texted reply: *Sorry that my dad died. Must be hard for you.*

If my father were still alive, would he offer similar advice? Warn me Jimmy had been through the wringer with his family and wasn't capable of love. That I'd fall for him only to get hurt. That he and his tattoos and motorcycle were nothing but trouble. My feelings for Gabe hadn't been born of love or lust. Seeing him had been me thumbing the system. Giving in to my attraction to Jimmy as an adult was a different animal. A primal beast, curious and hungry. But my father's last words swarmed my mind. Unable to clear my head, I let our silence linger.

That's when Jimmy's inquisition started.

CHAPTER 9

JIMMY

"You've met my ex and know I'm single, but I've seen you checking your cell plenty. Is there a man I should be aware of?" I patted the pillow she'd placed between us. "A reason you're keeping your distance?" I'd done enough sharing for one day. Never wanted to think about Sophia and her betrayal again. Time to unravel more of Rachel.

She smiled tentatively. "Are you jealous?"

"Yes."

She sucked in a breath at my honesty.

As soon as I'd acknowledged my deeper interest in Rachel to myself, the games stopped. I wanted her. Not just another night between the sheets (and on the floor and against the wall). I wanted a glimpse of that adoring look she'd leveled on me in the store, to stand together, her hand in my back pocket, my fingers in her hair, knowing she was mine. See if I could trust a woman again.

As a kid, I'd dreamed of being a professional soccer player.

I'd watch every major league match, imagining my father cheering me on. Determined to earn a spot on the coveted CRL —California Regional League—I'd played soccer day and night. My mother would have to drag me inside to go to bed. I'd stopped hanging with my friends. I'd made it, though. Played a few strong years, until girls and wine became more important.

My father only ever came to one game.

I figured it out then. My father may have withheld his affection, but if I wanted something tangible, lack of determination was my only roadblock. I aced my viticulture degree, traveled Europe to immerse myself in wines until I'd earned my Master Sommelier.

I planned to put as much effort into winning Rachel.

She dragged the first glass of Cabernet Sauvignon to the edge of the table, giving it a swirl. She brought it to her nose and inhaled. Instead of listing the aromas opening up, she said, "I don't have a boyfriend. I've been single for close to a year. The incessant cell noise is my mother. She's on the overprotective side."

I'd figured there was no other man, but it was nice to hear it. "You two are close?"

"She drives me insane at times, thinks every person she knows is a minute from catching an airborne disease, but I love her. You should have seen her at my high school art shows, telling anyone who'd listen I was her daughter, and wasn't I the most talented kid? Which was often followed by my childhood finger painting prowess, and the story about me and a naked Aaron Waxon covered in phthalo green."

"Sounds sweet." As was the way Rachel glowed, her memories lighting her from within.

"More like mortifying, but she always means well. My brother can be an ass, too, but we're close."

"Younger or older?"

"Physically, he's two years younger. He's twenty-five. Life-wise...definitely older."

Her voice thinned, insecurity in the hunch of her shoulders. She may be an adult, living on her own, but her self-worth was still tied to her family. Something I'd been well acquainted with until I shed that baggage. "What's wrong with your life?"

She replaced her glass on the table, untouched, and fell back onto the sofa. "I've held an obscene number of jobs since college. I can't figure out what to do with my life, like I'm in one of those movies where I'm left floating in space and can't find my way back to Earth."

That would explain her quotes on the wall, the searching. She was a fine wine, developing, exploring her depth. I wanted to help uncork her. "What was the worst one?"

"Worst one what?"

"Worst job? If you've had that many, some must have been painful."

She covered her face with her hands, like hiding would ease her embarrassment. "You have no idea."

"Let's hear it. I'd love to know the levels to which you've sunk."

She stole a glance between her fingers. "When you say it like that, how can I resist?"

I removed her pillow barrier from between us and scooted closer. "I'm dying of curiosity."

She didn't pull away, didn't shove that flimsy divider back between us. She uncovered her face and twisted toward me. "Okay, so, I don't even know why I'm telling you, but I saw a classified ad that read 'Must love animals.' Next thing I knew, I was on the street in a poodle costume, waving a *Doggy Wash* sign."

My grin stretched so wide my cheeks hurt, and Rachel covered her mouth, attempting to hold in her laughter. It escaped anyway, a snicker that rolled into a sharp cackle.

"The worst," she said, dabbing at her eyes, "was my brother. He happened to drive by and see me, and he's never let me live it down."

A full-on snort followed, her head tipping forward as she gripped my thigh. Her whole body shook, and she nearly fell right into me. I lost it, too, everything about Rachel's silly humor infectious. That ridiculous sound. Her willingness to embarrass herself. The way she could flip from sultry to fun to feisty on a dime.

When we'd taken the ass photo, she'd laughed even harder. She would try to pose, then she'd tip over on her side, slapping the floor and cracking up. I'd have to walk around, my abs aching, my throat dry from laughing so damn much. When we finally nailed it, she shuffled toward me on her knees and kissed me while smiling, branding me with her joy. I'd never kissed a woman like that—both of us grinning, small laughs tumbling against each other's tongues.

Rachel was one of a kind.

She was also lost.

When our breathing regulated, we slouched into the couch, side by side, the edges of our hands touching. "You know what I find infinitely interesting about you, Ray?"

Her fingers twitched, a spark sent from the back of her hand to mine. "What?" she whispered.

"You have this wild innocence about you, on the surface. Looks like you work hard to keep your apartment neat. Keep things in order. You're sexy as hell in everything you wear, but your outfits seem calculated. It reminds me of how I used to be, trying to fit into a certain mold. The girl I met that first night was wild, and I'd bet there's more of her in you than you'd like to admit."

She snatched her hand away and clutched her thigh, avoiding our touch. "I don't think my psychological assessment figured into our deal."

I knocked my boot against the gray coffee table. Clean lines. Compact. Probably Ikea. "Am I wrong?"

She settled heavier into the cushion, her body no longer rigid. "I don't know."

"Trust me, I do. I'm older and wiser and speak from experience." I pushed my palm under hers and clasped our fingers, bringing her knuckles to my mouth for a soft kiss. "I *see* you, Sunshine. Now what do you say we rock this tasting?"

I sat up, pulling her with me, the warmth between our palms snapping across my skin. Until we both let go. She kicked off her heels and crossed her ankles. Her skirt rode up, exposing the curve of her knees. That stretch of smooth skin had my mind back on our first encounter and everything I wanted to see again.

"I'm ready," she said.

I leaned in, our noses an inch apart. "Ready…meaning I can flip you over and eat your pussy now?"

Her cheeks burned the color of our Cabernet. "Incorrigible."

"Honest."

"Stick to the tasting."

"That's what I'm trying to do." I zeroed in on her prim thighs, pressed so tightly together. Her denial of our pull only incited my craving. That was fine. She was worth the effort.

With two fingers on my chin, she flicked my attention away. We turned our focus to our wine tasting, but the barrier between us had lifted, truths shared clearing the way.

We swirled the glasses and listed the scents opening, inhaling the aroma of a crushed blackberry, then repeating the exercise, comparing notes. I pushed her to close her eyes and bite the green pepper, chew its tough skin, describe the layers of taste from bright to vegetal to bitter. The exercise was a decent one, but mostly I loved watching her jaw work, her tongue darting out to wet her lips, her soft hum as she sifted through the flavors. The moment it clicked, when she linked that vegetable to the aroma in her glass, she grabbed my knee and squealed.

It sent my pulse thundering.

I had a rip in the knee of my jeans, and her thumb dipped inside. I placed my hand over hers to still her movements. One brush, and I was ready to tug her on my lap and explore the dirty side she kept locked up.

She slipped her hand away. "I've done classes, spent hours at my father's tastings, but Cabs were always elusive. It clicked tonight. So thank you."

I shrugged. "Told you I'd uphold my end of the bargain. And that's nice—that you and your father share wine." No matter my effort, mine was always too busy building his business to enjoy a glass with me.

"*Shared*," she said, her downturned eyes as sad as her voice. "He died five years ago."

The admission sunk an anchor through my chest, taking my heart with it.

Unable to keep my distance, I threaded my hand into her hair and dipped my head to her level. "I'm sorry."

There wasn't much else to say. No words eased the blow loss dealt. I'd loved my mother's father more than my own, and when my *pappous* had passed, I'd hid in the vineyard for hours, picking unripe grapes from the vines and crushing them with my fists. He'd kicked a soccer ball with me, had taken me by the hand and told me tales of the Greek gods as we'd walked our land. Hopefully Rachel saw understanding in my eyes.

She leaned into my hand. "The more time I spend with wine, the closer I feel to him. He loved it."

The more time I spent with wine, the farther I felt from my family. But I was glad for her.

We stood, our tasting and time over. I offered to help clean up, but she waved me off, an end to our night.

I grabbed my jacket and paused at the door. "Give me your number."

"Shouldn't you ask, not demand?"

"If you remembered our night together, you'd know I'm more of the demanding sort." I couldn't resist another glimpse of her indignation.

It didn't come. "How demanding?" Her voice purred with curiosity.

I stepped closer. "Very."

Her eyes lit up, a breathy sigh escaping her lips. "I wouldn't remember."

"But you want to know, don't you?"

She inched backward, until she hit her hallway wall. "Yes, but..."

"What's stopping you, Ray? Because this quote..." I gestured to the one above her head: *Aim for the moon. If you miss, you may hit a star. ~ W. Clement Stone.* "How do you know I'm not that star? I'm burning pretty hot for you. What's to say I'm not the thing you've been missing?"

There was little space between us—me hovering over her, her head tilted to search my face, determine my worth. She flattened her palms on my stomach and my abs tightened. If this was her keeping me away, it was having the opposite effect. But hesitation rippled from her.

I pressed closer, my lips a breath from hers. "I think I scare you. I think you can't imagine yourself with me, or me in the life you've pictured, and you think I'm after a quick fuck. You'd be wrong on all accounts. Life is what you make it, and I can find a thousand quotes to hang on your walls to that effect. But it only falls into place if you honor who you are. I'm more comfortable in a dive bar than a yacht club. I get off on body art and speeding on my Harley. I'd also wager having you on the back, gripping me with your thighs and clutching my chest would kick the experience up a notch. I want to spend time with you, not just prove I can make you come with my tongue. Although I want that, too."

Riled up and high on her scent, I brushed my lips against hers. Just a tease. She whimpered and eased her lips open, a small distance, enough for me to swipe my tongue along her bottom lip, stealing the tiniest taste. I pulled back, but her eyes remained closed.

"What's going to happen now," I said, my voice deeper than I'd ever heard it, "is I'm going to give you my number, and when you think you're ready, you're going to call. Until then, I'd prefer if you don't ignore me when we're at Crush."

Her iPhone was the same model and color as mine. I grabbed it from her hall table and tapped her screen. No lock in place. I entered my details, smirking as I chose a name for my listing. She blinked at me the whole while, lost in a haze. I was having trouble functioning, too, that tiny bit of contact jumbling my senses. All but one.

Desire.

She'd call me. Of that I was sure. Question was when, and if I could wait that long.

"Until next time," I said, and she bit her lip.

As I turned, she said, "I've never met anyone like you. You have me all twisted up."

Jesus.

I glanced back, and my heart gave a kick. It was like we were back in the grocery store, her eyes full of nothing but me. She may have been twisted, but the need in her voice had me contorted in knots. "When you're ready, I'll untie you. We're not in a rush."

The intense moment lingered, agonizing seconds filled with scorching heat as we stared at each other. I was a heartbeat from pinning her back against that wall.

Instead I left. It would take a long, fast ride to subdue a fraction of my sexual frustration. But it was more than that. The urge to lock us in her apartment for a week, wine tasted and stories shared, was potent. The past two years had been nothing but time to stew while I excavated the edges of who I really was. Rachel made me laugh and challenged my wine knowledge, a gift for the time I'd endured. Like walking into Vesper had been fate.

I still had no clue what led me to the club that night, but fuck if I cared. I had Rachel now, even if she didn't realize it yet.

As I reached my bike, my cell rang. Maybe I wouldn't have to wait long, after all. But I frowned at the screen. *Alena*

Giannopoulos. My mother's name had lit my phone often lately, a barrage of appeals I'd ignored. I did the same again.

Growing up, my mother would cook mountains of food for family gatherings. She'd tut over our cuts and sprains, always going out of her way to praise my accomplishments. She also worried over my father's heavy-handed ways, but never interfered. Not even when he gave me the ultimatum to break things off with Sophia or lose the winery. Not even when he followed through, and I lost both. My mother's meek acceptance of his authority hurt worse than his betrayal.

They could all go to hell—them and their lies tainting our family wine and my grandfather's legacy. The only call I planned on answering was from Rachel, a woman who spoke truth and offered innocence and oozed the promise of sin. Until then, I'd live off the meager taste I'd stolen.

CHAPTER 10

RACHEL

ONE OF THE benefits of working reception at my gym was the free membership. It meant I could work out *gratis*, often with Ainsley and Gwen. Today my shift ended later than usual, which meant the girls had come and gone, and I had to squeeze in cardio before I met them for drinks—more like me begging for the outing and them agreeing.

My motto since Thursday night had been to keep on the move, socialize as much as possible, all systems *go, go, go.*

The girls and I didn't normally do Sunday nights out, but keeping occupied was my prime directive. Bad Boy's number had been burning a hole in my phone since he'd entered it three nights ago. That entire encounter had been a disaster. I'd stood there, useless, while his lips touched mine, his tongue teasing a seductive line, his ballsy predictions whispered in my ear. When I'd pulled up his number and saw what he'd written as his name, I unleashed my famous cackle.

Six. The guy had some nerve.

I'd scheduled every minute since then—bird watching, buying M&Ms and separating them by color, framing and hanging a new quote.

"The question isn't who's going to let me; it's who is going to stop me." ~ Ayn Rand.

All endeavors helped force that phone number to the back of my mind. Briefly. I was on the treadmill now, vision hazy, once again fantasizing about Jimmy.

Us on the floor.

My mouth around his cock.

His scruff dragging across my thighs.

I upped my treadmill speed, but I couldn't chase away the sexual desire Jimmy had awakened. To my right, a guy—Matt, I think—hopped on the treadmill. He nodded my way, and I forced an answering smile. He was blond and fit, his suctioned tank top accentuating the work he'd put into his body. His clean-cut image and golden boy smile should have had my pulse buzzing. Except his skin was too plain, his hair too coiffed.

He wasn't *Six*. I ran harder.

As I neared my last five minutes, an older man stepped on the treadmill to my left. I'd met him recently, the grumbly sort who was forced to exercise for his health. When I'd asked him to fill out a new member questionnaire, he'd scanned the sheet, mustache twitching. His bushy eyebrows had framed his scowl.

"Emergency contact," he'd muttered, his words thick with disdain. "A ridiculous question." He'd scrawled his answers and shoved the page back to me, nothing on it legible.

Except for his emergency contact person: 911.

911 scowled at his treadmill, jabbing at buttons, curses garbled under his breath. My father had run marathons, trained indoors and out. He'd worked his heart like a maestro. It wasn't enough, but his time at the gym had prolonged his life, and any extra days with him were a bonus. At this man's age, it was even more important.

I slowed my treadmill to a fast walk, grabbing my towel to

swipe at my chest and neck. Breathing easier, I hit stop and faced 911. "Can I help you, sir?"

He ground his teeth, as though chewing leather. "The machine is broken."

I may not have been an electrical engineer (although I *had* sold lamps during my interior decorator phase), but the light displays were working fine, all necessary buttons aglow. Broken, the machine was not. The man reminded me of my grandfather, though, preferring to drive in circles rather than ask for directions. Tact would be needed.

I slung my towel over my shoulder. "Let me see what I can do."

I jumped to the floor, followed the mess of wires, found his, unplugged it, then plugged it back in. Electrical engineer genius. I stood and dusted my hands together. "Let's give it a shot now."

Leaning over him, I hit the Start button…and the platform moved, *of course*. He grumbled, lifting his feet like the time I'd forced my mother's schnoodle Stanley into doggy boots. The man was uncomfortable. Gyms, with their electronic equipment, weren't exactly senior friendly. But heart health was important. If I'd waltzed over and pressed the one button he couldn't find, 911 could have gotten frustrated and left.

I leaned over his dashboard. "These arrows control speed. Click up to go faster and down to go slower. These arrows"—I dragged my index finger to the incline—"tilt the base up, like walking up a hill. I'm Rachel, by the way."

His reply: "I am not a child."

That he was not. His sour expression had been excavated with age, the creases around his mouth sinking underground, his nose and chin pushed prominent. A face that had endured. "Just trying to explain the treadmill," I said.

"As though I am a child."

A child in need of a time out. "Anyway, I suggest you stick to a flat incline and speed up gradually. Next time, I can show you the programs."

"I can do it myself."

A time out *and* no dessert. "Don't push me, old man. An attitude like that will land you in detention."

With a harrumph, he ignored my teasing, and I patted his frail shoulder.

I hurried home and showered, in a daze the whole while. Because *Six, Six, Six.* I nearly dialed him three times, until I pulled up my father's message and let his soothing tone tamp the urge. It also heightened my confusion. Hopefully drinks with Ainsley and Gwen would offer more distraction.

———

Drinks with Ainsley and Gwen were *not* a distraction. The first words out of Ainsley's mouth when we sat down were, "Did my advice work? Did you tell Lone Wolf he was a shitty lay?"

Gwen frowned. "I thought she didn't remember the sexcapade?"

"She doesn't, but he's in the wine contest with her, getting all flirty."

Gwen leaned back in her seat. "I'd forget my dating sabbatical if it meant tapping that."

Ainsley fanned her face dramatically. "Tell me about it. She's nuts."

"You guys know I'm at the table, right?"

They grinned.

Ainsley clicked her French-manicured nails against her wineglass. "So, spill it. How did he take your brush off?"

I drummed my thumb on my thigh. I stretched my neck. I wiped an invisible crumb off the table. "It's busy here for a Sunday, don't you think?"

"Oh." Gwen rubbed her hands together. "This is gonna be good." She plunked her elbows on the table, chin in hand. "Open the vault, Rachel. We need details."

And I needed to dampen my Jimmy infatuation. This club

was more casual than Vesper, with small groups gathered at wooden tables, white-washed brick walls surrounding us. But I couldn't help imagining him here. I was in the same tight jeans and heels I'd worn the fateful night I'd met him, but my fitted black blouse didn't have a dip in the back. There was no place for Jimmy to lay his hand if he were here, ready to buy me a drink.

If he appeared, would I say yes this time?

I rolled the edge of my cocktail napkin through my fingers. "I *may* have flirted with him and helped him deal with a sticky situation with his ex, and he *may* have come over to my place to taste wine afterward. He also may have kissed me and asked me to go out with him."

Ainsley pursed her lips. "Sounds very hypothetical."

Gwen wasn't impressed, either. She shifted on her seat and tousled her bobbed hair, while staring me down. "Sounds like we need to order you more drinks to loosen your tongue."

I pressed my hand over the top of my glass. "No more wine. Excessive wine leads to poor choices." I'd for sure drunk dial Bad Boy.

"Okay," Gwen said, "but this 'might have kissed' crap won't fly. Is he as good as he looks? Assuming you *remember* this time."

Did I ever. The promise of his lips. The bite of his scruff on my cheek. "If I'd actually kissed him back, I imagine it would have been unreal."

Ainsley crossed her arms, her ample cleavage spilling forth. A group of three men looked our way, but she was focused on me, intent on dredging up every agonizing detail. "This game of twenty questions is getting tiresome. I'd like specifics before our next birthday."

My phone rang, saving me from their inquisition. I pulled it from my purse, only to be faced with my mother's name. Still preferable to dissecting my boy drama.

I exhaled and answered. "I'm out with friends, Ma."

"This won't take long. You remember Jonathan Richter, Joanna's son?"

Again with the setups. "Yes, I remember Jonathan." I'd last seen him three years ago at a housewarming party. He'd cornered me for an hour, his foul breath nearly melting my mascara.

"Well, he just moved back to town and is opening his own dental practice. Running the whole thing. He even has a play-room for kids and TV screens for patients. Very new age. I ran into him and asked him over for dinner next week."

"Ran into" was code for "stalked the man to his place of work." The woman had no shame. And, *God*, I hated how desperate she made me look, even to a man I had no interest in dating.

Ainsley mouthed, *Blind date?*

I nodded and whispered, "*Jonathan Halitosis Richter.*"

She proceeded to fake choke herself, complete with bugging eyes and extended tongue. Gwen jumped in on the game, sticking her finger down her throat and pretending to dry heave.

I giggled. "That's nice of you, Ma, but I'm not interested in Jonathan." If he still looked the same, his stiff posture, parted brown hair, and tweed vest would fit right in with my mother's crown moldings and opulent carpets. A chess piece carved to match.

I imagined Jimmy in her immaculate living room. Tattoos. Wild hair. *Dare Me* shirt. His toned body draped over a Queen Anne chair.

My mother would faint at the sight.

"I can't cancel, Rachel." Her exasperated tone grated my eardrum.

"Then I hope you have a nice dinner. Invite Mitchell. They were friends in high school." Dating Jonathan Halitosis Richter would be so much easier than falling for Bad Boy, but I was done with her random set-ups.

When I managed to end the call, Ainsley grabbed my cell and placed it on the table. "As fun as that was to watch, let's get back to the kiss that didn't happen. Explain yourself."

From one ambush to another. My phone lay on the table, Jimmy's number tucked inside. The number I'd like to sneak away and call right now. I had it memorized. I'd hummed the digits in time to Michael Jackson's "Bad" all freaking day.

"Here's the deal," I said. "I was close to caving in and hooking up again, but I've gotten to know Jimmy since, and truth is…I like the guy. Like, *really* like him. And he's talking about more than a fling. I just don't see how we could work."

Gwen stayed silent, assessing me.

Ainsley wasn't so subtle. "So you're, like, into him, but you won't go out again? You've dated umpteen guys, always upset when the sparks don't fly. What am I missing? And if you go out with Jonathan Halitosis Richter, I will unfriend you."

"*That* you don't have to worry about."

Gwen's vigil ended. "She's terrified of her mother and can't picture Jimmy and his tattoos in her tidy life."

Damn her observant self. "Something like that."

At twenty-two, I'd have reveled in taking Jimmy to one of my mother's luncheons, watching her face turn purple at the sight of him. At twenty-seven, I wasn't so sure. That very thing had pushed my mother and me apart once, an outcome that would devastate me today. No matter her overbearing tendencies, she was my last living parent. I needed her in my life.

Gwen's dissection of my psychological behavior didn't end there. "Is the Gabe Factor an issue, too?"

Ainsley's blue eyes narrowed, as though she'd caught her stylist applying the wrong highlights. "I still say we should have painted his motorcycle pink."

I hadn't accepted that particular offer, but the three of us never hesitated to volunteer our payback services. When Ainsley had confessed that her ex had cheated on her, Gwen and I had filled his door lock with expanding foam.

"Aside from the rough-and-tumble thing," I said, "Jimmy isn't like Gabe. He has baggage, though—an ex and some family drama that really messed him up. So it's a lot, I guess. He's hot as hell and we have fun, and he has this lost-puppy vibe that's hard to resist, but simple relationships are hard enough. Add in all this other...*stuff*, and it just seems too hard." My father's saved message added weight to my turmoil. More complications tangling my mind.

Gwen didn't blink. "Dating him doesn't mean you have to marry the guy. I get that you're after something serious, but maybe you need to let loose for a change. You've spent the last five years keeping your mother happy. Never stepping out of line. Gabe was a dick, but dating him was you testing yourself. When you drink, and your inhibitions unwind, a different Rachel comes out to play. I think she's more the real you than you'd like to admit."

"Do I have to pay for this shrink session now, or can I trade it for wine later?" I could joke all I wanted, but the blunt truth stung, as it had when Jimmy had suggested something similar.

Had my life deteriorated to such an extent? Leapt out of my control? I'd raise hell to see my mother happy and healthy, as well as keep us on good terms. Was losing myself in the process worth it? If I wasn't careful, I'd wind up as her shadow—big brooches, bigger shoulder pads, football-helmet hair.

My plethora of jobs had been desperate attempts to tap into the elusive something that made me tick. But I'd always come up short. Even now, with the sommelier possibility, doubt crept in. I wasn't just good at the contest tastings, I was *great*. Not so with the service exercises. Each loathsome task massaged my insecurities. The whole point of quitting and starting over was to find *The Job*. The one that would fulfill my resolution by following my dreams, so I could discover if the blackout that night had really been magical and would catapult the rest of my life from fine to sublime.

As much as I loved the tastings, executing a busy night at

Crush and running between tables didn't sound sublime. It didn't sound like *The Job*.

But I was too far in, my options too limited.

My wardrobe didn't appeal to me, either. It was necessity, function over form. Even Jimmy had called me on it. *You look sexy as hell in everything you wear*, he'd said. *But your outfits seem calculated.*

He'd also said I'd been wild the night we hooked up.

The more I replayed his words, the more curious I became, longing building in a steady rise. Jimmy could be my ticket. He could help me explore myself, push my boundaries. I just didn't know if I could offer him more. "*If* I call him, what would I even say?"

Gwen picked at a callus on her palm. "Set some ground rules. Tell him you'd like to hang out, but you don't want anything serious. No guy on the planet would say no to that. Then figure things out as you go. No pressure."

"I don't know…" But my body did. Anticipation tightened my lower belly, heat gathering. Still, I didn't make a move.

Ainsley, however, did. She snatched my phone from the table.

I shoved my upturned palm in her face. "Give it here, Ainsley. I'll call him when I'm ready."

"I'm staging an intervention and calling now. And if you don't want people going through your phone, you should lock the thing." She squinted at the screen. "You did say his name was Jimmy, right? Because it's not here."

Things just kept getting better. "He used a different name."

She twitched her button nose. "What name?"

Why, why, why did he have to be so persistent, programming *Six* and toying with my mind? I could tackle Ainsley and reclaim my phone, or feign ignorance, but she had on her "don't mess with me" face. I wouldn't win this battle.

"Six," I said.

"Six?"

"Yes. Six."

"Like the number?"

"Exactly like the number."

Gwen plucked the phone from Ainsley, the two of them intent on cracking Jimmy's code. "Is he like a divergent? Like Four? What's with the number?"

Lying and diverting their attention tempted me again, but they'd caught the scent of juicy gossip, the hint of my drama like tossing a live chicken to wolves. "He claims he made me orgasm six times."

Gwen sipped the last of her wine, placed the glass down, and slid it aside. "Honestly, the fact that you don't remember that night is a travesty. We need to remedy this situation." She raised my phone, but hesitated. "Does that mean you came from oral?"

If there was a God. "Supposedly, and give me my phone. I'll text him."

"Damn," was all she said, and handed it over

I could back down, stash my cell and make a break for it, but these two hound dogs were out for blood. And fighting the urge to see Jimmy again was a losing battle.

My text was short and sweet: *Are you around?*

His reply came quickly: *At work. Get off in an hour. You should come by.*

I chewed my cheek and flexed my toes, then I wrote: *Sure.*

Time to discover the woman I was meant to be. Once he sent the address, I stuffed my phone away and faced the girls. "I'm meeting him at work."

Ainsley clapped. "Excellent. When should we leave?"

Come again? "I must have heard you wrong, because it sounded like you said *we*."

Her bright eyes shone with glee. "If we leave this in your court, you might chicken out and do your overthinking thing. I also think we should suss him out. Make sure he's not messing with you before another round of Naked Twister goes down."

On that note, I stumbled after them, unsure how I'd lost control of the night.

CHAPTER 11

JIMMY

The bar was winding down, Sundays never busy. I kept glancing at the entrance, waiting for Rachel to show, unsure what the hell to expect. Her messages were short. Nothing flirtatious. No mention of the name I'd programmed into her phone.

I shined a glass, then stared at the door. I stocked the beer fridge and snuck another glance.

Rudy's Tavern was more dive than bar, the wooden floors roughened by herds of work boots. The women drank as hard as the men, the pool tables home to soured bets and raised voices. Rock anthems played on repeat. Conservative Rachel would be quite the sight in here, sitting all proper on a wonky stool. A sight I'd happily drink in.

My phone buzzed, hopefully not her backing out. It wasn't, but seeing my mother's name was just as frustrating. A text this time. I'd deleted her emails, considered blocking her number. She could beg me to visit their new apartment all she liked, but I wasn't stepping within a mile of the place.

A few more customers left, only the diehards lingering. A crew from the neighborhood talked over one another as they finished their pints. Rick, the ironworker, was talking shit to Mel as she bussed tables, a tango they'd perfected. It usually ended with her flipping him the finger, and him begging for a date. She was thirty years his junior.

As I wiped down the bar, the front door swung wide. I straightened, fisting my towel and crossing my arms. No one entered. A few second passed, then a few more. I was about to stride over and poke my head outside, when Rachel stepped in. Her eyes darted from the classic rock albums on the wall to the ceiling fan that looked a minute from falling. She brushed at her jeans, tugged down the edge of her black top. Her brown hair fell loose around her shoulders, her freckles not as visible in the dim light. She was a vision.

A vision who wasn't alone.

Two escorts followed on her heels, flanking her like body-guards. I remembered her friends from the night we'd met, but hadn't paid them much attention. Not when Rachel was all I could see. The tall one with the shorter hair and bangs looked tough enough to take Cris Cyborg in a fight, her tank top showing off toned arms. Her face was all business as she studied the room. The other one had Rick's jaw hitting the floor. She was shorter, cleavage and curves for days. Mile-high heels. All she was missing was a Chihuahua tucked into her purse.

The tough woman took the lead, arms swinging as she headed for me. "Jimmy?"

"As I live and breathe."

She held out her hand, her expression stern as she waited on me. I tossed the towel and gave her hand a shake. She caught my fingers in a vise grip. "I'm Gwen, this is Ainsley, and you of course know Rachel. We thought it would be fun to get acquainted."

Looked more like an ambush.

Ainsley fluttered her fingers. Rachel was a fidgety mess. I

fanned a hand toward the bar stools, inviting them to sit. Better to face the firing squad head on.

Ainsley and Gwen sat in front of me, Rachel to the side, but as Gwen opened her mouth, Rick sauntered over and leaned on the bar, facing Ainsley. "My Malibu is parked outside. How about a ride, beautiful?"

Ainsley flipped him the bird. "How'd you like to ride this?"

He sighed. "I'm losing my charm." He plunked down his empty glass and dragged his sorry ass to the door.

"He's harmless," I said.

Ainsley cocked her head at me. "He's old enough to be my grandfather."

"He just likes to talk to the ladies. Makes him feel young."

"If I wanted to hear an asshole speak, I'd set up residence in the bathroom."

Chuckling, I leaned against the back counter and slid my attention to Rachel. "Having a nice night?"

"Peachy," she replied, her top button quivering with her shaky breaths.

I didn't know how the current situation had transpired, what had gone down for Gwen and Ainsley to show up at my work, too, but if it brought me a step closer to ripping off Rachel's clothes, I was all in.

Until Gwen said, "Are you a player?"

The gloves were off. "I don't gamble, if that's what you mean."

"You know what I mean." The woman didn't mince words.

I could have claimed I was too busy and spent the next forty-five minutes closing the bar, waiting them out. I could have asked to speak with Rachel alone, gotten to the bottom of the ambush. Those were both easy outs. But I'd been serious when I told Rachel I wanted more, and that came with the truth. "I've had a number of one-night stands, but the women I've been with always knew the score. So I'd go with no, I'm not a player."

The next shot came from Ainsley. "Do you have a girlfriend?"

I shook my head. "Single."

Then they alternated fire.

"Are you on any dating websites?"

"None."

"Has a woman ever slapped you?"

"Not that I recall."

"Have you ever hit a woman?"

"What the fuck kind of question is that? And the answer is *hell no*." I lowered my hands over my nuts just the same. These girls weren't messing around.

At least Rachel's friends cared. When Sophia had left me and my life imploded, my acquaintances had thinned, until none were left. They'd either tired of my sullen moods or weren't genuine. It made me more self-sufficient, a state of being I craved. Or used to, at least. I was glad for Rachel, though. Happy she had people in her corner.

The next shot came from her. "Have you ever shoplifted?"

Not the question I expected. "Once. A pair of sunglasses on a dare." That's what happened when sixteen-year-old boys had beer and too much time on their hands.

Rachel's third degree continued. "Do you do drugs?"

"Does getting high on you count?"

"Have you ever been in jail?"

"I'm in purgatory now, waiting on you."

Ainsley snickered. "I like this guy."

Rachel rolled her eyes.

It was time to start steering the conversation. I gripped the bar and leaned toward Gwen and Ainsley. "Why is Rachel fighting my advances?"

A smug smile slid across Gwen's face. "You're not exactly her type."

Finally, we were getting somewhere. "What is her type?"

Ainsley held up her hand and ticked each finger. "Smart.

Driven. Un-inked. Family man. Great job. She basically wants to date her dad."

Rachel waved from her seat. "Remember me? The girl you're gossiping about? I'm sitting right here."

I ignored her, the intel too juicy to quit. Not that Ainsley's descriptions surprised me. The way Rachel worked at life—her pens lined up, wardrobe appropriately conservative, careers tried and failed—she was forcing a square peg into a round hole. She needed to tap into whatever it was that drove her, fed her soul, or she'd chase her tail forever. Her "type" needed an over-haul, too. She'd reacted to me the other day, deeply. She just couldn't admit it.

I slid my forearm on the bar, angling my back to Rachel. "I am clearly not her dad. So how do you suggest I get her over to my place?"

Gwen's face lit up with amusement, then she studied me, narrowing her eyes as the moments passed. She opened her mouth to reply, but Rachel beat her to it. "I'm not after anything serious. If we hang out, you have to promise it's casual."

I spun to find her sitting taller, chin raised, confidence in her strong posture.

I'd pegged Rachel as a relationship girl, only dating to find Mr. Right. Either my instincts were off, or this was her testing the waters. Feeling me out before opening up. I still didn't know if I could trust a woman fully, not after Sophia. Giving someone your heart only to find out she'd been using you was a hard pill to swallow. Rachel didn't seem the type, but my character assess-ment had proven shitty once.

Still, I'd thought about her since Thursday, restlessly, imag-ining our kiss deepening, instead of her holding stiff. I'd stroked myself to the memories of our one wild night. I wanted to hear her ridiculous laugh, feel her thighs bracketing mine as we toured wine country on my bike. Sit with her under the sun, wine sipped, cheese nibbled, her hair tickling my neck.

I wanted *us*.

If that meant agreeing to a casual affair, so be it. The sex had been unreal, and once I jogged her memory and had her gripping my scalp and screaming my name, she'd have to admit our connection was deeper than a fling. If not, I'd at least get another taste.

I slapped the bar. "Done. We hang out, nothing serious, just two people having fun." I shifted toward Rachel, her lips within biting distance. "That good with you, Sunshine?"

She crossed her legs. She made me wait for it. Finally, she said, "Deal."

I grinned. "Excellent. Can I get you ladies anything for last call? Drinks are on me."

"Something colorful in a martini glass," Ainsley said.

"White wine," Gwen replied.

"Red?" I asked Rachel, and she nodded.

I fixed Ainsley a cosmo and poured a glass of white for Gwen. I chose our only decent Cabernet and slid it in front of Rachel. Her fingers brushed mine, and my thighs tensed, electricity passing between us. She held my stare, neither of us moving, both breathing fast, until duty called. But my mind was an hour ahead, to us groping each other, our clothing littering the floor. Damn, did I want her.

The regulars filtered out, leaving only Mel helping me close up and the girls chatting. Rachel nursed her wine, heated glances shot my way. I had half a mind to kick everyone out, lock the doors, and bend her over a table. I settled on teasing the little minx.

I approached her from behind, collecting the pretzel bowl beside her and bending toward her ear. "You're coming home with me tonight. I will undress you and lick your pussy and fuck you hard, and then you can decide if you want to sleep over or leave. But make no mistake, I will be inside you tonight."

I bit the bottom of her ear, and her answering moan sent my dick pressing against my zipper, eager for more. The next twenty minutes couldn't go fast enough.

CHAPTER 12

RACHEL

Jimmy had the dirtiest mouth I'd ever heard, and it turned me on. Like *whoa* turned me on. I didn't know dirty talk got me hot. Everything about him jacked up my temperature: the roughness of his ripped jeans, his tattoos, the brush of his callused fingers against mine. Jimmy sent my pulse thrumming, and the past ten minutes had ticked by too slowly.

Ainsley sipped the last of her cosmo and perched higher on her stool. "So, Jimmy, have you ever seen *River Monsters*?"

He stood from organizing something below the bar and scratched his neck. "Is that the fishing show?"

Gwen's smirk was all mischief. "Yeah. They travel all over to find terrifying species of freshwater fish. Have you ever seen the Candiru episode?"

"Never seen any. Don't watch much TV."

I swallowed my laugh, knowing what was coming. A few months ago, when I'd texted the girls from a horrific date, they showed up, feigned surprise at the sight of me, and had proceeded with their Candiru performance. My date, Liam, had turned a shade of green I can only describe as rotten avocado, then made an excuse about having to get home.

I sat back to enjoy the show.

"So anyway," Ainsley said, "they found this crazy species of fish called a Candiru. It's a thin, slippery little sucker."

"And it's attracted to urine," Gwen continued, her face glowing with excitement. "In this one episode, there was this guy urinating in the river, and the fish"—she paused for effect—"swam up his penis."

Jimmy paled.

"If it gets too much," I said, "just tap out."

He shot me a worried frown. "It gets worse?"

"Much."

"I can take it."

The man was a trooper.

Gwen swirled her wineglass, always one to accept a challenge. "The fish has these gnarly spines, so once inside it anchored itself to him. Sucked his blood. Gnawed on his flesh. He tried to pull it out, of course, but the things are slippery as a wet bar of soap. It wouldn't budge."

Jimmy went from pale to ashen, his jaw clenched tight.

Ainsley leaned on her elbows, dropping her voice to a whisper. "They raced the guy to the hospital, and he was there for, like, two hours. The fish just hung on. They debated cutting him open to retrieve it, but decided on inserting pincers through the tip to—"

Jimmy shot his hands in the air. "Tapping out!"

He gave a shiver and strode away, muttering to himself.

Ainsley called after him, "I have a friend in marine biology. Mess with Rachel, and you'll regret it."

He didn't glance back, but I cackled.

Man, did I love my girls.

Once they'd said their goodbyes, I waited for Jimmy to finish, my last few minutes spent in a lust-induced haze. His dirty promises echoed in my ear.

Undress you. Lick your pussy. Fuck you hard.

Please, and thank you.

My body was alive with want, awareness pulsing through my blood. My calves tingled against my jeans, the breeze of the ceiling fan like feathers through my hair. Even my fingertips prickled. I sensed Jimmy behind me before I felt him. He ran his hands down the outside of my thighs, his heat flowing over me. "Sorry it's taking me so long. You okay?"

"Yeah." My voice was nothing but a whisper. "I'm okay."

His concern melted something in my chest, though. I could no longer deny my pure *need* for Bad Boy, but the gentleness in his soothing tone threatened my plan. Our time together would be research and nothing more. I would explore my sensuality and take pleasure for myself. I wouldn't fall for him.

He squeezed my legs. "I'll be done soon. And for the record, your friends are terrifying."

I would have laughed, offered a witty reply, but my rising body heat burned a path up my lungs. He kissed the top of my head and returned to cashing out.

Breathless, I waited.

Ten minutes later, his hand was on my lower back as he guided me toward his Harley, all that black and chrome glinting with danger. The bike I'd always wanted to ride, with the guy I would be *riding* shortly. He passed me a helmet and stared a beat too long. "You really are beautiful."

I almost dropped the helmet.

He straddled his bike and nodded for me to join him. "You better hold on tight."

And never let go, I thought. A notion I needed to extinguish. Every second with him became riskier, his compliments and gestures planting roots in my heart. I slung my leg over his metal beast and plastered myself to his back. There was that scent again—leather and spice with a hint of gasoline. Unadulterated man. My mother would have fainted at the sight of us. He paused, tightening my arms around him and resting his hand over mine. My belly dipped. It was an intimate gesture, sweet. Something a boyfriend would do.

Then he revved the engine.

The kissing began before we made it into his apartment. He slammed my back against the wall, one hand anchoring my neck, the other branding my hip as his lips crushed mine. And the sound I made? I'd never been so filled with longing, so utterly undone. That motorcycle ride had flipped my bad-girl switch—wind in my face, Jimmy between my thighs, the roar of the engine. The trip to his place had been both too fast and too slow.

And we hadn't made it past his hallway.

I'd never groped a man in a public space, let him suck my neck and squeeze my breast and rock his erection into my belly, but I was lost. Entranced. Absorbed in the feel of him. I latched one leg around his, palmed his ass, whimpered into his mouth. Heat scorched my core. An answering groan rumbled from his chest. His tongue stroked mine, his lips hard yet soft.

"Inside," he murmured.

"Not yet," came my reply, because I liked this. I liked that we could get caught. Any moment, someone could happen upon us, all roaming hands and gasping as we explored each other. It only made me hotter. Regular Rachel would never have been so bold; that was a job for Reckless Rachel. With only two glasses of wine in my system, my abandon wasn't alcohol induced.

I was drunk on Jimmy.

He kissed me harder, his cock like steel against my hip. *I* did that to him. I was driving the man wild. With a grunt, he gripped my shoulders and pushed away, his full lips puffier and glistening from our kiss. He eyed me hungrily. The thick line of him stretched his jeans, and I gripped his length, stroking and squeezing through the worn denim. He rocked, unsteady on his feet.

Two strokes later, he gripped my wrist, stilling my greedy movements. He shoved his hand into his front pocket and fished out a key. Working quickly, he led us in, then kicked the door shut, crushing his mouth back on mine.

I tugged his hair.

He bit my neck.

We devoured each other.

He pulled back long enough to toss his jacket and undo the top button of my blouse, but he fumbled, an impatient *"Fuck"* following. He growled and ripped it open, plastic buttons pinging against his floor.

There went piece seven in the ensemble. "That was an important part of my wardrobe," I said, bra exposed, goose bumps spreading across my stomach.

He stared, eyes hooded. "Seeing your tits was more important than saving that shirt."

The man had a way with words.

His apartment came into focus then. It looked the same as last time, just as barren. And lonely. As vacant as the room was, the shadows of what we'd done in here still teased me. I replayed Jimmy's stories, picturing us uncorking the Screaming Eagle and laughing together, him taking that ridiculous butt shot. We'd had fun, he claimed, and I sensed it, the ease with which I lost myself around him proof enough.

His hands gripped my waist, warm and rough, and I jumped at the contact. He sucked a path down my neck and tugged my bra cup lower, just below my nipple. I dropped my head back on a sigh. His scruff scratched my sensitive flesh... and Jesus, he *bit* me. A subtle sting, surprising in its pressure. Surprising in how good it felt. He moved, walking me backward, his mouth busy on my breast, my hands in his hair, until the back of my legs hit his bed. With a light shove, I fell onto his mattress, but he didn't join me. He toed off his boots and pulled off my heels.

Then he looked.

And looked.

He rubbed his hand over his jeans, stroking his cock through the fabric, soaking me in like I was a porn star splayed for his amusement. I wanted to touch myself, too. In private, I used my vibrator (the Dildo Incident had its plus side), but I'd never masturbated in front of a man. Now my fingers drifted across my ribs, a slow drag toward my jeans. But I chickened out. I couldn't do it. Couldn't be as bold as Jimmy, who was basically jacking himself off at the foot of the bed.

"Take off your jeans," I said, eager to see the length of him. Watch him stroke himself.

His blue eyes turned molten, and his jaw slackened. "Not yet. First, I'm going to peel off *your* jeans and taste you, and you're going to come on my tongue."

Yep. A way with words.

Men had gotten me hot before, turned me on, but the second their heads were between my legs, I'd lose the edge of my desire. The burn would slip into a dull ache that would vanish. Easy come, easy go. I'd stress about keeping my abs tight, in case the guy looked up. I'd worry about the position of my legs, if I should touch his head or grip the sheets or groan to show support. (Good job, buddy!) Once, in college, I spent the time reviewing for a test.

Jimmy promised more.

Before he stripped me bare, he covered my body with his. "You're so fucking hot," he said. His next kiss was deep and wet, sending me to oblivion. "All that innocence hiding this wild woman. When I'm inside you, I want to hear you scream."

If he didn't do something soon, I might have screamed then and there.

I didn't have to. He reached behind me, unhooked my bra, and dragged it off. His mouth fell to my breast while his hand cupped me over my denim. I rocked into him as he pressed harder. "This needs to happen," I said, desperate.

"Patience, Sunshine."

His use of my nickname spurred my desire, as though I were his. A woman he took care of, in the bedroom and out. He worked my body over, lavishing my breasts with attention, sliding lower, kissing my belly, nipping my hips as he dragged off my jeans. He tossed them to the side, never breaking contact. He kissed me over my underwear, his hot breath working me into a frenzy. By the time my cotton thong hit the floor, nuclear war could have been declared. The last iceberg could have melted. As long as I had Jimmy and that tongue and those hands on me, the world could crumble.

His first lick was slow. Divine torture. I let my legs fall wide, not caring how I looked. I threaded my fingers through his hair, the dark strands tangled in my grip, and I rocked toward him, unabashed. Need in my movements. Little moans escaped me. Not on purpose. Not as a way to speed things along. Everything I did was involuntary. I was his marionette, pushed and pulled and lit on fire.

He spread me wide, his tongue flicking over me, the rhythm building. A symphony nearing its crescendo. I dug my heels into his sides, and he groaned, sinking one, then two fingers inside me. The room disappeared. *I* disappeared. Nothing remained but that one point of contact, all my nerve endings gathered in a tight bud.

Then I exploded. A cry wrenched from my throat, the sound unfamiliar, my body alight. He pushed me further, took me higher, until I was nothing but sensation. Pulsing light. His final lick, slow and languid, had me pulling away, too sensitive to be touched.

He kissed my inner thigh. Even that subtle press made my stomach clench.

"Tell me, Ray, do you still think I lied about the six orgasms?" He knelt over me, fully clothed, caging me with his hands. His lips were wet with my taste. He was deliciously disheveled. All that hair tousled, impossibly thick eyelashes, dark eyebrows set off by blue eyes, slivers of gunmetal swirling at the edges—the man was magnificent.

"I can't be sure," I said. "I need to do some further studies. Cover all the variables." I traced the veins up his inked forearms until my fingers coasted below his cuffed sleeves. "Take this off before I rip the buttons."

He jumped off the bed and pulled me with him—into him, my naked body pitched against his jeans and belt. The contrast was sinful. "I prefer you to rip," he said.

Well then. I gripped the edges of his shirt and yanked. Or tried, at least. The thing snagged and didn't budge. "I'm ruining the sexy," I said.

He chuckled. "Let's go with the buttons."

Impatient, I reached for his jeans instead, unlatching the large belt buckle. If I lifted that sucker, I'd get a killer workout. Next came his button, the slide of metal through frayed denim teasing, too close to what I ached to see. What I *had* seen but couldn't remember. I dropped to my knees, undid his zipper, and slid his jeans and black briefs to the floor.

That's when I said, "What the hell is that?"

"*Now* you're ruining the sexy."

"No. Seriously. What *is that*?"

"In case you weren't aware, those are the last words a guy wants to hear when a girl pulls down his pants."

He sounded amused, and he must have removed his shirt, because the gray plaid pooled beside me, but I couldn't look up. I could only stare at his cock, thick and hard and standing at attention. "Did you know you have a piece of metal through your penis?"

His answering laugh had the piercing catching the light and winking at me. "I have a vague recollection of getting it done. I'm also having déjà vu. We had this whole conversation last time we hooked up."

He stepped out of his jeans, but I stayed put, entranced, the floor digging into my knees. He was thick and long. His shaft curved up, the taut skin flushed deep red, and there, on the underside, just below his swollen head was a bar through his skin, a silver ball on either end. I reached for it, but drew my hand back. "Does it hurt, if I touch it?"

"In the best way," he said, his voice low and rough.

I looked up. He was fit and muscular, not bulky. More tattoos decorated his ribs, but his flat stomach and the broad planes of his chest were ink free. There was more metal—two hoops through his nipples, his silver chain hanging between them. His bad-boy factor just tipped the bad-boy scale.

And I was a minute from coming again.

I slid my fingers around his thick thighs and licked the piercing. He gripped my hair, a guttural sound following. Apparently he liked that. I took another taste, the metallic sting sharp on my tongue. Moving one hand around his shaft, I slid my tongue in circles, each pass landing on the barbell, giving it a gentle tug.

His hold tightened on my hair. I sucked him deeper, always finishing on the tip, exploring his piercing. His groans escalated, as did his dirty words.

Love fucking your mouth. My dick is so hard. I can still taste your pussy.

My fascination gave way to hunger, the rush so thick my mind blurred. I wanted him. No, I *needed* him inside me. I needed to feel that barbell dragging along my sensitive walls.

I circled my tongue once more, then stood. "Sex has to happen."

He pulled me close, his erection pressed to my hip. He coasted his lips over my jaw. "I was counting on it."

I dragged my fingers between his pecs, enjoying the softness of his chest hair, finally touching his nipple rings. "Have you been tested? Are you clean?"

He stilled. "Yes." He dipped his head to catch my eye. "What's going on in that mind of yours?"

"I want to feel *it*. Feel you inside me. No condom. I've been tested, and I'm on the pill," I added, like that was the only thing stopping us.

I'd only had unprotected sex with my last boyfriend, my mother's fear of disease ratcheting up my caution. I trusted Jimmy, though. I didn't know him that well, but my intuition said he'd never hurt me. And I was drunk on the man.

His hips rotated, mine joining his rhythm, a subtle rocking of our naked bodies. "I've never been bare in a woman. My ex had an issue with the pill, and it never happened. I've been tested, too. But I'm not sure this is a good idea."

I slid my hand between us, gripping him. "Aren't *you* supposed to be the wild one?"

My recklessness knew no bounds.

He made a pained sound at the back of his throat, then he pressed his forehead to mine. "Do you trust me?"

"I do."

"Does this mean you're staying over?"

I stilled my movements. Staying over sounded better than sipping another Screaming Eagle Cabernet, his hard body tangled around mine divine. But sleeping over led to feelings, which led to commitment, which led to entrenched lives. An outcome I wasn't ready to entertain. "No. It's too much. You said you were okay keeping it casual." To convince him, I stroked him again, his erection like silken steel.

He shuddered. "You are dangerous." Then he gripped my hips. "This is how it's going to go. I'm going to fuck you and come inside you, *bare*. I'm too turned on and can't be gentle. You probably won't come, but the next round will be all about you. That work for you, Sunshine?"

All I could do was nod.

He lifted me up and carried me to the middle of his bed, all pretense gone. Then he seized my ankles, anchored them on his shoulders, and wrapped his hand around the base of his cock, guiding it toward me. He didn't push in, just moved the head around, over me and toward my entrance, the slide of his piercing dizzying. I canted my hips, coaxing him. Asking for it. A muscle in his jaw ticked, the only sign he was holding back.

Until he wasn't.

He pushed into me, a long drag that had him dropping his head forward, a pained *"Christ"* rumbling from his chest. His pause didn't last long. Neither did the slow pace. He dug his fingers into my hips and pounded into me, his gaze locked on where we were joined. My focus was glued on *him.* The ripple of his abs as he contracted. The veins on his neck, tight with exertion. His thrusts rocked me, so forceful I couldn't move. I could only take. *And take.* My pleasure coiled, the nudge of his piercing teasing me.

Then he exploded. "Fuck. Fuck. *Oh, fuck."* His orgasm was forceful, a storm unleashed, and my lust spiked.

Him unhinged was a beautiful sight, and I took him there.

His guttural sounds brought me closer, but not to the brink, as predicted. He eased my ankles from his shoulders and lowered his body, until we were flush. His dangling chain tickled my collarbone. "Is this what you wanted to feel? My hard cock inside you?"

The storm had passed, his movements as smooth as the tide. "Yes," I said.

I loved his dirty words, but couldn't reciprocate. Couldn't voice how I *liked* him fucking me. How the roughness turned me on. When he cupped my breast and pinched my nipple, I didn't scream *yes* and *harder*. I simply moaned.

He softened inside me, the fullness less acute, but he kept moving, shallower glides, in and out. Until he thickened again. It didn't take long, each roll of his hips deepening. His lips captured mine, our kiss as languid as his movements, and my heart swelled. It shouldn't have swelled. We were having sex. *Fucking.* Not making love. But being joined to him, nothing between us, was more dangerous than sleeping over.

I turned my head, focused on his boxing gloves hanging from

his closet door, the red leather scuffed in spots. I gripped his shoulders, moving with him. Up, down. Together. Hips connecting. Him so full inside me, and that bit of metal. He pulled out farther, making sure it nipped my entrance, then slid back in. *So, so good.*

He shifted onto one elbow, one of his hands sinking into my hair. His other pushed between us, touching where we were joined. "Rachel."

I closed my eyes, lost to the feel of him.

"Rachel," he said again. "Look at me."

I couldn't comply. Agreeing to this fling wasn't his first choice, and he was testing me. Calling me on my bullshit, knowing I was falling for him. I could deny it all I wanted, but a lump built in my throat, worsening each time our hips met. One look, and he'd see it. Everything I denied. But I couldn't have sex with him, bare, and shut him out, as tempting as it was.

So I looked.

His gaze was fierce, locked on me, like he was memorizing my face, and my heart burned up. My chest constricted, my eyes a watery mess. I bit my cheek, keeping my emotion at bay. This man who had no one in his life, had invited me in. And I offered him scraps.

He rode me and I raised my knees, forcing him deeper, pretending the steel in his blue eyes didn't cut. The faster I moved, the harder he thrust. I was close. So unbelievably *close*. I kneaded his shoulders and arched my back, our gazes connected. One last stroke was all it took.

Light danced behind my eyes, an endless parade of explosions rocking my core. I clenched around him and bit his shoulder to muffle my cries, both of us coming together.

There was no doubt Jimmy and his six orgasms were fact not fable, and sleeping with him again would be dangerous.

CHAPTER 13

JIMMY

No fucking condom. Not sure what I was thinking, letting that go down. Following Rachel's rule and sleeping with her, no strings attached, had the potential to mess me up. Doing it bare pulled the rug from under me.

I stilled, breathing hard, all that heat and wetness surrounding me. I ached for another round, but Rachel turned in on herself, wrenching her gaze away. For a moment, she'd been with me. Feeling our connection. There was no hiding the emotion in her big, brown eyes. Then it was gone.

"So, wow," she said. "That was pretty unreal." She slipped out from under me, pushing me to the side, when all I wanted was to pull her closer. "And that head," she went on, a regular Chatty Cathy, "you certainly know what you're doing down there. Since we're in agreement, and I was sober for the fireworks, we don't have to do this again. But it was fun. The next girl you're with will be very lucky." She gathered her jeans and underwear, holding them over her body. Then she bit her lip.

"Do you have a T-shirt I could borrow? My blouse didn't survive intact."

Neither had my heart. Still, if she wanted to pretend we hadn't shared something intense, I'd play along. I'd promised her as much. It didn't mean I had to make it easy.

I strode to my dresser, naked, and pulled out a gray T-shirt. I sauntered toward her and held out my offering, but when she reached for it, I tugged it away. "You sure you want to leave? I was just getting started."

Her gaze dropped to my dick, and she licked her lips. "Yeah, no. Probably best if I go. I have an early shift at the gym, and I like to be punctual. Get there early, actually."

"I could wake you up. I'm really good at wake ups." I hid the T-shirt behind my back, and her focus stayed on my dick. "I also make killer pancakes."

Her determination wavered. "Your cock?"

I squinted at her. "My cock?"

She waved a frantic hand as she blushed. "*Cook*. You *cook*. Not your cock. Jesus. I just can't picture you *cooking*." She pursed her lips and reached around me, snatching the shirt from my hands.

"Like a five star chef," I said. "Spent time at a restaurant in Italy. I make pasta from scratch."

Ignoring me, she marched into my bathroom and slammed the door, but I shouted, "I often cook naked, so you can still look at my cock."

"Such a comedian," she called.

I chuckled and pulled on a pair of sweats. I should have stayed pissed, frustrated that her fears drove her actions, but I had my own demons to slay. A woman like Rachel deserved a man willing to risk things for her. A man with a future, and I'd had one, once upon a time. I'd had a winery and would have been able to offer her everything. If I wanted Rachel, I needed to get my shit together.

The sooner I forced my family to fix their wines, the sooner I could move on. If their deceit came to light down the road, it could hurt me. Tarnish my reputation and prevent me from returning to the wine world. This way it was under my control. I'd give my real name at the final round, claim I'd just learned of the fraud, and let the drama unfold. If it happened by my hand, I'd rise above the scandal. Distance myself from it until the mess blew over.

Find some peace.

But queasiness clogged my throat, those grapevines tied to who I was, at my core.

My grandfather and I had tended them. Gave them life. When he'd started our winery, he'd struggled to make ends meet. If someone gave him a sob story about their money woes, he'd practically give his wine away. If customers claimed they'd fallen on tough times, he'd tell them to pay him in a week or a month, but the money never came. My father took over the operation and called him a fool. I called him smart and generous and loving.

Destroying the vines, even by reputation, was akin to destroying my grandfather's memory, killing a piece of myself. But I was floundering, my options always circling back to my plan, a way to forget the cruel things my father had said to me. To forget that my family had put me in this position.

Until that time, better to focus on Rachel.

Our next sommelier session was in two days, but I'd wager my Harley she'd text before then. I looked for her purse in the living room. I fished out her phone and changed my name to *Eight* in her contact list, chuckling to myself.

Seconds later, she hurried into the room, my paint-stained T-shirt hanging over her jeans. She snatched up her purse, but hesitated. "I just want to make sure things will be fine on Tuesday. I don't want it to be weird."

"It won't be weird."

"Okay. Good. Thanks."

"Especially since we'll be doing this again."

She fisted her hands. "It's not a good idea."

I crossed my arms and leaned against my couch. "It's a brilliant idea."

"Jimmy, you promised this was casual."

"I didn't propose marriage. I just suggested you'd be so desperate to fuck me again you'd be begging for another round. So it won't be weird. Sitting in Crush's cellar, imagining me taking you from behind, will be fun. Don't you think?"

Her slender fingers drifted to her neck. She stared at my bare chest. "Maybe…"

"Definitely?"

"God, you're annoying." She hurried toward the door.

"I aim to please. And Ray," I said, as she was one step out, "I changed my name in your phone. Thought you should know. Don't want you freaking out when you can't find my number."

"I won't be using it."

"You will."

Her breathing escalated, a deep rose coloring her cheeks. Like at the bar, her brown eyes went hazy, everything about her telling me she wanted this, too. Then she blurted, "I have to go," and left.

Thirty minutes later, my cell buzzed. Rachel's text read: *You're coming over tomorrow.*

I nearly fist-pumped. *Sure thing, Sunshine.*

My phone buzzed again, my grin widening as I checked it, but the name that popped up had me scratching my head. *Owen Phillips?* I hadn't seen Owen since we'd played soccer in high school, the fucker always one move ahead of me—his passing slightly stronger, his ball handling a notch better. Last I heard, he was working at some Washington D.C. finance firm, married and living the life. I hadn't seen him in twelve years.

Got your number from your folks, he texted. *Just moved back to San Fran. Wanna grab a beer sometime?*

After Rachel's quick turnaround, Owen's message brightened my mood further. It was nice to smile again, to think about a future that didn't involve me alone in my shell of an apartment. Moving around Rachel in a kitchen, flour on my hands, her hips brushing mine, sounded pretty fucking good. Having a drink with an old buddy was appealing, too.

Name the time, I replied.

CHAPTER 14

RACHEL

JIMMY HAD BEEN a relentless flirt all week. We'd spent three nights at his place and three at mine, always naked, always with him asking for a sleepover, always with me saying no. He'd then ask for dinner, and I'd say no. He'd ask for a movie night, a walk, an *ice cream date*…and I'd decline. I'd remind myself he was just a fling, a portal to my other dimensions. I'd also given us a time limit.

At the end of the sommelier contest, we'd be done.

My insistence on keeping us casual didn't stop his flirtatiousness. Our contest group had thinned after recent eliminations, so our corner had become even more remote. The man took advantage. Today's service component involved us decanting wines in pairs. As I poured his glass (*expertly*), he said, "I can see down your top."

He was one move shy from getting voted off the island.

Still, I didn't botch the decanting, and the Chardonnay tasting went smoothly. I swished the wines around my mouth, taking time to note the layers. *Pineapple. Banana. Buttered toast.* If I did as well as I thought, I'd be one step closer to the finals, winning the contest, and never seeing Jimmy again.

My stomach curdled, but I wasn't sure if it was the prospect of securing the job or losing Jimmy that soured my insides.

As we waited for the last few contestants to finish, Bad Boy's hands roamed freely, copping feels at random, like he was my boyfriend.

"Touch my thigh again," I said, "and I'll purple nurple you."

"Touch your thigh like this?" He pressed his leg to mine, even that bit of contact echoing along my skin. "Or like this?" His fingers traced a path up my pants' inner seam, stopping a millimeter short of his goal.

I slapped his hand away. "I told you. Save it for the bedroom."

Or the bathroom. The floor. The couch. Any available surface.

After another triple-O (Olympic Oral Orgasm), we'd had sex twice last night—once against my wall, then with me sitting on my stove. I sent him packing afterward with a smile and a thanks, like he'd stopped by to fix a leaky faucet. It was a game. One he allowed me to play.

He'd caught me staring at him enough to know more than lust turned my eyes into swoony pools of mush. I was falling for him. I wanted to open up, eat ice cream with him and walk hand-in-hand. I wished I wasn't so afraid of his past and my mother's reaction to him. Wished my father were here to meet Jimmy and predict if he would hurt me or love me, like he had with Gabe.

But I was on my own.

"That puts a wrench in my plans," he said.

"What plans?" A hint at something alluring, and I was putty in his hands.

"I bought some cheese and pâté and was planning a ride to Napa on Friday. Find a secluded spot to enjoy the day. Guess I'll have to ask someone else." He focused on April across the room, and I tried to burst her head with my mind.

She was blond, like his ex. She was curvy, too. Pink lips, sexy wrap dress, high heels. She was sweet, but often glanced at Jimmy, probably fantasizing about slumming it. I frowned, hating that I'd been doing the same. Using him.

But dammit, his jealousy plan worked. "If you ask someone else, I will pull out your piercings with my teeth."

"Go with me, Ray." His deep voice melted into honey. "Let me take you on a date. Tour the valley together. Have some fun. I make a killer picnic."

He also made a killer sales pitch. The idea of lounging in the grass, wine sipped, the sun on our skin was too tempting to decline. "I *will* go, but I haven't decided if it's a date yet."

He slid his hand back between my legs. "Anything I can do to convince you?" I was too turned on to reply, so he added, "In case you were wondering, I changed my name in your phone again."

If my calculations were correct, he'd be listed as *Twenty-seven*. My mouth dried like I'd sucked a bushel of grape skins. "If you don't move your hand, I'll have to switch seats." I wasn't sure if I wanted him to move it away or move it...*around*. My ability to concentrate was nose-diving.

"Where will you sit? Next to the Schnozinator? Who, by the way, is killing it. If he keeps acing the exercises, you won't be in the finals."

"Me?"

"Yes, you."

"What makes you think you'll beat me?"

He released my thigh and raked his hand through his hair, the dark strands falling across his forehead. "I'm a Master Sommelier, Ray."

Come a-fucking-gain? My jaw nearly hit the floor, any hope for winning the contest out the window. Becoming a Sommelier was a hard-earned title. Becoming a *Master* Sommelier was as likely as sprouting wings. People invested years studying viti-culture, perfecting their palates, and considered passing akin to being knighted. Less than three hundred people in the *world* could list that credential on their résumé. And Jimmy was one of them?

The cool, damp air thickened in my throat, the wines lining the walls taunting me, telling me I was an imposter. Becoming a sommelier for three restaurants, *without experience,* was a joke. A recent article had said as much. It blasted the Adriano brothers for turning this contest into a circus. Consider me the acrobat swinging without a net. The Nose would for sure make it to the end and, apparently, so would Jimmy.

My landing wouldn't be pretty.

"Hey." Jimmy leaned in front of me and ran his hand along my back. "You okay?"

"I shouldn't be here."

"Says who?"

"Says me. And why are you even in this contest? Why the hell would a Master Somm take part in such a farce?"

The knowledge still floored me. We'd explored each other's bodies, had been sweaty and vulnerable in each other's arms, but he'd neglected to mention he'd earned his title.

Resentment surfaced. Not that I had the right to be mad. I was the one who'd forced our relationship into the casual zone. A classification up for reassessment. I wanted to learn where he'd gone to school or if he preferred mustard or mayonnaise, reading or watching movies. I'd kept him at arm's length, a self-imposed distance, but denying my curiosity was getting harder.

The gray-blue lines of his plaid shirt reflected his eyes. He blinked repeatedly, worry crinkling his forehead. "Because I knew you'd be here?"

I laughed, but he'd have to do better than that. "Seriously. I don't get it."

His hand was still on my back, his thumb rubbing the same spot. Like he was stuck in a thought pattern. His focus dropped to the floor, seconds dragging into minutes. Then, "The past two years have been about starting fresh. I didn't want to do anything related to the old me and my family. I'd avoided wine until now, but when I read about the contest, I realized I missed it. It sounded fun. Just like being around you made me realize I missed having someone in my life."

His honesty struck a match behind my breastbone, ribbons of heat tickling my ribs. *He wants me to be his someone.* If I gave in, he could answer all my unasked questions. I could stop lying awake, pretending he was at my side, holding me. Nights had never been so long, the days leading to our sexcapades tortuous. I kept thinking I'd kick my infatuation, sure this wasn't the man I should date. I was existing on slice after slice of denial pie.

Unable to address my flurry of emotion, I focused on his absurd claim. "You probably studied countless hours to pass the Master's exam, and you're doing this because it's fun?"

He shrugged. *Shrugged*, like it was nothing.

Unlike him, I didn't have choices. If I lost, I didn't have a fancy title that would allow me to write my own ticket at top restaurants and wineries. All I had was a drawer full of diplomas I'd like to burn, and a future job talking to dead people. I was destined to fail.

He nudged my knee with his. "I'd like to make it to the final round, but we could always break into a lab and spike the Schnozinator's water with a flu strain. If we clog that nose before the last week, you'll be golden." When I didn't smile, he dropped his voice. "You're good at this, Ray. *Great*. Wine is in your blood. If you don't win, we can figure something out."

My heart skipped. *We.* He'd called us we. I wanted to wrap that word around my shoulders and nuzzle into its comfort. I wanted him, and us, and I was getting tired of my fear. Tired of floundering, my choices too often a reflection of those around me.

I faced him, our lips too close to be decent. "Thank you. I'm looking forward to Napa."

He leaned back, taking in my face as though I'd offered him my kidney. "Glad to hear it. And that piercing threat? You can tug on them all you want."

Such a bad boy.

––––––––

Although I'd worked the morning at the gym, I hadn't had a chance to exercise, so I left Jimmy and his dirty mouth to meet the girls. We'd been working out together for years. Or more specifically, I'd do basic exercises while Gwen would lift weights heavier than my body, and Ainsley would do eyelash reps, batting her mascara-laden lashes.

Grunting, Gwen dropped her barbell. "Ainsley, will you pass my water?"

"I could use my towel, too." I placed my eight-pound weights next to Gwen's bar, like a pea beside a pumpkin.

Ainsley fixed her ponytail. "When did I become the errand girl?"

Gwen blinked at Ainsley's sports bra and leggings, not a drop of sweat marring the hot pink ensemble. "If you actually worked out, we wouldn't use you as our gofer."

Ainsley gawked and flung her arm toward the back wall. "I did the leg machine. I could crack a walnut with my thighs. And anyway, someone has to keep watch. There are dodgy guys here."

The weight room was usually bustling with meatheads flexing for the mirrors. Not tonight. More women than men were working up a sweat, the few guys ignoring us. One of them dropped a weight, and the clang vibrated through the room. "I think you're waiting for yoga boy," I said.

She tossed my towel at my face. "*Emmett* isn't a boy. He's a specimen of manly perfection."

Gwen sucked back water. "Who doesn't know you exist."

Ainsley swatted the air. "He's playing hard to get."

"More like you're dying to get him hard," I replied.

She fanned her face. "You have no idea. Have you seen him with his shirt off? The guy makes Chris Evans look like the Stay Puft Marshmallow Man."

I rubbed my towel over my forehead, then used it to flick Gwen's butt. We were both in capri leggings and fitted tanks—mine black, hers splashed with a CrossFit logo. We'd both worked out for an hour. Somehow her loose hair had that sexy, disheveled look, while my lifeless ponytail was plastered to my sweaty neck.

"It's smoothie time," I said. "Let's call it a night."

Gwen checked her watch. The thing was some minicomputer that calculated her heartrate and steps taken…and probably the number of times she blinked. "I'd like to do another round of cardio. I'll meet you after."

I put away my weights, then Ainsley and I ordered smoothies and sat in our usual spot—one of three tables facing the cardio room. Towels were strewn by the treadmills, the disinfectant spray bottles half empty. There would be lots of work tomorrow.

Good thing I had those college degrees!

"I read an article about your contest," Ainsley said, "by some restaurant critic blasting the thing, saying it's nothing more than a lame attempt to increase business."

I sucked my straw, blueberry and banana swirling on my tongue. "I read it, and it totally is. I'm not even sure what I'm doing there. Actually"—I pressed my wrists to my cup, hoping to cool down—"I know exactly why I'm there. It's a delay tactic."

She adjusted her sports bra. "I don't follow."

Since Jimmy's Master Sommelier revelation, I'd been stewing over the contest and my place in it. Realizing I wouldn't win didn't upset me as much as I'd imagined. Frustration weighed me down, but not the way it had on impact. I'd jumped on this opportunity because I'd quit yet another job and had no clue where to turn my focus. With the birthday wish taunting me, wine seemed like the right move.

But the thought of winning, as hopeless as it was, had me breaking out in hives. It wasn't what I wanted, but that left me at ground zero, sifting through the internet for inspiration, *again*.

"I'm in a holding pattern," I said. "My mother has pushed me forever to work for my uncle's funeral home, and I'm running out of options. I'm not sure this sommelier position is for me, but if I hang on until the end, she'll back off. That gives me a month to figure something out."

"And to flirt with Jimmy?"

The heat flushing my chest had me placing my smoothie against my neck. "I've fallen hard for him. I still question things, thinking I'm nuts to pursue him, but my excuses are drying up."

Ainsley pushed her straw around. "Is he a player?"

"I don't think so." A player wouldn't own his discomfort when confronting an ex. He'd shared bits about his family, had admitted the contest was a way for him to ease back into the land of the living. As was dating me. He'd never been anything but honest.

"Are you attracted to him?" she asked.

"Is that a real question?"

She smirked. "Do you have fun with him? Does he make you laugh? Do you think about him when he's not around?"

I bit my lip, and the truth spilled out. "Yes. Yes. And all the time."

"Then stop worrying about the rest. Enjoy him. Open up. I bet your mother will surprise you. She might love him."

I stared at her, wide eyed.

"You're right," she said. "She'll hate him. But it doesn't matter. The only one who has to live with him is you."

That sent my mind to Jimmy and me sharing an apartment—something small and tasteful, warmer than his, with new quotes on the wall. Sayings about love conquering all and opposites attracting. I'd hang my pencil skirts next to his ripped jeans, and we'd cuddle on the couch, wine in hand, talking about our days. Days that hopefully wouldn't include discussing the benefits of open versus closed caskets. I blinked the vignette away.

Unless I got over myself, that daydream would never happen.

Ainsley fiddled with her straw, a stirring motion that sloshed her kale smoothie. "Do you ever think about our birthday? About the blackout after our wish?"

More than I cared to admit. "Sometimes. It was pretty nuts."

Her stirring sped up. "It's just, I've thought about it lots. My wish was a big one, something that's been on my mind. I don't believe in ghosts or mind reading or fortune tellers, but I felt"— she sighed—"*something* when it happened. Was it just me?"

The air had swelled that night, all right. My arms had prickled, too. I'd dredged up the memory countless times but hadn't voiced my whacky belief that bigger things were at play. The possibility that my father had somehow orchestrated the encounter. Just thinking it made my heart hammer faster than when on the stepmill. "No. It wasn't just you. I don't want to say my wish out loud, and I don't want to hear yours, but part of me thinks if we fulfill our resolutions, the rest of our lives will fall into place. Like a domino effect."

My pulse didn't slow, but calm descended. Hearing I wasn't alone reinforced my resolve. I *had* to find the right career. Had to move heaven and earth to make it happen. Fighting for something better could give me the confidence to figure out this Jimmy situation. It would help me escape my mother's shadow. If I found *The Job*.

As I sipped the last of my smoothie, both of us lost in our thoughts, an old man stepped onto a treadmill and stood there, stabbing at the buttons. Even from behind, I could tell it was my favorite grumpy gym member, and I grinned. At least he hadn't given up.

"I have to help a guest," I told Ainsley. "I'll catch up with you later."

She barely acknowledged me, and I paused. Ainsley didn't get down and moody; she got angry and sarcastic. I hesitated, but letting 911 drown in his frustrations could cause him to quit exercising. Next time we were out, I'd ask Ainsley what was up.

After giving her shoulder a squeeze, I approached the old man slowly, worried I'd scare him off. His grumbling had other guests casting frowns his way. I tipped my head into his view. "Looks like the machine is acting up again."

He stabbed his index finger some more, hitting every button on the screen. "It is broken."

I could have run through the same routine, unplugging and plugging in the treadmill, but that wouldn't help him the next time he showed up. I did the next best thing. I hopped on the machine beside his and hovered my finger over the program key. "It could be broken, or maybe it's jammed. I just did a workout with my friends, and I was planning on finishing with a cooldown. So I'll just hit the Start button here"—I made a show of pressing the middle button—"and walk for a bit, until my heartrate slows."

He side-eyed me, scrunching his large nose as my walk began. "I am not an idiot," he said abruptly. "I was waiting."

Waiting, my ass. But he copied me. He hit the Start button, lifting his feet like last time, and I bit back my grin. The crotchety man was too cute.

Exaggerated in my movements, I pressed the upward arrow, increasing my speed. 911 grumbled under his breath, but followed suit. Next I raised the incline a notch. His treadmill mirrored mine. I picked up speed. As did he. A few minutes later, I brought the platform level with the ground, and he copied my move. Since he hadn't offered his name last time, I tried again. "I'm Rachel, in case you didn't remember."

"I am not senile."

His tone was stiff and formal, the tiniest accent under his tongue. That didn't stop me. "Do you have a name? In my mind,

I keep calling you 911. So if you have a name that *isn't* 911, I'd love to hear it."

He pressed the arrow key (on his own!), but didn't acknowledge me. A minute later, he said, "George."

Houston, we have progress. "Well, George, it's nice to have someone to chat with while working out. Helps pass the time."

He stomped along, his Frankenstein impression spot on. "You are too skinny. Women these days are always too skinny. You shouldn't exercise so much."

My cackle escaped, the birdlike squawk ricocheting off the walls, and I clamped my jaw shut. It was my nervous laugh, the kind that hid the emotion clawing at my throat. My mother had often said I was too skinny. Then my father would jump in and tell me Marilyn Monroe's curves may have driven a generation of men wild, but Twiggy had decorated every high school locker in the sixties. He'd said I was exactly as I was meant to be. He had been a one man pep rally.

And I missed him.

I swung my arms faster, needing to keep George talking, moving. Pumping his heart. Keep mine from shriveling. "I exercise to keep healthy, not lose weight. Looks to me like *you* could stand to slim down." I looked pointedly at his belly, the solid bulge stretching his white T-shirt and keeping his sweatpants from circling his waist.

He tried to stop marching, but the platform didn't slow, sending him jogging to catch his stride. He slowed and shot me a look. "My wife is an excellent cook."

"Must be nice. Do you have kids? Grandkids?"

His breathing seemed labored, that quick run pumping his lungs too hard. I slowed my treadmill, hoping he'd do the same. He did and took a few cleansing breaths. "I have one son," he said.

He didn't elaborate, but talking kept him exercising. The next best option was to blabber about myself. "I have a brother. And a dog. Our family's dog, actually. Stanley. She's part schnauzer, part poodle, and all adorable."

His mustache twitched. "She?"

"She has a beard, white fur on her muzzle. Stanley suits her."

He grunted.

My mother had bought me our schnoodle when my father died, hoping the furry friend would lift my twenty-two-year-old heart. When I'd moved out, I made her keep him. *Because I don't have room*, I'd told her. *Because she needs the company*, I'd thought.

Mom pretended it was a burden.

I loved Stanley, though, and didn't trust people who wrinkled their noses at dogs. I'd bet Jimmy loved animals, too. He probably sponsored the Humane Society and fostered iguanas, had a farm for injured llamas. Before today, while fighting our connection, I would have told myself he hated cats and dogs and spent his free time kicking puppies. I'd have invented stories, pathetic attempts to reverse my growing affection for him. Anything to forget the way he'd cupped my cheek one night, looked into my eyes, and said he'd dream about me.

I had to find the strength to mute my father's last words and trust my own judgment. Stop revolving my life around my mother's preferences, worried she'd cut me off again for dating the wrong guy.

I snuck a glance at George. What was left of his gray hair had frizzed up, giving him that old-and-wise look. "So…George," I ventured tentatively, "if your son dated a girl you didn't like, like *really* didn't like, but he seemed happy, would you be upset?"

As he was about to answer, he stubbed a toe and tripped over his feet. I jumped off my treadmill and slammed my palm onto his Stop button. 911 wouldn't eat dirt on my watch. He gripped the handrails until his erratic breaths evened out. His eyes were glassy, though, the exertion too much.

"Maybe you should walk slowly awhile."

He nodded, his hand still over his heart. He pressed Start on his own and resumed a leisurely gait. I returned to my treadmill, walking beside him, ensuring he was okay.

I assumed my question had been forgotten, but a moment later, he said, "Children are impulsive. They do not think ahead. As parents, we must be firm. If my boy dated the wrong girl, they would not be welcome in my home."

It was my turn to stumble over my feet, his harshness tripping me up. My hackles rose, along with my indignation. "That's ridiculous."

He tutted me. "Lust can be confused for love." Then, although I'd asked a theoretical question, George added, "This man in your life may not be what he seems."

Our conversation had veered from hypothetical into *oh hell no* territory. "The guy, for your information, is one of the most caring, thoughtful people I've met. He's smart and funny, and I'd be lucky to have him, even if my mother disagrees." My vehemence surprised me, and part of me wanted to slap George for being so old-fashioned and stubborn, but I'd asked his opinion.

He grimaced, probably unsure why I was gifting him with too much information, but a drum pounded in my chest, the tune confirming my decision. My reaction to George's overprotective, and frankly *dictatorial*, comment had been nothing but pure emotion. The heart of my heart. And my heart wanted Jimmy.

On the outside, Jimmy may have read *tabloid*, scandalous and tempting, provocative but lacking substance. Inside he was all romance novel, thick with sweet words and sweeter kisses, tortured hero and all. He irritated me, but in that adorable *I want to jump your bones* way, and my need to defend his honor to this crotchety old man surprised me in its ferocity. Jimmy and I laughed together, and our chemistry was off the charts. My smile grew, my list of things I loved about Jimmy growing with it, topped off with the most important point: he'd always been honest with me.

My father's final voice message still looped in my mind, but Jimmy wasn't Gabe. He may not have been the man I'd imagined for my future, and my mother might stroke out at the sight of him, but pretending I could keep away was a full-time job. Another career I was thinking of quitting. Our Napa Valley trip was in two days. That gave me forty-eight hours to buy something cute (that didn't belong in an ensemble), and figure out the best way to tell Bad Boy I was ready to claim him.

CHAPTER 15

JIMMY

GRAVEL KICKED under my tires and wind blasted my face as I leaned my bike into a turn. The speed and freedom when riding always helped me zone out. I'd forget the onslaught of messages from my mother, the winery I no longer called mine. I'd lose the chip on my shoulder and be one with my Harley. Adding Rachel to the equation took the experience to another level.

Instead of seeking oblivion, her presence anchored me. Her thighs bracketed mine, her hands pressed to my abs. My senses flared in response. I could practically taste the birth of new grapes seeking the sun, almost *feel* the rows of vines beneath my hand, rough leaves dragging along my fingers.

Most of all, I felt Rachel—each shift of her hips and squeeze of her arms. Her heat seeping through my leather jacket. I could have driven until the world dropped from our feet.

Except Rachel yelled, "*Stop.*"

We'd just turned down a dirt path, and I braked fast, the two of us jolting forward. "You okay?" I called over the motor.

"I want to drive."

I killed the engine and leaned my bike on its stand, but neither of us moved. The simmering motor gave way to the buzzing hum of nature, a tune I hadn't heard in ages. I liked living in the city. Great food. Cool hangouts. The hustle and bustle always offered something new. But I was still a country boy at heart and returning here was bittersweet. It brought bad memories with the good, but with Rachel around, I had less room for the hate.

She pressed her head to my back, and I closed my eyes as more warmth spread through my limbs, filling me up. Crowding out the things that normally wound me up. I didn't question why I'd fallen for her so fast, didn't care to understand the how or when of it. I was a thirsty man desperate for a drink, and she was a woman parched for danger.

I threaded our fingers and kissed the back of her hand. "You sure you can handle all this power between your legs?"

The little minx extricated her hand and dragged it down my chest and abs. She slowed over my dick, gave it a squeeze, then splayed her fingers over the motorcycle seat. She slapped the leather. "I think I'll manage."

I groaned.

When the heat fisting my balls ebbed, I kicked my leg over the seat and stood. "You ever driven a bike before?"

She shook her head. "Only been on the back. But I've always wanted to."

She was exploring her deeper urges, sampling which itches needed to be scratched, and she trusted me to help her. "Rules are as follows: you go in a straight line. No fancy spins or turns. Just a smooth ride forward. Sound good?"

She bounced on the seat. "Perfect."

Keeping the kickstand down, I pointed out the foot pegs, shifter, clutch, throttle, and brakes. Her attention was rapt. If I had to guess, I'd say her pulse was buzzing louder than a jet plane. Mine had on my first ride. When getting my first piercing, too. That first tattoo. Each experience had been thrilling, and I was gifting this to her.

She shifted her weight, settling on the seat and gripping the handlebars. "I think I'm ready."

I raised the kickstand, making sure she was steady before letting go. "Keep your fingers on the clutch," I reminded her. "Release it slowly, get the bike rolling, then apply the throttle."

Her helmet bobbed as she nodded. "Got it."

She turned on the engine, my beast of chrome and metal humming below her. Sexy as hell. Then she released the clutch. She squealed as she rolled forward, but promptly jolted to a stop. She teetered before finding balance. "Did I break it?"

Just my heart, I almost said, unsure why my head had gone there. A place it had been visiting more often these days. Each time she'd snubbed a date request, it stung a little more. Her fear may have shone through each rebuke, but every minute with her had me sinking deeper. Eventually, getting out would be a bitch.

"Everyone stalls out when they start," I said. "You released the clutch too fast. Slow and steady wins the race." Exactly how I'd been pursuing her, but my heart was bound to stall, too. Everything with her was moves and counter moves. Admissions of feelings by me lowered her defenses. Give her too much time to think, and her walls shot back up. The picnic was my grand master plan, one I hoped pushed us from fuck buddies to fuck *couple*.

She set her jaw and tightened her grip. "Let's try again."

"Slow," I repeated. "Wait for the sweet spot, then the throttle."

She was in the zone, body taut, her posture pitched forward. The engine thundered to life. She waited a beat, long enough for me to second guess letting her drive. Motorcycles were danger-ous. One wrong move, and she could end up with serious road rash, or worse. Maybe this was a bad idea.

But she was gliding along the dirt path, past the point of me stopping her. The throttle roared. The sound set up residence in my chest, vibrating through me. When the bike shot forward, I pictured her losing control, her slim body pinned under all that crushing weight. Panic pushed my legs into a run. *She better not fucking fall.*

She rode a perfect straight line.

Breathless, I reached her as she stopped. Her grin hit me like a blast of fireworks. "That was *unreal.*"

I gripped the handlebar and killed the engine. Too bad I couldn't silence the hammer pummeling my chest. "You're a quick study, but I'd feel better if you had some lessons before your next ride."

Unconcerned, she thrust her arms into the air. "I am such a rebel."

An adorable rebel. "That you are. Now scoot back. We have a picnic to enjoy."

I parked my bike farther down the path, grabbed my backpack and blanket, and guided Rachel to a shaded area protected by tall grasses and a towering willow tree. Growing up, my brother and I had hiked these mountains and explored the creeks and rivers, branches in hand, as we waged war for our kingdom. Kings of the land. It made for quite the wonderland as kids, but I also found hideaways, secret places I'd keep to myself. Like the secluded pond ahead of us.

Rachel shrugged off her jean jacket and peeled off the leggings she'd worn for the ride, practically skipping to the water's edge. She kneeled down and dipped her fingers in. No pretense. No worry about muddying her sandals. The yellow straps of her sundress were nothing but strings, the loose fabric shifting over her tanned skin. Add the freckles and long hair, and she was the picture of summer.

I shook out the blanket and spread it on the grass. "Nice to see you in something other than black, gray, or white," I said.

She grasped a handful of water and flicked it at me, missing by a mile. "Is that your version of a compliment?"

"No. It was an observation. If I wanted to pay you a compliment, I'd tell you you're the most genuine woman I've ever known. I also might add that your beauty makes it hard to breathe."

Her hand stilled in the water, the warm air shifting between us. "That was an improvement."

"Did you want me to go on?"

She bit her lip and nodded. I could have continued for hours. Mentioned how her laugh filled my empty apartment, how her freckled curves brought me to my knees, how she was kind, and her impressive wine knowledge made me feel like she shared a connection to my happiest childhood memories. Instead I walked over and crouched in front of her, the birds, the frogs, the crickets all singing her praises. "You, Ray, make me feel alive for the first time in ages."

A small squeak escaped her lips, her brown eyes a mirror of the sparkling pond.

Damn if it wasn't true. She also made me want to be better. Admitting I was a Master Sommelier and wasn't using my skills had coated my gut in inadequacy. I may have chosen my clothing and tattoos and piercings, but I could do a hell of a lot better than working at Rudy's Tavern. For myself, sure. If someone like Rachel were in my life, I'd do it for her, too. Be proud of my work. Proud to be her man.

Before everything went to shit, I'd toyed with the idea of organizing larger events for the area, shining lights on smaller wineries eking by. I could still do it.

After I forced the winery carrying my name to right its wrongs.

I brushed her hair from her face and tucked it behind her ear, stealing a slow kiss. Just a taste. An *amuse-bouche* before the main course. "Now get your ass over to the blanket, so I can lay my bounty at your feet."

"Bossy, aren't you?"

"You love it."

She didn't admit it, but she didn't disagree. A hint of progress.

She sat on her hip, tucking her legs and purse to the side. I spread out our feast: Manchego cheese, Castelvetrano olives, duck pâté, prosciutto, dark chocolate, sliced apples, and quince paste, all on a small wooden board. I'd wrapped two wine-glasses in T-shirts, and Rachel unrolled them as I lifted a surprise from my bag. Nestled in a cooler sleeve was the 2010 Marcassin Chardonnay—perfection in a bottle.

When Rachel saw the label, she lowered the glasses and yanked it from my grasp, reading it as though it were a bible. "Would it be wrong to press this to my breasts?"

This woman was too much. "Don't let me stop you."

She actually smothered it between her tits, ecstasy on her face. Sometimes a guy just wished he were a bottle.

"I don't want to open it." She held it at a distance, her expression still dreamy. "Can I take it home and spend some time with it? Maybe open it in a week or two?"

"It's wine, Ray, not a date. You don't need to buy it dinner before popping its cork. Wine is meant to be enjoyed."

"But"—she glanced at me, then down at her dress—"I should have worn something celebration worthy. This wine deserves black tie."

I had on my motorcycle boots, ripped jeans, and a faded Rolling Stones T-shirt. Most people opening a Marcassin would be in slacks or a tux, piano playing in the background, a five-star meal about to be served. But this? The rustle of the willow branches, Rachel's sundress, the glow of her freckled cheeks—it put that snobbish shit to shame. Instead of replying, I leaned back and yanked off my boots, tossing them and my socks to the side. Rachel smiled and kicked off her sandals.

I stood and helped her up, then led us to the grass. "Feel that?"

She wiggled her toes. "What?"

I flexed my feet, letting the blades wedge between my toes,

cool and fresh. "*Life.* Everything out here is alive. Not just the birds and insects. The grass, too. How often do you let yourself slow down and feel it on your skin? Remember what it was like to play as a kid, stains on your pants, mud under your finger-nails. We didn't care, back then. Having fun was more important than wearing the right thing or driving the right car. As far as I'm concerned, being out here *is* a celebration."

She stepped closer, until her toes covered mine. "Then let's celebrate."

I cupped her cheeks, feeling the grass below me, the blue sky above, Rachel in my hands. "Sounds like a plan."

I didn't kiss her. One more touch and I'd be hiking up her dress and pressing her back into a tree. I slapped her ass instead. She jumped, rubbing her bottom with a playful scowl. We sat back down, and I picked up the Chardonnay, only to realize I'd forgotten the most important thing. "Shit."

Rachel froze. "What?"

"No corkscrew."

She smirked. "Well, *Master Sommelier*, it's a good thing you brought me along." Shifting on her hip, she tipped over her purse, spilling its contents onto the blanket.

How everything had fit inside was a mystery. "Remind me to bring you if I get stuck on a deserted island."

She sifted through pepper spray, a few tubes of cream, small scissors, tape, paper, a whistle, Band-Aids, thread and a needle, mini flashlight, batteries, Advil...

I'd never understand the relationship between a woman and her purse.

I held up what looked like a bell. "Is this in case you lose your voice, the whistle breaks, and you need to hail a cab?"

She cackled, sharp and abrupt, the sound infectious as always. "It's a bear bell. You know, in case grizzlies invade San Francisco and I need to ward them off. Always best to be prepared."

When I chuckled, she added, "It's my mother's fault. She

gives me all this stuff, worried I'll rip a skirt and have to repair it, or that I'll get kidnapped. *Or* aliens might land, and we'll discover they can be killed with cortisone cream." She held up three tubes.

"Seems plausible," I said drily. "But why carry it around? Just tell her you don't need the stuff."

She pulled a Swiss Army knife from the pile and played with the attachments, opening and closing the corkscrew. "I know it's silly. I'm twenty-seven. I shouldn't do what my mother says or care what she thinks. It's just, family's important to me. Since my dad died, my mother's anxiety has gone a bit nuts. If carrying this crap calms her, what's the harm?" She passed me the knife, tossed her phone next to mine, and re-stuffed her purse.

"It's nice that you care about her," I said.

It's also why I'd lied to her the other day.

I busied myself cutting the foil and twisting the corkscrew, guilt coiling with the movement. I shouldn't have lied to Rachel, but if I'd told her the reason I'd joined the contest was to leak my family's deceit, an act that would sabotage their winery, she'd have shut me down. Family was everything to her. I'd have to tell her eventually. If she stopped fighting our pull and things moved forward, there couldn't be secrets. But she'd already been searching for excuses to cut me off. No point handing her the knife.

The cork eased out with a quiet *pop*, and Rachel clapped like a kid about to inhale cupcakes. She held out the glasses, and the golden liquid sloshed up the sides as I poured.

I loved the ritual of wine. The dance of man and nature— vines tended, grapes crushed, fermentation coaxing the fruit into greatness, and *this*. The moment of decision. Pass or fail.

Good, bad, or perfect.

I smelled the cork and Rachel did the same. Next we swirled the glasses, breathing in their bouquets. I didn't want to sip mine yet. I preferred watching her lips touch the crystal, the flush of her cheeks and pleasure in her eyes as she swallowed.

"Holy shit" were the first words she managed. Then, "Like, *holy shit*. My mouth just had an orgasm." She inhaled, taking in the sundrenched pond and blue, blue sky. "It tastes like this place."

I resisted the urge to taste the wine on *her* lips, instead sipping from my glass. It really was a mouthgasm. "Lemon peel," I said, the first taste on my palate.

She took another sip and shook her head. "Lemon *meringue*."

Always the competitor. I swished my next taste, and there, *just there*, was the candied sweetness she noted. "Apricot marmalade," I said, then we alternated suggestions.

"Chamomile."

"Brioche."

"Green apple."

"Quince."

She scrunched her nose. "Quince? Nope. More apple than quince."

"Shall we wager?"

She traced circles on her knee, scenting her wine periodically. "What's on the table?"

I could have backed off, not pushed her to drop this charade and admit she was falling for me, but I was only digging myself deeper. Better to force the issue than wind up at a tattoo shop a month from now, covering the pain left in her wake. "A sleepover."

She nearly spilled her wine. "If I'd dropped this on the blanket, it would have been grounds for murder."

"I'd like to see that stand up in court."

She clutched her glass to her chest. "Your house or mine?"

I picked up a square of dark chocolate and let it melt on my tongue. "I'm not picky."

She looked at me, then at the wine, her gaze darting back and forth again. "Fine. Sleepover. My place."

I'd have expected her to suggest mine, a location she could

leave on a whim. Hers was even better. I'd make the wakeup so good she'd want to stay indoors all week.

I opened the quince spread and dipped my finger in it, bringing the jam to her mouth. "Want a lick?"

Her doe eyes flashed and she scooted closer, the board of delicacies between us. "Don't mind if I do." She parted her lips and took my finger in, rolling her tongue around as she sucked, releasing me with a drag of her teeth. And, *fuck*. My dick lengthened, jealous of my goddamn finger.

As she savored the jam, she repeated my move, dipping her finger in and placing the quince on my tongue. I groaned, the tease of her and the added sweetness sending my mind to her straddling my face and rocking her hips. I got harder. With a final lick and kiss, I released her finger. We sipped the Chardonnay next, savoring its complexity.

She huffed and dropped her head back. "You're right, of course. I taste the quince."

"I liked it better on your skin," I said.

She rolled her eyes. "I bet you did."

I poured more wine, the two of us drinking and eating, alternating bites, talking about everything and nothing. One hour passed. Then two. I admitted I sang in my school choir. She confessed her teenage love for NSYNC, complete with posters on her wall. She grilled me about my rise to Master Sommelier, and I relived every detail, another reminder I was an idiot for denying that part of myself.

"I envy you," she said.

I moved the remaining food aside and pulled her bare feet closer, the wine and conversation casting a lazy spell. "Because my life circled the drain and I work at a dive bar?"

She kicked my thigh. "*No*. Because even if you're taking a break, you know who you are. You wanted to become a Master Sommelier, and no matter the hours or how hard it was, you went after it. You had a path."

A path that had led me to a messed-up place, but she was

talking about her life, not mine. "What was the job you quit, again? Before the contest?"

"Loan officer, which basically meant I was a telemarketer. Constant cold calling, trying to convince people to borrow money. It was soul sucking."

"And before that?"

"Thai massage."

"And before that?"

She sipped the last of her wine and placed the glass on its side. "You'll make fun of me."

I lay my empty glass next to hers and pulled her foot toward me. "Now I need to know." I dug my thumbs into her arch, steady rhythm, eliciting a hum from her.

She leaned back on her hands. "I can't tell you. It's ridiculous."

I released her foot. "My hands are cramping. Not sure I can continue this massage."

She grumbled, then huffed out a breath. "Fine. Tattoo artist. I wanted to be a tattoo artist. I never followed through, but that was the plan."

I gawked at her. Walking into a shop to find Little Miss Proper at a station, tattoo gun in hand, would have been quite the sight. "But you don't have a stitch of ink."

"First, get back to the massage." She kicked my thigh, and I complied. "Second, I do have ink."

My thumbs froze. "No, you don't."

"Yes, I do."

"In case you weren't aware, Sunshine, I've explored every inch of your skin. If you had a tattoo, I would have seen it. Unless you got something in the past four days, in which case, you better undress right the fuck now." Tattoo or not, getting her naked was sounding better and better. The perfect dessert.

Color bloomed on her cheeks. "It's on my hip. When I told Gwen my new job plan, she said I couldn't ink people without knowing how it felt. She forced me into a shop."

My eyes roved over her, picturing the freckled skin below her yellow dress. No way did she have a tattoo. "And?"

"*And* I'd drawn an image. I mean, the only reason I'd considered tattooing as a career was because I could draw and didn't have to do more school. So I drew this really beautiful anchor for my dad—he had a boat and loved fishing." She smiled at the memory, a fleeting thing that squeezed my heart. "The stencil was on, the gun buzzed, but I have a pretty low pain threshold."

"This is too good," I said, sensing where the story was headed. I crawled over her, until she was on her back, my knees on either side of hers. I grabbed the bottom of her dress and lifted. "Keep going, Sunshine."

Her throat bobbed in a long, slow slide. "He did one mark, and I screamed bloody murder. I flew off the table, created a scene, and ran from the shop. Gwen, the instigator, ran after me, doubled over with laughter."

I would have paid good money to see that, but I needed my eyes on her skin. "Which side?" She pointed to her left, and I pushed up her skirt. Above her skimpy underwear a tiny mark decorated her hip, nothing more than a pinhead. "I thought this was a birthmark."

"Nope. I ride motorcycles *and* I'm inked, like the badass I am."

Badass and cute as hell. I gave the tattoo a kiss, then planted another one below the white lace. Then one on her inner thigh. My dick throbbed, the day nothing but an aphrodisiac. I could have slipped her underwear down and dragged my tongue up her pretty little pussy, but finding out why she was so lost was important. Rachel was important.

She shifted restlessly, and I moved up, caging her shoulders with my hands. "Why so many jobs?"

Her eyelids were heavy with lust, but she said, "Because I don't know who I am."

It came out softly, a whisper on the breeze. I lowered my voice, too. "You're a girl with a wild side she's afraid to explore, and you need wine as much you need oxygen. I've seen it before, the look you get when you swirl a glass, right before you take that first sip. It's what you're meant to do. Not some stupid contest and serving at restaurants. Being a part of the process. That's where the magic is. Why not explore that?"

A squirrel scurried up the willow tree, its noisy chatter drawing our attention. Rachel kept her focus there. "I got into wine after my dad died. Never considered it more than a hobby. As my interest grew, I looked into it. Checked out the requirements to be a winemaker." Her left cheek hollowed, probably from biting it. A habit when she was stressed. "It's daunting, starting over. It would take years, and I'd probably have to move back home, when relying on myself makes me feel strong and independent."

Her gaze drifted to my hand and up my arm, landing on my face. Her brown eyes glazed with sadness. "My parents paid for school for my brother and me, and I ask for things from time to time, but letting my mom support me now doesn't sit well. I don't want to go backward. And it's like"—she wrinkled her nose as if her words scented the breeze with sourness—"each time I fail at something, I'm disappointing my dad. He had nothing and worked hard to build a life for us. He believed I'd be a success. So it's like he's watching me steamroll through life, shaking his head."

This woman. So honest and so *good* and desperate to please everyone around her, gone and alive. She needed to focus on herself, though. Be the woman she was meant to be, even if it meant sucking up her pride. "Not following your dreams, for whatever reason, is the only thing that would be a failure. And not exploring yourself is criminal. For instance, when I do this"—I placed my hand on her ribs, over her dress, my thumb grazing the swell of her breast—"what are you hoping I do next?"

Pupils blown wide, she tried to wriggle lower, get my hand to move, but I held firm.

"Do you want it slow and sweet, or rough and hard?" I asked. "I could spend an hour kissing and sucking your breasts, or I could grab your *tit* and take your nipple between my teeth. Either will make me a happy man, but what do *you* want?"

The rise and fall of her chest quickened, and her throat bobbed. "I want it rough. I like when you bite. I like when you pull my hair."

Her words spilled out, each one chasing the next, and *Jesus*. To hear her say it, ask for me to push her boundaries? That level of trust tugged at my primal instinct to call her mine. Protect her. Learn every lick and touch that would make her buck.

It also sent a punch of lust to my groin.

I nudged her knees apart, and my hips fell on hers. My erection dug into the valley between her thighs. The thrust that followed had her arching her back, and I squeezed her tit. She gasped, short and sharp, fueling my desire. All I wanted was *her*. Those incoherent sounds. To know I was taking her places she'd never been.

Leaning on an elbow, I shoved her dress above her bra, my jeans thick and rough against her lace underwear. Exactly how she liked it. I didn't unclasp her bra, didn't have the patience. Instead I tugged the cups down, and her breasts pushed up, small and perfect, light pink nipples puckered in tight buds.

I fucking loved her tits. And she loved it wild, like me. I squeezed and licked and bit and sucked, while grinding against her. Her fingers dug into my back. My thighs were on fire. She writhed under me, one hand tangling with my hair, forcing our lips together. The kiss wasn't pretty. It was need and urgency and hunger. It was the pressure of our lives and all we wanted but weren't sure we could have.

It was us.

I couldn't wait. The urge to slam into her had me undoing my belt buckle and shoving my jeans past my ass. She shimmied out of her underwear, and then I was in her, all that tight heat beckoning me closer, as though I had a home. A place in Rachel's life. Her bra was below her tits, the straps of her dress down her shoulders, my jeans at my knees. My hips slammed into hers—hard, sharp, greedy thrusts. She met me each time. I wanted her messy, letting go of her inhibitions. Taking for herself.

"God, *Jimmy*." Her face was a display of sensual abandon, her nails on my ass, forcing me deeper.

Hell yes.

"You're an animal," I growled. "Exactly how I like you. So fucking hot."

An animal who pushed a hand up my shirt, found a nipple piercing, and gave it a twist. Heat shot down my spine, my orgasm building. With each thrust, I rubbed against her, pulling out far enough for my barbell to tease her opening and then slamming tight. Harder. *Rougher*. It felt too good. She felt too good. Dammit if I wasn't losing my heart to her.

The thought caught in my chest, tangled and twisted, driving my movements. She was on the brink, her pussy clamping around my cock, and I shot off like a rocket. Her spasms followed, both of us riding the wave.

Something crossed her face then, a softening of her eyes, moisture gathering in the corners. Her lips parted, like she was about to speak. Instead she swallowed, and her expression dimmed—her internal light flickering, its power source weakened.

Mine damn near blew out. If this was her closing off again, putting up her walls, it would gut me. I couldn't keep drifting with her whims. Not after today. Not after this. To me, she could never be a fling.

CHAPTER 16

RACHEL

JIMMY WALKED into the forest to pee before leaving, and I was still high as a kite—the sex, the picnic, the Chardonnay. *The sex.* The conversation, too. All that school and wine talk had set my mind spinning. I'd stopped considering winemaking as an option, but here it was again, a seed planted, courage growing. The pros and cons unfolded, because of Jimmy.

He'd also unlocked Reckless Rachel in doses. Manageable pieces I could incorporate into my life. I could still feel the roar of the motorcycle under me, the perfection of Jimmy between my thighs.

If I wanted to honor myself, understand what truly made me happy, in the bedroom and out, I'd have to start here. With my bad boy. Not get nervous like I had a moment ago and chicken out from confessing my feelings. I had to forget my concerns and trust that he was ready for a relationship. No more games. No unnecessary complications. When he came back, I'd look him in the eyes and tell him I was all in. I'd take him up on every sleep-over offer and add a few suggestions of my own.

I pulled on my leggings for the ride and gathered my jean jacket. As I packed up the food, my phone rang. I'd ignored my mother's calls the past two days. So jumbled with thoughts of Jimmy and my stalled career, I worried I'd let something slip when I wasn't ready for the head-on collision. If it was her and I ignored her again, she'd slap my face on a milk carton.

I dropped to my knees and hit Talk. "Hello?"

Whoever was on the other end sucked in her breath. "Is Jimmy there?"

The female voice was sharp and strong, *not* my mother's, and unease slicked my gut. Jimmy and I both had black iPhones—the same black cases, neither of us having chosen unique ring tones —which meant this wasn't my cell. It wasn't cool to answer Jimmy's phone. It was intrusive and rude and something I'd never do. With the conversation I wanted to have, this wouldn't be a great start. If I hung up, he'd never be the wiser, and the person would think they'd dialed the wrong number.

But as I pulled the phone from my ear, the woman said, "I'm his mother, Alena. I know Jimmy doesn't want to speak with me, but he won't return my calls. I'm not sure who this is, or if there's anything you can do to help, but we've let this go on too long. We want our son back."

My breathing spiked, and I searched the trees, worried Jimmy would return any moment and catch me talking to his *freaking mother*.

Why did I answer the phone?

Or maybe I was supposed to, another twist of fate, like my father's final apology, my birthday wish, the blackout, and seeing that sommelier poster. Destiny unfolding.

By the sounds of things, Jimmy would have ignored the call, but I'd seen how lonely his life was, how hard it had been for him to sip his family's wine. I didn't know the gory details of their fight, but he hadn't moved on, and they clearly wanted to make amends.

Steeling my voice, I said, "I'm Rachel"—*his girlfriend? Fuck buddy? Play thing?*—"his friend. He's just stepped away, but I can talk to him for you, if you'd like."

She exhaled heavily. "Well, Rachel, that would be appreciated. I'm not sure how well you know my boy, but all the Giannopoulos men are stubborn mules, my husband included. But this business has poisoned our family. I'm concerned about my husband's health. The stress is wearing him down."

My stomach cramped, the notion of Jimmy's father being unwell hitting home. If something happened to the man before they reunited, it would haunt Jimmy. My final argument with my father tortured me to this day, as did the little things—a birthday of his I'd forgotten, the dinner I'd cancelled because I wasn't in the mood. Stupid stuff, but tiny bumps became moguls, hills became mountains.

"I'll make sure he gets in touch. Or"—I searched the trees, nerves buzzing—"if you wait, I can put him on the phone."

Her answer was delayed, until, "I'll wait, but he might not want to speak with me."

I was intimately familiar with Jimmy's stubbornness, and I could only imagine his father. Even his mother's voice was a solid thing, her businesslike tone demanding my attention. But to not speak with her? After hearing his dad was unwell? It seemed preposterous.

The man in question walked from the trees, taking long strides, focus on his feet, like he was deep in thought. I hesitated. I'd have loved nothing more than to tell him I was all his, not mar our perfect day with stress, but this was important. This was family.

When he glanced my way, he frowned. "You okay?" His attention settled on the phone burning up my hand.

Sweat gathered along my spine. "I didn't mean to answer it.

Our phones were next to each other, and…I thought it was mine."

He stopped dead, arms limp at his sides. "Who is it?"

I held the phone toward him. "Your mother."

A muscle in his jaw ticked. He shifted on his feet. "I have nothing to say to her."

I stood and stepped closer, covering the mouthpiece with my thumb. Alena didn't need to hear this. "I don't know what happened, but she wants to talk and fix things." I touched his forearm. "She's reaching out. She's worried about your father's health."

He didn't flinch. His body nearly turned to stone. "Not interested. You can hang up."

Excuse me? I reviewed my words, wondering if they hadn't come out as planned. But my brain was functioning. He'd heard me just fine. "This is your family, Jimmy. How could you not want to speak with her and make sure your father's okay?"

Instead of replying, he wrenched the phone from my hand, hit End, and tossed it on the ground.

My pulse thundered, blood rushing in my ears. "What is wrong with you?"

"There's nothing wrong with me, Rachel. It's them who have the problem."

Rachel. He called me Rachel. Not Sunshine or Ray. It was detached, cold. This was the Jimmy who'd spent an hour flirting with me only to tear off and leave me in his dust. Here I was, about to pour my heart out to him, tell him I was ready for us to move forward, and he was calling me *Rachel*.

I poked at his chest. "You're the one with the problem. Your father might be sick, and your mother called to bridge the gap between you. I don't know the details of what tore your family apart, but this is your chance to make it right. If you ignore them, you'll regret it."

He shook his head. "This isn't like what happened with you

and your dad." His fist swallowed my finger, ceasing my stabbing. "My family is nothing but poison."

His blue eyes had never been so frosty, the silver at the edges sharpening into icicles. With a flare of his nostrils, he dropped my hand and turned away, jamming the rest of our stuff into his backpack. My throat burned. Gone was the man who'd told me I made him better. Disappeared was the lover who'd loosened my inhibitions. This cold-hearted imposter turned a blind eye to his pleading mother, and I couldn't process the change.

When he got the bike loaded up, he planted his hands on the leather seat and slumped forward. "I'm sorry," he said, defeat in his voice.

His apology eased the sting behind my eyes, but we so weren't done here. "You hung up on your mother, Jimmy. You're not some angsty sixteen-year-old. She needs your apology, not me."

He spun around. "You don't understand. My father said things to me a son should never hear, and she let it all happen. They ruined my life and made some brutal choices. Let's just…" He scrubbed a hand down his face, shook it off, then approached me. My arms were crossed, my spine straight. He dipped his head to my level. "Can we sit and talk about this? I'll tell you what happened. The whole sordid mess."

Tenderness laced his tone, and I softened, but this was bigger than Jimmy and me and our fledgling relationship. "Will you call your mother back? After we talk?"

He flattened his lips and jammed his hands into his front pockets. "No. I'm done with them. As far as I'm concerned, I don't have family."

My abdomen cramped, stealing my breath. He had a mother reaching out and a sick father, but he *didn't have family?* So many things about Jimmy didn't fit into my world, most of them superficial. Still, I'd decided to overcome my reservations, because he was worth it. This wasn't superficial, though. This was the meatier stuff, the thing that made a man tick, and our clocks were set to different time zones.

How could I love someone who'd rather nurse his anger than make amends?

My head warred with my heart, a dizzying battle that had me shaking. I dug my toes into my sandals. "I'd like to go back, if that's okay. We can talk tomorrow." I needed space. Time to process and make sure my feelings were more than infatuation. That he was the man I believed him to be. I probably needed a glass of wine, too.

Silence built between us, an extended pause that worsened my turmoil. He huffed out a sad laugh. "You know what? There's no need to talk to this out. This is all an excuse for you to continue keeping me at a distance. We're just casual, like you wanted. I wouldn't want to mess up your tidy life, anyway."

His reproach hit hard, knocking the wind from my chest. He had no clue what I'd nearly confessed. That I was going to jump in with both feet, stop fighting our connection. Finally open up. Or…was I? I'd given him such a hard time recently. Playfully maybe, but he'd put himself on the line, and my rebukes must have hurt. Still, if he was the guy for me, how could everything be undone by a phone call?

Tears stung my eyes, a headache setting in, along with a lump in my throat. If I hadn't answered that phone, we'd be tucked together on his bike, planning our week. Our sleepovers.

Now we couldn't look at each other.

He plunged his hand through his hair, then strode to his bike. Like he was finished with me. I bit my cheek, barely containing my tears. My mind kept flitting between his anger, his mother's plea, his sick father—*my* father, forever taken from me—to our perfect day, and the way my body had responded to his, landing on my selfish choices the past weeks.

Unsure how to unravel it all, I did the only thing I could —*nothing*. I climbed onto his bike, held on, and spent the ride trying not to cry.

CHAPTER 17

JIMMY

RACHEL WAS the girl for me. I knew it in my bones, felt it in the ache constricting my chest. But I was tired of her games. The ride back to San Francisco was torture. Her thighs hugged mine, her hands gripping my sides, but she wasn't present. Her reaction wasn't surprising. She didn't know about my plan and the ruin it would bring to my family winery, but denying my mother was a big fat X in her books. A checkmark in her undateable column —next to tattoos and bartender.

She may have been the girl for me, but I was done trying to be the guy for her.

When I pulled up to her apartment, she didn't move. Her chest wasn't pressed to my back, but I could feel each of her inhales and it hurt. It was too much, she was too much, and I *felt* too damn much. Two hours ago, we'd had the best sex of my life, raw and open and *real*.

Now we sat like strangers.

She pushed off my bike and paused on the sidewalk.

"Thanks for the picnic, and the wine. I..." She trailed off, turmoil in her fidgety stance. "I'm sorry for how it ended."

I was sorry, too. Sorry I'd lost my temper and that my mother had shoved her way back into my life. Sorry I wasn't enough for Rachel, but it was time to let her go. It had taken me years to be comfortable in my own skin. I needed a woman who respected that.

Gripping my handlebars, I wrung my hands around them, tamping the urge to strut over, carry Rachel up to her apartment, and remind her how *good* we were together. But her indecision was palpable and getting in deeper wouldn't end well for me.

At the least, she needed to know the truth of it. "I'm not perfect, and my family situation is a disaster, but I'm not the bad guy here. If I thought you'd have listened, I would have explained things, but you've had me running in circles. I can't keep on like this. It sucks you can't see what we have. It sucks how hard I've fallen for you. But I..." I revved my engine, unable to go on. "It's better if we end things."

I peeled out the second I said it and didn't glance back. *Couldn't* glance back. If relief had flooded her features, it would have cut deep. If she'd looked crushed, I would have said fuck it and grabbed her and kissed her and apologized for being such a dick, only to wind up back here the next time she freaked out.

Lose-lose.

I drove for an hour, gut twisting, cruising the streets in search of peace that didn't come. Just as my life was turning around, my family had to mess it up, *again*. Get in the middle of another relationship. Rachel could cope with me having estranged parents, but one hint they wanted to mend fences, and she saw me as the asshole in the equation. The troublemaker.

My path was clearer for it. I had to cut them off, once and for all. Bring their lies to light, clear my conscience. My mother would stop trying to reach me, and they'd all leave me the hell alone. Maybe then I'd meet a woman who could accept me as I was.

I pulled over by the ocean. Salt stung my nose, the expanse of the Pacific a welcome sight. Cars rushed behind me, waves rolled ahead, birds coasting above. I blinked through the darkening light, envious of the seagulls and the simplicity of their existence.

Fly. Fish. Eat. Repeat.

My phone rang and I gritted my teeth, unsure if I should check it. If it was my mother, I'd probably toss it in the sea. If it was Rachel, I'd probably toss it, too. Then I'd jump in after it.

Unable to resist, I pulled it from my pocket. *Owen Phillips.* An unexpected name, but one that had me relaxing. We hadn't connected since his first text. He'd asked to hang out once, but Rachel was coming over, and I'd been greedy for her, unsure how many nights we'd have.

Not enough, in the end.

I hit Talk. "Owen Phillips."

"Last I checked," he said. "Wondering if you wanted to grab that beer."

I could drive around for the night, or stare listlessly at the horizon until the sun came up, but clouds were rolling in, dark with rain, and none of it would make me feel a damn bit better. It certainly wouldn't help me forget I'd have to see Rachel in four days and pretend I was over her.

"Sounds great," I said.

Thirty minutes later, I walked into The Blue Door. My gaze cut to the stools Rachel and I had sat on as I coaxed her into a no-strings affair, clueless to what I'd started. It was probably stupid to revisit this place, but it had a cool vibe, and the familiarity was comforting. Cameron stood behind the bar, and I spotted Owen at one of the cramped tables, spinning his tumbler of amber liquid. He glanced up as I came in. His eyes skimmed over me, past me, then darted back. A grin split his face.

I ordered a beer from Cameron, then made my way over to Owen. He clasped my hand and pulled me into a hug.

"Been a long time," I said.

He thumped my back. "I'll say. Barely recognized you."

I wasn't the only one who'd changed. Owen was still taller and broader than me, but the eighteen-year-old I'd chased around the soccer field had worn jeans and running shoes back then, his shirts often from Goodwill—he'd showed up at school once, an old top of mine on his back. That kid had hidden behind a mess of sandy hair. He'd been the first to throw a punch if it meant protecting a friend.

This thirty-year-old man seemed cool and collected: trim hair, gold watch, pressed dress shirt and slacks. Like me two years ago.

"You join a biker gang?" he asked as we sat.

"I heard membership came with health insurance." We shared a grin, and I gestured to his business attire. "What about you? Did a millionaire mug you and swap out your second-hand clothes?"

His straight posture relaxed. "I had a meeting, hence the clothes. And if my friends in D.C. saw my teenage self, I'd have gotten laughed out of the city."

A bead of moisture dripped down my bottle. I spread it around with my thumb. "Heard you were living there. Married. Working some fancy finance gig. Why'd you guys move back?"

He swirled his drink as low murmurs rose from the half-filled room. Blues tunes strummed from the speakers. Owen tapped his finger against his glass. "I moved back on my own. Left everything behind. The wife. Job. All of it. Consider me starting fresh."

"Jesus. Anything you want to talk about?"

"Yeah, actually. Would probably do me some good, but it's a messy divorce, and the judge assigned to the case has a thing about us airing our dirty laundry. My lawyer advised me to keep my mouth shut. My soon-to-be ex-wife is an attorney herself, and she can be"—he took a healthy pull of his drink, then crunched on an ice cube—"aggressive."

"Well, I'm around if you want to unload. My life took a

header off a cliff a couple years back. You'd be preaching to the choir."

"That header have something to do with why you don't talk to your folks?"

I gripped my beer so tightly my rings bit into my skin. Last thing I needed was more family talk. "Not something, everything. And how'd you know we were on the outs?"

"I called them to get your number. Your mother jumped all over me, demanding I talk some sense into you, convince you to call them." He shook his head. "That woman always scared the crap out of me."

I huffed out a laugh. "She has a way with words. Remember when she picked us up from that soccer tournament in San Diego and caught us sharing a beer under the bleachers with the Ellis twins?"

He coughed around his next swallow, pounding his chest and clearing his throat. "What did she say again? 'If you're not in the car in two minutes, you'll never need a protective cup again.' My nuts crawled into my stomach."

"The Ellis twins were worth it."

The memory settled, the first positive one I'd had of my mother in ages. Others surfaced too: her singing me to sleep when I was sick, her tears of pride when I'd earned my Master Sommelier. The moments tugged at the frayed edges of my heart, guilt surfacing the way it did at times. A pang that didn't last.

Her interference with Rachel had singed all residual fondness. As did the memory of our last argument. When it mattered, when my future hung in the balance, she'd turned a blind eye.

Owen nudged my foot under the table. "There something *you* need to get off your chest? I may be under a gag order, but I can listen."

We hadn't seen each other in twelve years. No phone calls. No Facebook chats. I didn't know the first thing about his work or the woman he was set to divorce. In school, we'd picked up girls together and drank beers underage, sweating it out on the field with our teammates. We'd since grown into men, but underneath we were still the same boys, finding our way through life one fuck-up at a time. "There was this girl," I said.

"Isn't there always?"

"Pretty much." I ran my tongue over my teeth. Rachel's taste still lingered. As did the feel of her lips, her skin. *Always* a girl. But this mess had started before her. "Her name was Sophia, and I met her after college. Her family bought the property next to ours. That winery on the hill?"

He nodded, and I went on, ready to purge the story. Get it out. Eviscerate the guts of it. "Her father and mine didn't get along, something about pesticide usage seeping onto our grapes. My folks were pissed when I asked Sophia out. Not that my father giving me a hard time was new, but it wasn't cool. Then Sophia's dad found out our property division line wasn't accurate. He sued my father for a section of his vines, and the bastard won."

Owen let out a low whistle. "That must have burned."

"More like set off an explosion. By then I'd been with Sophia two years and planned to propose. But I was given an ultimatum. End things with her or lose the winery. Lose everything I'd worked toward. So I chose the girl, assuming he was full of shit. The man had always been stubborn, but I was his son, right?"

"Wrong?"

I clenched my fists. "The fight we had could've been heard for miles. The whole business landed in my brother's lap and I was disowned. But the best, the fucking kicker, was when Sophia found out, she turned down my proposal. I lost Offshoot Winery for her, and she dropped me like a rock."

Two years later, I could still barely choke out the words.

Owen winced. "Man, that's harsh. Your dad was always stubborn, though. Maybe it's his age. Some old-fashioned views on family."

My father was twenty years older than my mother. So

focused on the winery, he'd married late, and my brother had often joked she'd end up as his nurse. A joke that had lost its humor.

I mulled over Rachel's words today, that he might be unwell. It was likely a ruse. A trick to get me on the phone. If it were serious, Alena Giannopoulos would have shown up at my place and dragged me out by the ear. Still, I couldn't tell if the possibility made me sad or worried or protective. It was hard to feel much under the ache of losing Rachel.

I lifted my beer in salute. "To the women who ruin us."

"I'll toast to that."

I didn't mention how rough I'd been, or how I'd met another woman, one who was *real* and *beautiful* and had opened my eyes to the world. That not driving to her place and convincing her to give us a proper chance was killing me. Righting the wrong my family was intent on denying would be the only bright spot in my near future.

We finished our drinks, another round ordered as we caught up, painting the broad strokes of our lives. Turned out Owen was tired of working insane hours and planned to get into carpentry, a skill he'd developed since school. He wanted to make furniture and volunteer on some Habitat for Humanity projects.

Talk of giving back to the community played over in my mind, bringing with it thoughts of running viticulture events. Rachel had prompted the idea, her presence in my life shifting my thinking. Even before her, I'd grown tired of slinging drinks at Rudy's Tavern, and the contest had reawakened my love of wine. I could have denied it all I liked, but it was in my blood. Just like it was in Rachel's. My ray of sunshine.

On cue, my ribs tightened.

Ready to get home and end this shitty day, we said our good-byes and made plans to meet again. Unloading felt good, having a friend to grab a beer with even better. But neither lifted the weight from my chest.

By the time I got outside, the rains had unleashed, curtains of water draping the city in mist. I didn't flinch or run to my bike. I let the downpour wash over me. Puddles grew; cars splashed sheets of water onto the sidewalk. My heart was as heavy as my sodden clothes.

At home, I parked my bike and grabbed my backpack and helmets, everything a reminder of what I'd lost. Two steps toward my apartment, I stopped. My heart migrated to my throat. I blinked, sure the rain had blurred my vision, but a figure was hunched on my stairs.

A figure that looked a hell of a lot like Rachel.

CHAPTER 18

RACHEL

I COULDN'T BE sure how long I sat there. A light drizzle fell, my harried pulse slowing as the cool liquid drummed on my head, my arms, my legs. My jean jacket soaked through quickly, my sundress and leggings sodden. I didn't care. Jimmy had ended things. He'd called me on my erratic behavior, had admitted how hard he'd fallen for me, then he'd driven away.

With my heart.

It was all clear, suddenly, how I'd let us derail. Jimmy had apologized for his abrupt behavior, had asked for a chance to explain, but I'd clung to his indiscretion, allowing it to taint my mind. All to make pushing him away easier. I'd sabotaged our relationship from the start, holding back, taking instead of giving, so many stupid fears feeding my actions. But I was unprepared for him to end things, each word cutting deeper than expected. Watching him drive away had been worse, my chest caving the farther he got.

And I needed to get him back.

The rain pounded the pavement, tires spraying water as cars rushed by. I wrapped my arms around my legs, lay my chin on my knees. I wouldn't move from this spot until Jimmy returned and I apologized for my cowardice. I'd live here, if need be.

An eternity later, a familiar voice, deep and rich, said, "Rachel?"

My head snapped up. Jimmy's hair was as soaked as mine, his clothing, too. We stayed immobile, as though the sky hadn't opened up, dousing us with its fury. I dragged a hand across my face, unsure if tears were mixing with the rain.

This time I didn't hesitate.

"I'm so sorry. I want you. I want to listen to you, understand you and your life, and I want us. I was scared and stupid, too many family issues holding me back." My words fell as fast and hard as the downpour. "Yes, hearing you dismiss your mother like that and getting angry at me was hard, but I don't know what you've been through. It was wrong of me to judge. And you may be frustrated with me, tired of my games, but I'm done playing. I think about you all the time, wondering what you're doing. Hoping you're thinking about me. You made today perfect, and I ruined it. And I'm just—"

"Ray."

My heart hitched. He'd called me *Ray*. Not Rachel. It could have meant nothing. It could have meant everything. I bit my lip to keep it from trembling.

Then he said, "Get over here."

My belly dipped and I jumped, opposing forces that had me shooting into his arms. We clawed at each other, everything soaking wet. Our mouths, wet. Our clothes, wet.

Salty tears dripped over our lips. "I'm sorry," I said against his mouth.

"Shut up, Sunshine."

We broke apart, long enough for him to grab his pack and helmets, then we ran upstairs. He slammed his apartment door behind us as we toed off our shoes. We left puddles in his living room, his bedroom, until we were in his bathroom, the shower-head spraying against the glass walls. We walked in clothed, and his hips pinned mine to the tiled wall. His cock was hard as granite in his jeans.

"You're shaking," he said, forehead pressed to mine.

Warm water sprayed over his head. I was still cold, my clothes locking in the chill, but the quiver in my limbs was all Jimmy. And we had too many layers between us. "I need you," I said.

His nostrils flared. Eyes locked, we struggled with his T-shirt, the fabric suctioned to his body. We tossed it over the shower door, and it landed with a wet *squiltch*. My jacket and dress went next, leaving me in leggings and my bra, and him in jeans. His nipple piercings and silver chain rose with his shallow breaths.

We paused, not touching, ribbons of water dripping along Jimmy's cut shoulders, over his tattoos, down his defined chest. So beautiful. So *not* what I'd pictured as the object of my desire. An image I was happy to overhaul.

My tears leaked again, the burn building as I acknowledged the mistakes I'd made. I placed my hand over his heart. "I won't let you down again, but…I'm scared. I feel so much with you."

His eyes searched mine—blue and gray, hard and soft. His dark hair was slicked back, those full lips inching closer. He kissed my cheeks, smoothed my tears with his wet thumbs. "This is how it's supposed to feel. Kind of terrifying. And we still have stuff to talk through…but I want you, Ray. I'm all in."

I reached around him and dragged my fingers down the grooves of his slippery back, knotted muscles shifting below my fingers. "Are you sure? I can be kind of anal. I mean, I like things tidy, and if we're serious, you'll have to meet my family."

He pressed a finger to my lips. "I love anal, so that's not an issue." He winked. *Such a bad boy.* "Tidy makes messing things up more fun. As for us—I would love to meet the woman who raised you. I may look like a thug, but I can be charming."

He sure could.

"Now get out of those leggings so I can fuck you in this shower."

He could also be dirty.

We peeled off our layers, adding them to the river rising on his bathroom floor. His large hands gripped my ass and lifted as I wrapped my legs around his hips, all that male power pressed between my thighs. Power I had to touch.

One hand on his shoulder, I fisted his shaft with my other, reveling in the feel of him, so hard and thick, because he wanted me. I slid my hand up, root to tip, my thumb toying with the barbell under his swollen head, then I ground into him, pressing his length and piercing against me. Gone were my inhibitions, my reservations dripping down the drain with my tears. This man was all mine.

I swallowed my shyness. "Fuck me." I dug my knees into his sides. "Hard."

His pupils dilated, a low growl rumbling from his chest. He didn't hesitate. He pulled his hips back until the tip of his cock dragged down my belly and lined up with my entrance. His thrust was forceful, slamming me against the wall. The raining water was hot, the tiles at my back cold, my body so full with Jimmy. With *us*. He kissed my collarbone. His teeth scraped my skin, water coasting over my open mouth as I groaned.

"You're mine," he said, wet sounds of slapping skin echoing in the small space. "Don't push me away again."

"I won't." I pulled his hair, drank from his lips. "I'm yours."

I think he said *mine* again, but his gravelly voice disappeared in our hungry kiss, our tongues tangling as they slid against each other. I met his thrusts, my eyes rolling back. Electricity hummed along my skin. The drag of his cock, in and out, fanned the sparks. Hotter. Wilder.

I apologized with my mouth, sucking a path down his neck, over the hard bone of his shoulder, sinking my teeth in when he pushed deeper. His fingers dug into my ass, possessive and hard enough to bruise. It spurred my lust.

"I'm so close," I said.

"I'm right there. You make me fucking crazy."

He changed our angle, freeing a hand to squeeze my breast and take my nipple into his mouth. My whole body clenched. Wet from the shower and his mouth and *him*, heat pulsed through me, sharp shocks that shook me to my core. His orgasm chased mine, both of us chanting *fuck* and *yes* as we stole our pleasure.

My limbs slackened. We traded lazy kisses as he pulled out of me and eased my legs to the floor. "I love your pierced cock," I said against his mouth.

We swayed under the water, dancing to an unheard song. He rolled his tongue around mine in a long, sensual stroke. "I love your tits. The perfect handfuls."

"I love the dimple in your chin." I pressed my lips to the spot. "I only just noticed it, under all that sexy scruff."

He lifted my left leg by the knee and coasted his fingers up my thigh. "I could spend a week worshipping your legs, and I fucking love your badass tattoo." He released my leg and slapped my hip.

"Nipple," I said, circling the flat of his with my thumb, trailing the piercing.

"Neck." He tasted my skin.

We named each body part we loved, punctuating the claims with a lick or kiss or nip, the water unrelenting, my chill extinguished, everything deliciously warm. We didn't say we loved each other. There was still too much vulnerability between us. Too much uncertainty. But we said enough.

Then his face was between my thighs. I came on his tongue, shuddering until I sank to my knees, too. More kissing. More groping. I pushed him to his feet and took him in my mouth, pulling a long, hard orgasm from him. I'd never enjoyed giving head as much as I did with Jimmy. The power. The control. His thickness in my mouth and piercing on my tongue.

Later, we sat cross-legged on his bed, Jimmy in his black briefs, me in his Harley-Davidson shirt, a bowl of red grapes between us. I popped one into my mouth. The sweet juice mixed with the tannic skin. "When you were a kid," I said, "what did you want to be when you grew up?"

He plucked a grape and spun it through his fingers. He grinned, boyish and sweet. "A professional wrestler. Like in the WWE, not the Olympic kind. I was addicted to the shows, had all the action figures. Even had a name picked out for my wrestling persona."

I flicked his ankle. "Spill it."

He leaned closer and lowered his voice. "The Grisly Greek."

I tried to stifle my laugh, but picturing a young Jimmy puffing up his chest and reenacting wrestling scenes as the Grisly Greek was too much. "Wow, yeah. I think you missed your calling."

"Your turn, smart ass. Aside from your endless list of jobs, what did seven-year-old Rachel want to be?"

The title *winemaker* pushed to the tip of my tongue, but we were talking about childhood dreams and fantasies. There was my ballerina phase, but it hadn't lasted long. My other wish was a lot more embarrassing. "I don't want to say."

"You brought it up."

"I'm changing the topic."

His hair had started drying, wavy black strands standing on end, a glorious mess framing his handsome face. If he really were a wrestling star, I'd name him the Heartthrob.

"Not a chance," he said.

The Stubborn Heartthrob.

I picked up a grape and peeled its skin—a habit that drove my brother nuts—one thin strip at a time. "Fine. But this stays between us. Gwen and Ainsley would never let me live it down."

He rolled his hand, coaxing me on, and I sighed, slipping the naked grape into my mouth. "Big Bird," I said.

"You wanted to be a big bird? As in fly?"

"No, like Big Bird. From *Sesame Street*. I wanted to be Big Bird."

He tipped his head back, laughing. "Oh, babe, that's priceless. I'll be in charge of Halloween costumes this year."

"Not on your life." My cheeks heated, and when his comment sunk in, they positively burned. Halloween was in five months. Jimmy was imagining us together...in five months.

Why had I fought this feeling so long?

Still chuckling, he wrinkled his nose at my grape peelings and grabbed another, chewing slowly. "What's your greatest fear?"

The mood sobered, intensity in his gaze. We hadn't spoken of our argument yet, but it was there, below the surface, under the lines etched between his dark eyebrows. If nothing else, I owed him my honesty.

"Disappointing my family. When my brother got in trouble for leaving his room messy, I'd run to mine and check that my clothes were put away. Mitch has always been smart and driven, but he pushed his boundaries—skipping classes and winding up in detention. The more he rebelled, the tighter I toed the line. Like I had something to prove, maybe. The one time I colored outside the lines was with a guy like you."

"Like me?"

"Not *like you* like you, but the dangerous kind with blue hair and ink and a collection of punk albums. Dating him drove a wedge between my mother and me, and it ended in a huge fight with my dad, which was the last time I saw him. So all this stuff"—I gestured between us—"the way I've put you off and have been difficult was tied to this fear of mine. Letting my parents down again. Especially my father." I rubbed at a dry spot on my heel.

He placed two fingers under my chin and forced my eyes on

his. "You're a strong woman. Independent. You have friends who love you, and you care about your mother and brother, more than most people I know. He'd be proud."

Tears threatened again, a familiar wave of regret and sadness and longing for my father. A day didn't pass where I didn't think of him or silently ask his advice. When I opened my heart to the pain, it became hard to breathe. Even now, five years later, his loss had the power to break me.

I grasped Jimmy's hand from below my chin and kissed his palm. "What about you? What's your greatest fear?"

He threaded our fingers together. "The opposite of yours. Ending up like my father. Cold. Bitter. Stubborn. Having kids and never showing them affection. I'm scared I'm just like him." Turmoil thickened his voice.

He may have been a stubborn mule—exactly how Alena had labeled her husband—but Jimmy was as far from cold as a man could be. "When I'm with you, you make me feel sexy and precious. That's a man unafraid to show affection."

He untucked one of his feet and placed it by my hip, settling his inked elbow on his knee. He ran his fingers through my damp hair. "You do crazy things to me, Sunshine."

I purred at his admission. "The feeling is mutual. And I know you're angry at your family, but that's because you care. Apathy would be worse." I touched his toned calf, dragged my nails through his dark hairs. "What happened? I want to know, and I won't get mad. I just want to understand."

Drawing a deep breath, he stretched his neck and exhaled. Then he spoke softly, the story binding us closer. We could share our hopes and dreams all we wanted, but the ugly truth was the iron that branded lovers. He started with Sophia, a name I was starting to loathe.

Meeting her in the grocery store had itched at me, but that was *before*. Now Jimmy was mine. My jealousy was irrational, but here I was, playing that name game in my head, rhyming Sophia with *Banana-fana fo-phia* like a schoolyard bully. Pulling her hair and kicking her shins would have felt better. Still, I listened. His hand was in my hair, mine on his leg as he bled it all out: Sophia's family, the land dispute, and the ultimatum dished out by his father. The worst was the argument.

"The bastard tried to hit me." Jimmy practically spat the words. "I was bigger than him, stronger, but he was so mad he raised his palm to backhand me across the face."

He pulled away, releasing my neck to scrub his own. His body bristled with anger. "When I caught his wrist, he was livid. Called me a mistake. A disappointment. Told me no son of his would marry an enemy. The whole thing was surreal, like we'd spun the clock back to the sixteenth century. But he meant every word, and my mother listened to the whole damn thing. Aside from yelling at him once to stop, she let it play out. Neither of them called afterward, not that I would have answered. I had Sophia and, as far as I was concerned, she was enough. Until she fucked me over, too."

He dropped his head, as though the weight of his confession pressed on his shoulders. When he looked up, his eyes were a river of pain. "They discarded me like trash. Who does that to their kid? And why does it still hurt?"

Heart breaking for him, I pushed the bowl of grapes aside and straddled his lap. "Because you still love them. They're your parents, your family, and you still care." I pulled his head to my chest and pushed my fingers through his hair. "You might not be ready to forgive them now, but maybe in time, you will. Maybe, if you have a family one day, you'll want your kids to meet their grandparents."

He fisted the back of my shirt and buried his face in my neck, but he didn't reply.

My lingering guilt bloomed. He was right, earlier, saying he wasn't the bad guy. My father had loved me. We may have had arguments, and I'd thrown a tantrum or fifty growing up, but I'd never questioned my place in my family. To be told you weren't wanted could push anyone over the edge. Add losing your livelihood and love, and it was no wonder Jimmy shut them out.

If his mother called now, I'd probably give her a piece of my mind. Nice Rachel would let Reckless Rachel loose.

But there'd been regret in Alena's voice. She missed her son, and his father might have come around, too. It was still possible for her to ease Jimmy's pain. For that, I would help any way I could. Jimmy couldn't be pushed, but if the situation presented itself, I'd find a way to bridge the gap between them.

There was still one question left to ask. Something that had been gnawing at me. "Sophia…" I said hesitantly. "Did you ask her to marry you because you loved her, or were you trying to upset your father?"

Jimmy pulled back and stiffened. His hands ceased coasting along my spine. "Why would you ask that?"

"It's just, I don't—"

"Forget I asked," he said, cutting me off. His cheeks hollowed, shadows darkening his face. "Sophia is in the past. We're over. What happened is done."

Like after the grocery store incident, he was shutting down, unable to relive that time of his life. It was unhealthy, and if I had to guess, I'd say aggravating his father had had something to do with that relationship. I'd walked the "provoke your parents" path. Dating Gabe had intrigued me, but he was more of a symbol. A way to prove my independence. If my father hadn't died, if I hadn't spent the last five years living the life I believed he and my mother had wanted, I'd probably look a lot more like Jimmy—riding a motorcycle, piercings hidden under my clothes.

Bad Boy and I were more similar than I'd realized.

He would need to face what had happened eventually, maybe own some part of the disaster. A mountain we'd climb another day. Our night had been intense enough, and I still had apologizing to do. With my body.

I shifted my hips, a subtle rocking that had him gripping my sides and pulling me closer. He thickened between my legs, and air hissed through his teeth. We lost ourselves in each other. Our fight, my job stress, his family drama, and all he couldn't face—everything faded, the only tangible feelings being our connection. And desire. And a pinch of *ohmyfuckingGod*.

CHAPTER 19

RACHEL

I WAS A NEW WOMAN. Well, not *new*, new. I still had my wash-and-wear wardrobe. My straight hair hadn't gained unexpected volume. There was still no career on the horizon. But my hips swayed when I walked, a perma-smile plastered on my face. I was sickeningly happy.

The treadmill pushed me into a slow jog, my arms pumping at my sides. Ainsley and Gwen were finishing their yoga class, and I was humming along to One Direction (because I was twenty-seven going on sixteen), my mind on the man responsible for my current state of bliss, Jimmy *Bad Boy* Giannopoulos.

It had been two weeks to the day since we'd fought and kissed in the rain and gotten dirty in his shower. Two weeks of (holy hot) sex and (heart melting) talks and (delicious) sleepovers. We flirted openly at the contest sessions now and held hands on the street. The more time we spent together, the more I craved, never questioning my feelings, never caring if I slipped from proper to wild. I hung out with him at Rudy's Tavern; he picked me up on his motorcycle from the gym. We'd effortlessly slotted into each other's lives.

"The boy situation, looks like things are good."

I started at the gruff voice and gripped the handrails. "George. I didn't notice you."

911 was on the treadmill beside mine, a common occurrence these days. We'd built a friendship of sorts. I'd berate him for not dieting, and he'd ask me about my "boy." Never pushing his opinion on me, only passing the time. I had a tendency to over-share. I'd told him about Jimmy's love of wine and how we could talk for hours or not talk, and how Jimmy surprised me with another picnic last week—that one on my apartment floor, blanket down, fresh pasta made by his strong hands. I didn't share how my bad boy had pushed up my skirt and used his talented tongue until I was incoherent, but George had become an unlikely confidant.

"What makes you think things are good?" I asked.

He started the machine himself, even using the incline. He increased his speed. "The look in your eyes. That is the look of love."

I couldn't fight my giddy smile. "Maybe," I said, unwilling to analyze the extent of my happiness. I hadn't even told the girls how hard I'd fallen for Jimmy. My feelings were intense, but something kept me from sharing those three words with him. Fear, maybe, that the second I let it all flood out, it would drown me.

George marched, his focus on the windows in front of us. Pedestrians strolled by. "Nonsense. I may be old, but I know love. Thirty-two years ago today, I married the most beautiful woman in the world."

Reverence coated his voice, love for his wife evident in his husky tone. "It's your anniversary, then?"

He nodded, and I slowed my treadmill, matching his speed. Each year on my parents' anniversary, my father used to book a hotel room. He would buy my mother flowers and treat her to a fancy dinner. She would walk on air for a month afterward. He died a week before their twenty-fifth year. When the hotel emailed to confirm the booking, my mother's keening could be heard across the city.

I blinked rapidly and steadied my breaths. "What have you planned for the occasion? Flowers? Chocolate? Wine?"

He waved a dismissive hand. "I am not an amateur."

For a grumpy old man, his sweetness was endearing. "What does a *professional* husband buy his wife to celebrate their love?"

"A weekend away from me."

I choked on a laugh. "You booked your wife a private getaway for your anniversary?"

Smug, he increased his incline. "Of course."

He obviously knew the woman. If a pampered weekend alone would make her happy, more power to them. "I'm sure she'll love the gesture," I said.

He harrumphed, clearing his throat as though it were lodged with rocks. "I cannot gift her the one thing she wants. It is the next best choice."

"What does she want?"

He paused briefly. "To reverse time."

His wife must be one of those obsessive women, fighting age, filling her face with creams and Botox. I caught my reflection in the window, a transparent view of myself. I had my gran's freckles and her slender build. My straight brown hair was all my father, along with my large eyes. The bend in my nose matched my mother's, as did my fuller bottom lip. I was a living puzzle, my pieces shaped by my family. Altering even a bit of myself would be unthinkable.

Plus, Jimmy said he couldn't wait to add laugh lines to my eyes.

As George and I walked in silence, I imagined Jimmy's reflection next to mine—so different, so rugged. Yesterday, during our contest session, his hotness had distracted me. His hotness *always* distracted me, but this time I botched the tasting. The basement cellar had felt cavernous, only eight contestants left before the final round next week.

Mr. *Master Sommelier* was a shoo-in. Jimmy never broke a sweat, the tastings and serving tests like taking candy from a baby for him. I had my money on the Schnozinator for his competition. Although the blond, April, seemed competent, too. She nailed every service exercise, making me feel like I'd sprouted extra thumbs.

The tastings had been my strength, until yesterday. Not just because of how Jimmy's T-shirt had clung to his biceps. My palate had been off. Glasses of Syrah were lined up before us, a grape I'd always admired. I should have discerned the acidity and earthiness of the old-world wines no problem, noted the fruit-driven qualities of those from Australia and the U.S. Instead the flavors melded, my answers more guesses than fact. It had been worse than my multiple choice psych exam back in college. I'd spent that painful hour circling letters based on the women present, guessing their bra sizes.

Any minute, I expected a termination email in my inbox.

But another impending disaster loomed larger: Jimmy's meet-and-greet with my mom in a few hours.

My belly churned, the prospect of her horrified face souring my mood further. George and I walked at an even pace, both lost in our thoughts. He grunted in exertion, and I eyed my new friend. He was straightforward and as old-fashioned as they came. Maybe his opinion could prepare me for the worst.

"Can I ask you something, George?" He gave a sharp nod, and I swallowed. "Remember that advice I was after, about approving of your son's girlfriend?"

His mustache twitched, but he didn't reply.

"You made your opinion pretty clear. One I don't agree with, by the way"—I shot him the evil eye—"but I'm taking my boyfriend to meet my mother tonight, and he's the exact opposite of who she imagined me with."

"Is there a question?"

I snickered at his snarkiness. "Yes, *there is a question*. What can I do to soften the blow for my mother? Anything that might help her get past the superficial stuff."

He continued his soldier march, his paunch practically hitting the machine's console. "Do you care for this boy?"

"I do," I said quietly.

"Does he care for you?"

"Yes. I mean, I think he does. He says he does." A flush crept up my neck, like I was in high school, whispering about a secret crush. "I've never felt like this about someone. I'm nervous I'll mess it up. Worried my mother will scare him off. He's really special, and he's estranged from his family. They hurt him badly. So I guess I want my family to love him. Remind him what that's like. He deserves it."

My newfound fears lodged in my stomach. I'd gone from being afraid of rocking my familial boat to worried my mother would be so awful Jimmy would have second thoughts. Even if she hated him and couldn't see past his tough exterior, I'd stand by my man. Shoulders back, head high, I'd prove how happy he made me. Still, the prospect of dealing with her dramatics was daunting. She would never cut me off like his parents—not permanently, at least—but her superpower was just as scary: Maternal Guilt.

Which meant Jimmy could face more parental rejection.

George slowed his treadmill until it stopped. I followed suit, waiting on his wisdom. The man could have nothing but wrinkles to show for his age, but I'd bet each line represented knowledge earned.

"Love is beautiful," he said. "It is the heart of life. Show your mother your heart, and she will understand." His eyes were a light blue, clouded with age, a red rim often at the edges. Today they glistened, as though he were choked up. Discussing my love life probably reminded him of his wife.

I also didn't contradict him and claim I was still waffling in the *maybe* love column. It would have felt like a lie.

"This man," he added, "he is lucky to have you, and my wife was right to send me here." He stepped off his treadmill and patted my arm, a sweet gesture I hadn't expected.

"Thank you," I said.

He offered a thin smile and left. I had no idea how his wife sending him to exercise figured into anything, but his touch eased my churning stomach, as did his words.

Until Ainsley bounded over and smacked my butt. "Two hours until D-day. You ready to puke yet?"

I rubbed my backside. "I was doing fine until a second ago. And is that sweat on your forehead? Did you actually work out?"

She rubbed her towel over her face. "Emmett was in the class, behind me, so I had to show him I'm into those stupid breathing exercises, and that I can *bend*." She winked.

"Did you ask him out?"

She tossed her towel around her neck and held each end. "Sadly, I did not. He left before I had the chance."

Gwen snuck up behind her and tugged her ponytail. "He rolled his mat in record time and bolted, to avoid her."

"Says you," Ainsley huffed.

"Honestly, you need glasses. Emmett is gay with a capital G, and Ainsley here"—she poked our friend in the side—"is in denial."

Ainsley scrunched her button nose. "I still think you're wrong."

"I am *not* wrong. Have you seen him eye other dudes? Totally scopes them."

"Whatever. Gay or not, drooling over him helps pass the time."

Gwen ran a hand up the back of her neck. "I'll give you that. Gay, straight, or bi, the man is fine. Speaking of fine men, have you prepped Jimmy for the interrogation he's about to face?"

The girls knew how to ratchet up my stress levels. "As much as I can."

"I'd love to be a fly on the wall when your mother sees him," Ainsley said.

"A video would be awesome." Gwen's heartfelt contribution.

"You two suck at pep talks, and if I don't get home soon, we'll be late. I need to start this night on the right foot."

As I pushed past them, Gwen said, "Tell him to wear a tie."

The image of Jimmy in a tie was ridiculous. And hot. Especially if he were shirtless. I fanned my face.

"Have him wear a cup," Ainsley added. "Your mother is skilled with her kitchen knife. One look at his tats, and she could 'accidentally' circumcise him."

My cackle exploded, a blast of sound that had all heads swiveling our way. "I'll keep that in mind." But my man *was* circumcised, and if I told them about his jewelry, they'd ask for photos and a life-sized sketch.

———

Jimmy threaded our fingers as we neared my mother's front steps. "I've always loved these houses. The Painted Ladies, right?"

I nodded. "My father admired them for years. It was a big deal when he bought it." The street was quiet, the pastels of the row houses blanching under the setting sun. My father had loved the nickname attributed to the Victorian homes. The day he'd bought our yellow and red slice of real estate, he'd popped a bottle of Veuve Clicquot and offered me my first sip of Champagne. It had tasted like sunshine.

We paused on the top step and Jimmy spun me to face him. "You ready for this?"

With his unshaven face and motorcycle boots, Jimmy was still Jimmy. But his jeans weren't ripped, and his black T-shirt didn't have band logos or sayings splashed across the front. He wanted to make a good first impression. The effort swelled my heart.

I shook out my silk tank top, hoping to staunch the gathering sweat. "Ready as I'll ever be. I mean, it's not like it'll change anything, right? You won't get freaked out and realize my family is nuts and decide you're not into me and erase my number from your phone and never—"

His lips landed on mine, a deep kiss following. He always kissed me like this. Like I was his oxygen. He nipped my bottom lip. "No matter what, nothing will change. I'm here for you."

Still, my nerves lingered.

Stanley was the first to greet us. She slammed into my legs and wagged her tail, grinning.

Jimmy sat on his heels and rubbed her cropped sides. "What's your name?" he cooed as he stroked her. His attractiveness jumped ten notches.

"Stanley," I said, although she looked like an imposter. She normally had crimped brown fur, like an eighties rock star, all of it a few inches long. My mother must have taken her to the groomers. Aside from her head, the rest of her was clipped so short, her skin shone.

He scratched her ears. "You're a cute boy, Stanley, even though your haircut is dog ugly."

Stanley wagged her tail, unconcerned by Jimmy's insult. "You just told my dog she was a boy and called her ugly. Great first impression."

He looked up at me, eyebrows raised. "You named your girl dog Stanley?"

On cue, Stanley shoved her nose in Jimmy's crotch. He grabbed her collar. "Hey, there, Stan. Maybe leave the boys alone."

Stanley liked what she smelled and dug her nose in farther. Smart puppy. "Did you put bacon in your pants? Because Stanley loves bacon and if you shoved some down there, she'll be glued to your nuts."

With one hand, he held Stanley at a distance. His other crept under my gray skirt, between my thighs. "You want to check?"

Did I ever. My passion for Bad Boy had only grown. One look, one touch, and I was one hot flash from mauling him. Unfortunately my mother's front hall was neither the time nor the place. Especially when she chose that precise moment to greet us.

"Rachel, I didn't hear you..."

Jimmy yanked his hand from under my skirt and stood. Stanley rubbed against his leg. I nearly fainted. My mother pursed her lips.

"Am I interrupting?" Her eyes danced the length of Jimmy, taking in his tattooed arms. Her expression soured, as though she'd chugged expired milk. Not a good start.

"Ma, this is Jimmy—my boyfriend. Jimmy, this is my mother, Lydia Kates."

He dragged his palm down the side of his jeans and stepped forward, extending his hand. "Mrs. Kates, it's a pleasure."

Her attention darted from his hand to his face to me, returning for another circuit. Color rose to her cheeks. "It's lovely to meet you." She offered him a limp handshake. "Rachel, do you mind helping me in the kitchen? Jimmy can join Mitchell and Cora in the living room."

The woman didn't waste time. I pointed Jimmy through the archway. He squeezed my hip as he passed—a gesture of solidarity. A bulletproof vest would have been preferable.

My mother strutted down the hallway, each slap of her ballet flats punctuating her distaste. I followed, steeling my nerves.

She'd renovated the kitchen last year, a project that had kept her occupied. Large windows filtered light onto the new seating area. She'd updated the appliances and had added gray subway tiles, the all-white cabinetry trimmed to match the crown moldings. My father would have loved it.

What he would *not* have loved was the tension hanging between us.

My mother gripped the center island with one hand. She

pressed the back of her other to her forehead, as though she'd sprung a fever. "What was that?"

Before answering, I closed the sliding pocket door to the dining/living area. I crossed my arms and faced her. "What was what?"

"That." She gestured wildly. "That *man*. When you said you'd met someone and wanted to bring him home, I was thrilled. Pleased you were moving forward in one area of your life. Then you show up with...him? Does he even have a job? Is he one of those street performers?"

My limbs locked, my teeth clamped so roughly my jaw hurt. "His name is Jimmy, not *him*, and yes, he has a job. He's a bartender."

"*Bartender?*"

"Bartender."

She swayed, a minute from fainting. "Lord, where did I go wrong?"

I inhaled until my chest hurt, then released my breath to the count of five. "He's a bartender, not a drug dealer. He's Greek and grew up in Napa Valley, but no, he doesn't have a fancy car or dress like Mitch and his friends. Jimmy's smart and sweet, and he makes me happy. If you give him a chance, you'll see that."

"Greek," she mumbled, as though unfamiliar with the term. Like our family trip to Greece had never happened. Like we didn't eat at Andros regularly.

"Yeah, Greek. You love Greek food. You order souvlaki all the time." And her not-a-Greek salad.

But I wanted to grab the nearest fork and stick it in my eye. This conversation was nearing the ridiculous, talking about Jimmy as though he were defined by his culture's food. My father had been Jewish, my mother was Catholic, my grandparents from Europe and the United States. We had family dinners on certain holidays, and I was told stories of my heritage, but neither background drove my choices. Apparently my urge to please those around me did. As did my need to prove myself successful. Unlike Jimmy, who owned who he was, regardless of what others thought.

Pride surged at the strong man he was.

My mother straightened, the soft drape of her cashmere sweater a contrast to her stiff posture. "Have you sampled his souvlaki? Is that what this is about?"

Oh my God. "Ma, keep your voice down." My cackle almost escaped, nervous energy and frustration bubbling up.

Her loud-nasal tone didn't abate. "It's like Gabe all over again—you rebelling, wanting to have fun with the boy from the wrong side of the tracks."

"You are impossible," I whisper-yelled. "He's from *Napa Valley*, and I wouldn't even care if he'd grown up in a trailer park. And he's nothing like Gabe. I fought my feelings for Jimmy at first, for the same stupid reasons you're judging him now, and I won't make that mistake again. He's the real thing. And yes, I've sampled his souvlaki." I rolled my shoulders back. "It's the best I've ever tasted."

"Honestly, Rachel." My mother fanned her face, unsure what to make of my outburst.

We'd rarely fought since Dad died. We quipped at each other, pecking like hens, but there had been no drawn out arguments, and we'd certainly never dissected my sex life. She'd gone too far, though, her inappropriate comments proving what I'd come to know.

I was in love with Jimmy Giannopoulos.

There was no maybe about it. No hesitation in my pounding heart. I wanted to fling my body over his, protect him from her negativity. This was not a fight she would win.

Her brown eyes welled, a look I'd come to dread. She was about to unleash the Maternal Guilt. "It's all my fault. The piano lessons I forced on you. The job for Uncle Charlie. The men I set you up with. You're rebelling because of me."

She was impossible. "It's not you. It's not the fact that I was bottle-fed or that you told me the Tooth Fairy wasn't real. I'm with him. That's the end of it, and I hope you find it in your heart to support me."

A vein in her left temple throbbed, her heated face nearly matching her pink lipstick, but she didn't speak.

I shook off my irritation and searched for my Zen. "Remember the day Dad was out of town and you rear-ended his car in our driveway?" Frowning, she nodded, and I went on. "I waited in the living room with you, and I'll never forget how foolish you felt. How terrified you were to tell him. Do you remember what he said?"

Chin trembling, she sighed. "As long as I get to spend the rest of my days with you, you can smash my car to pieces."

It was the day I understood what it meant to be in love.

I pressed my tongue to the roof of my mouth, suppressing the urge to cry. "I always admired your marriage. Dad supported everything you did. You made each other better. That's how I feel about Jimmy. What else matters?"

She flattened her lips. Whether to tame her emotions, like me, or in defiance, I couldn't be sure. But I'd said my piece. I swiveled and pulled the sliding door open, praying Mitch and Cora had more tact. If they were asking Jimmy about his freaking *souvlaki*, I'd claim adoption.

CHAPTER 20

JIMMY

RACHEL WALKED into the living room—cheeks flushed, head bent —like her butt shot had just gone viral. Mitch was sharing a priceless story about the time twelve-year-old Rachel had peed her pants on a family trip to Mexico. Their father's weak Spanish had led to him asking a waiter for *polla*, thinking he'd ordered chicken. Turned out, he'd asked for a "woman." The conversation that followed had Rachel laughing until she'd wet herself.

As much as I wanted to hear more embarrassing stories, her look of mortification deepened as the gist of our conversation sunk in. She gawked at her brother. "Seriously? The *polla* story? Can I still file for emancipation and sever ties with this family?"

Cora giggled, the airy sound matching her appearance. She had boy-cut blond hair and big blue eyes. Her pink dress hung loose over her sprite-like frame. She placed a dainty hand on Mitchell's knee. "You should stop. It's not fair to Rachel."

"Was it fair when Rachel told you about the pot brownies and my bathing session in Huntington Park fountain?" He quirked an eyebrow. When no one answered, he said, "Consider us even."

But the evil look in Rachel's eye as she sat next to me and glared at her brother said otherwise. She settled into my side, hand on my thigh. I shifted, stretching my arm behind her on the couch. Stanley took advantage of the move and tried to shove her nose between my legs, *again*. The damn dog was relentless. I held her off with a calculated knee shift.

"She must have a thing for souvlaki," Rachel murmured. Her maniacal laugh erupted, and she slapped her hand over her mouth.

Lydia entered then, a tray of dip in hand. Her face was an emotionless mask. "Contain yourself, Rachel."

Her reproach sent her daughter cackling harder, a sound that had me wanting to pin Rachel down until I kissed her raw. Lydia, however, was unimpressed—with her daughter and her daughter's choice of boyfriend. A situation I'd have to resolve. Winning Lydia over was important to Rachel, so it was important to me.

Rachel leaned into my ear. "My mother might take a while to warm up, and I don't recommend the dip."

I eyed the thick, white mixture warily and heeded her advice. Where her mother was concerned, I wasn't about to back down easily. "You have a lovely home, Mrs. Kates."

She sat opposite us, straight backed, her answering smile nowhere near pleased. "Thank you. Rachel tells me you're a"— she cleared her throat—"bartender."

A chuckle came from Mitchell, and my shoulders bunched. When I first met him, he'd seemed more genuine than his pressed shirt and gold cufflinks. He'd shaken my hand warmly and hadn't flinched at my ink. It didn't mean Rachel's brother wasn't judging me. I glanced his way now, braced for his disdain, but he was shaking his head at his mother, not me, like Lydia was a petulant child.

"Come on, Ma." Amusement laced his voice. "The Healing

Hearts luncheon isn't far, and you mentioned something about a bartending issue. You should hire Jimmy."

Lydia's eyes widened in fear, and I nearly laughed. Instead of watching her squirm, I jumped in to save her. "Not sure I'm the right man for the job, but I know the event. It's an impressive fundraiser, and a great cause. Must take a ton of work."

That won me a head tilt and closer inspection. "It does," Lydia said. "I've helped organize the event since David passed. Or, more to the point, Rachel forced me into it." She winked at her daughter, nothing but love in her eyes. "She was worried I'd lock myself indoors, which might have happened if it weren't for my kids. They were here daily for those first couple of years."

They all shared a sad smile, and I cupped Rachel's shoulder.

During some of our quiet moments, she would whisper stories, her voice melancholy as memories spilled out: her and her father snorkeling in Mexico, their father/daughter school dance, how his hearty laugh had filled a room. She'd been Daddy's little girl, and he'd likely been wrapped around her finger. His passing must have crushed her, but she'd held it together for her mother, had made sure Lydia pulled through. When things got tough, they'd banded together. As a family should. My father's property had been threatened, not his life, and all he'd done was lash out.

Rachel's phone buzzed, breaking the moment. Lydia turned her focus to Cora, asking about her teaching job. Rachel fished her cell from her purse and checked a text. Her face fell.

"You okay?" I asked.

She stuffed her phone away. "Yeah. Fine."

Except her left cheek hollowed. She was stressed. "Who was it?"

She slumped into me and lowered her voice. "Alonzo. I was eliminated from the contest. But I'm fine," she added before I could speak. "I was expecting it."

Didn't mean it hurt any less. Rachel didn't like to fail. No one liked to fail. Every soccer match lost as a kid had me cursing and pouting, until my grandfather had sat me down and told me real men used their frustration to improve. *Turn that anger into success*, he'd say.

I angled toward her and dipped my head to catch her eye. "You might not have passed that round, but you proved yourself in that contest. You have more passion for wine than anyone in there, me included. Please don't let it slip away."

The corner of her mouth curved up. "I have passion for *someone* in that group, and his jewelry, if that's what you mean."

One teasing word from her and my lust awakened, the jewelry in question ready for a tug. My dirty princess. "You're damn right you do, and the feeling is mutual. But don't brush this off. You're smart and your palate is amazing. We'll figure this out together."

She touched my cheek and said a quiet, "Thank you."

Guilt, familiar in its discomfort, coated my chest. And the way she looked at me? There was something deeper in her eyes, something I wanted to dive into. Bask in.

If I didn't need to end my family's lies, I'd bow out of the contest and give her my spot. Even if I won, I'd pass on the job. But it was more than putting things right. My parents had come between Rachel and me once, with nothing but a phone call. I wouldn't let it happen again.

The past week, Rachel and I had fucked and tasted every inch of each other, filling in the gaps with laughs and stories, sharing the details of our lives. The extent of my feelings, *my love* for her, floored me. And scared the hell out of me. I never thought I'd let myself feel this again, give someone the power to hurt me. But here I was, in love with this amazing woman. No way would I lose that. Not this time. Not her. She meant more to me than Sophia ever had.

I kissed Rachel's forehead, swallowing down my rising mix of emotions. I worried about where she'd go from here, hoping she wouldn't shy away from a career in viticulture like I'd ditched my Master Sommelier status. Something I needed to rectify. If I wanted her to chase her dreams, I couldn't keep avoiding mine.

I'd thought more about organizing events for boutique wineries, using my education and whatever contacts I still had to build a festival. Events highlighting smaller producers. Soon, I'd make plans, but Rachel and the contest came first.

I glanced up to find Lydia watching us…with longing? Her brown eyes were glazed, her pinched mouth softer. Her pearls rose and fell on a deep breath.

She scrutinized her daughter. "Everything all right?"

Rachel squeezed closer to my side. "Just some bad news. But Jimmy's helping me figure it out. Nothing to worry about."

Lydia studied us, long enough I actually ventured toward the onion dip. Bad idea. It burned the roof of my mouth, the thick mixture nothing but mayonnaise and raw onion. Eyes watering, I forced it down, preferring Lydia's withering glance to that horror show.

She nodded once, as though coming to a decision. "I'm glad you've found someone supportive, Rachel. It's lovely to see."

Rachel pressed her hand over her heart. "Thanks, Ma. That means the world."

Warmth crept over me, uncomfortable in its intensity. Lydia's acceptance shouldn't have mattered. I'd stopped caring what others thought two years ago. Still, heat flooded my cheeks like I was a kid again, glowing from parental praise. It felt *nice*. Better than nice. It was a reminder my family had stolen more than my future. They'd cheated me out of basic affection, but Lydia sent it rushing back. Even at thirty, I soaked it in…and an idea caught, a way to run with her approval and pull the shards of my life together.

I leaned my elbows on my knees, nudging Stanley away from my crotch. "If you're in a bind for bartenders, I might be able to help."

Lydia's response came slowly. "The company we hired went

out of business. We have a few others in mind, but the timeline is tight. Was there someone specific you'd recommend?"

"Not exactly. I've been wanting to promote smaller vineyards in the area. This type of event could be great exposure. You could market it as a 'diamond in the rough' thing. Let guests know they'll be sampling from the best boutique wineries. We'd have to spin it, maybe have them pouring from private collections at set stations, something to wow the crowd. Even do the wine tasting blind and have guests guess the grape, with prizes for the winners." I pushed my hand through my hair. "Sorry. Just thinking out loud."

Lydia didn't seem to mind. "Supportive *and* smart. I should have known better than to question my Rachel." She leaned back and clasped her hands. "I'd like to discuss this further, but I bet the girls would love the idea."

Pride rushed through me again, along with a sting of longing. If mending fences with *my* mother were as simple as proving I wasn't a selfish meathead, maybe I could suck up my anger and return her endless calls. Unfortunately, ours wasn't a trivial misunderstanding. *You were a mistake*, my father had claimed. A disappointment. She hadn't once stood up for me. No point wishing for the impossible.

But this, right now—my first taste of belonging in too long— was because of Rachel. Because she'd screamed pussy and had walked into The Blue Door and entertained my advances. Because she trusted herself with me. I'd have to do the same with her. Tell her about my plan and why I'd really joined the contest, but my excuses kept piling up. Delay tactics.

She would be pissed. No avoiding that. If hanging up on my mother had shoved a wedge between us, this stunt of mine had the power to ruin what we had. It all felt more fragile now. With my heart in the mix, it felt downright brittle. Like everything we had could shatter at any moment.

I'd still have to come clean, about the contest and the extent of my feelings. I should do it tonight. Get it over with and hope for the best. Neck tense, I sipped my wine.

Mitch whistled a low note. "If Mom came around that quickly to your biker boyfriend, it might be a good time to tell her Cora's pregnant."

That was unexpected.

Rachel squealed, the sound so jarring, I nearly spat out my wine.

"Mitch!" Cora buried her face in her hands.

Lydia frowned at her son. "Stop being a pot stirrer, Mitchell. That's nothing to joke about."

Mitchell didn't take it back, and Cora's hands dropped to her belly.

"Oh my God. How could you not tell me?" Rachel didn't wait for a reply. She was up in seconds, pulling Cora into a hug.

Lydia fanned her face. "A baby? But when? How? You're not even married."

Mitchell beamed at Cora as Rachel pressed her hands to Cora's stomach. He shrugged at his mother. "Yes, a baby. When—she's six weeks along. How—I could get into it, but Rachel might stick her fingers in her ears and sing songs like when she was a kid. As for the married part, we're not in a rush. We weren't expecting this surprise, but we're thrilled. The rest will come later."

Rachel jumped, chanting, "I'm going to be an aunt," while Lydia tossed more questions at the couple, shocked Mitchell hadn't proposed, wondering if they'd planned to move to a bigger place and where and when and listing all the ways she'd help.

Rachel may have been scared of her mother's reaction to us, but I'd bet Cora and Mitchell had been shitting bricks, terrified to break their news. Unnecessarily. Lydia proved she was a woman whose sun rose and set by her kids. She'd already started coming around to me, and she'd no doubt spoil her grandchild rotten, whether or not her son followed a traditional path.

I stood and shook Mitchell's hand, thrust into this nutty family. Everything with Rachel was a wild ride, but this was special. And tough. Some sadness would follow; her father wasn't here. He'd miss this important milestone, which meant tonight wasn't the best time to confess about the contest, or my love. Saying the latter wouldn't feel right with lies between us. It would all have to wait.

CHAPTER 21

RACHEL

"ARE YOU SURE THIS LOOKS GOOD?" Nothing about the leopard-print skirt hugging my legs would mix and match with my wardrobe. The black stilettos were dangerously high, the halter top flashier than I usually purchased, its greens and blues bright against my freckled skin. I still grinned, knowing I'd buy it all.

A hint of reckless just for me.

"If you don't buy it, I will burn your wardrobe and send you through the streets in a potato sack." Ainsley wasn't one for subtlety, but she was indeed the Style Whisperer.

The instant we'd walked into the all-white space, sparse décor adding to the posh vibe, she'd sifted through racks and had chosen two outfits for me. The second was a homerun. The woman was like a hound dog, sniffing out perfect ensembles. She'd already found a purse to match her pink pumps and had Gwen buying a jade scarf to highlight her eyes.

Gwen came up behind me and hung a silver chain around

my neck. "This would work, too." The attached sphere dipped into my minimal cleavage.

I touched the pendant, then ran my hands over my hips, imagining Jimmy's palms following the trail, strong and sure. He went crazy for my legs, an attribute this outfit played up.

"It will set me back," I said, "but it's worth it. And FYI, I'll be on a serious budget soon." I faced the girls, needing to share my news, get it out and make it real. "I'm going back to school."

Ainsley surveyed the store. Gwen wrapped her new scarf around her neck.

Neither acknowledged my comment.

I cleared my throat and tried again. "I'm going back to school."

"What's on tap this time?" Gwen asked. "Window washer? Dog trainer?"

Ainsley adjusted my skirt, smoothing out a side seam. "I saw online that a girl critiques dick pics. Like, breaks them down and analyzes the positives and negatives. You should do that. With our help, of course."

Gwen scrunched her nose. "I'm all for hot guy pics, but peen shots? Not sure."

That was a *no* for me. There was only one male specimen I cared to look at. One I'd swirled my tongue around last night until Jimmy had grunted my name and spilled into my mouth. I licked my lips. "If Jimmy's is the last I see, I'll die a happy girl."

"Is he big?" Gwen asked, nudging me. "He looks like he'd be big. And good."

The girls hadn't ceased prodding me, trolling for bits of information, trying to get me to share juicy gossip. I glanced around, worried the store owner could hear us. "I'm not talking about my boyfriend's *dick*."

"What else do friends talk about?" Ainsley piped in. "Since neither of us have men in our lives, we need to live vicariously through you."

"Not happening."

My friends, of course, started talking to each other, as though I'd vanished.

Ainsley tapped her chin. "I bet he's small."

"Or maybe he's all about himself," Gwen said, "and doesn't know how to please her."

"That would explain why she hasn't dished about him."

"Right? If he were good, she'd be all gushy."

Tired of their taunting, my harsh whisper rushed out. "He's the perfect size and rocks my world and knows exactly what to do, and he's *pierced*, which is ridiculously hot, and that's the last we're talking about my sex life."

Gwen held up a hand. "Back up, buttercup. Did you say *pierced*?"

Oh, crap.

Ainsley sighed. "Does he have a twin?"

Two women entered the store, browsing through the quiet space. Before my friends could grill me on details or my cheeks burned any hotter, I shoved the conversation back on track. "Like I said, I'm going back to school. Not to add another useless diploma to my collection. This time"—I inhaled deeply, memories of my phone call earlier today speeding my pulse—"I'm enrolling in the Napa Viticulture program. Not sure I can get in for the fall, but I talked to admissions and there's a chance. I can probably finish the course in two years, then I'd apprentice, so I'll be, like, thirty before I dive into the field, but I'm going for it."

Gwen looked ready to launch an attack hug. "Are you for real?" When I nodded, she flung her arms around me and squeezed. "This is the best news! But I thought the school thing was a hard no. What changed?"

She released me, both of us grinning like loons. "A bunch of things, really. The contest reminded me how much I love wine, but the service stuff wasn't for me. And Jimmy's been talking a lot about his family vineyard, what it was like being involved. I think *not* going for it would haunt me. I'd always wonder."

I didn't mention my birthday wish, still worried speaking it aloud would thwart my efforts. That my forward momentum was truly a result of that one fateful night. Everything with Jimmy was falling into place. Even my mother was on board with my plans.

After the Mitch and Cora bomb—the revelation bittersweet, knowing my father would never meet his grandchild—I figured returning to school wouldn't shock her. I explained how long it had taken to figure out my path. That my fear of failing again and delaying my life had held me back. She didn't cave right away, but she offered her support in the end. I *may* have pointed out my father was the reason I loved wine—a low blow, which made her cry—but she got behind my plan.

Sometimes a girl had to fight dirty.

"Does this mean you won't get to dress dead people?" Ainsley asked.

I shuddered. "My mother tried to force the funeral home issue, but she came around. Even offered to pay my tuition, which feels wrong at twenty-seven, but I'm done being stubborn. If she wants to help, I'll take it." Which meant she'd hold it over me every time she asked a favor. More Maternal Guilt in her arsenal. Painful, but worth it.

Gwen pointed to the fitting rooms. "Go change. I'm buying your outfit as a *congratulations you're moving on with your life* gift."

Ainsley clapped. "I'm buying the shoes and necklace. Jimmy will die when he sees you in that. And Rachel," she called as I turned, "that pierced conversation isn't over."

"Yeah," Gwen chimed in, "I have questions. We can have a whole sex ed night. You'll use your dildo to show us exactly how his jewelry affects your pleasure."

Damn them and their needling selves. But the thought of Jimmy seeing me in this mini-skirt put a bounce in my step. I hadn't told him about my school plans yet. As much as he'd pushed me to consider viticulture, the choice needed to be mine.

No outside influence. I had to make sure it was what I wanted this time.

The second I decided, though, I knew. I'd also bet my father was smiling down on me, pleased I'd taken the risk.

Suddenly I was desperate to share my news with Jimmy, and finally tell him I loved him. I'd been waiting, thinking we'd celebrate after tonight's final contest round. He and the Schnozinator would be serving top wine critics, both vying for the coveted sommelier position. Jimmy was sure to win, and I wanted the moment I shared those three words to be special, but I knew better than to delay important milestones. Losing my father had taught me that. The where or when or how of spilling my heart to Jimmy didn't matter.

Living without regrets mattered.

I had to drop by the gym to pick up my paycheck, then I'd run to his apartment and catch him before the contest. Tell him I was going back to school and that I loved him so much it turned me inside out. I'd give him the best good luck kiss in the history of good luck kisses. Maybe we'd have a quickie, too. My smile nearly split my face.

————

I reached the gym at four. Normally George and I would be on our treadmills by now, walking in time, him asking me about my "boy." I hated skipping our forty minutes together, time I'd grown fond of, but shopping with the girls and seeing Jimmy took priority. What I didn't expect was to hurry through the doors and practically walk into 911 himself.

I cringed, guilty for having ditched him. "Sorry I missed our workout. I hope you weren't waiting for me."

Instead of offering a signature gruff response, he touched the woman beside him. Her figure was slight next to his bulk. She turned and studied me, critical at first, a warm smile following. "Rachel?"

This woman was much younger than George. Thick black hair spilled over her shoulders, a turquoise pantsuit accentuating her trim frame. Something in her full lips tugged at me, the slope of her cheekbones and dimple in her chin subtle in their familiarity. She reminded me of a celebrity, maybe. Catherine Zeta Jones? Either way, she was gorgeous.

I smiled. "Yep, I'm Rachel. And you are?"

Her gold necklace rose as she inhaled. "I'm Alena—George's wife and"—her arms shook slightly—"Jimmy's mother."

"Jimmy's...*my* Jimmy's mother?" My hand shot to my mouth, and I stepped back, my gaze flitting between this stunning woman and the old man I thought I knew. George. *911.* The grumpy father figure I'd confided in. The man who'd asked me questions about my boyfriend, never letting on who he was, stealing information about his son. A violent storm set sail in my stomach. "I don't understand."

"Jimmy is my son," George confirmed, and my mind *reeled.*

Was there a hidden camera? Was I being punked? Maybe I'd slipped in those stilettos at the store, had hit my head, and was in a coma, the swelling in my brain causing hallucinations. I bit my cheek, tasting blood. Not a coma.

Somehow I found my voice. "You lied to me." And he was so old to be Jimmy's father.

"I did no such thing," George said, his snarkiness ever present. "If you had asked, I'd have told you."

"Excuse me?" The harshness of my tone had his watery eyes widening. "You said you only had one son."

His face hardened. "Family matters are complicated."

"Complicated?" My volume rose, but I didn't abate. This was the man who'd torn Jimmy down and ruined his life. A man who'd abused my trust. "We've spent hours together and you never, not once, mentioned who you were. But you had no problem asking me about my 'boy.' So you could what? Spy on him? On us?" My voice dropped, disappointment and sadness seeping through me. "I'd hoped Jimmy was wrong, that he could mend things with his family. Looks like I was being naïve."

Jimmy would also potentially lose his shit. I'd been hanging out with his freaking *father*. For weeks. How would I explain that? Suddenly ill, I sat on the nearby couch. Guests often sat here and picked through fitness magazines, killing time. I wanted to curl into a ball and block out this reality.

"What I did," George said, "I did for my family."

Alena said something to him about giving us space. I didn't watch him go, barely noticed her sit beside me. I was in khaki shorts, the black leather cool under my thighs. I fought the urge to press my forehead to the armrest, instead squeezing my eyes. *His freaking father.*

"I've been trying to reach Jimmy for a while, as you know." Alena's voice was soft but strong, the same as it had been on the phone. The day Jimmy and I had nearly broken up.

What was even happening?

"I found out where he lived," she went on, "and I stopped by a few times, but never knocked on his door. It was one thing for him to ignore my calls. If he'd looked at me with hate…it would have crushed me. But I'd watch him, from time to time. Not often, but when missing him became too much, I'd follow him awhile, to gauge if he was happy. That's when I saw you."

Lines creased Alena's forehead, sorrow in the depths of her eyes. Her despair was potent. "My husband is a good man," she said, "but even good men do bad things. What happened with Jimmy was wrong. What George said was potentially unforgivable, and my silence was equally as harmful."

When I didn't comment, resignation laced her tone. "At the time, I thought my interference would make things worse. I decided to give them space to heal. Then everything happened with Sophia, and it spiraled out of control. I gave Jimmy six months, hoping his anger would lessen. By the time I contacted him, he wouldn't speak with me."

I'd nearly chewed my cheek raw. "And you thought stalking him through me was the answer?"

She massaged her knuckles. "This family is on a thin wire. One more fight, and there would be no hope of patching things up. George can be difficult. He's fiercely stubborn and couldn't admit he'd been wrong. He also saw Sophia for what she was and believed losing Jimmy was worth saving our son from that woman. I'm glad Sophia is out of Jimmy's life, but things were said in the heat of anger that weren't true. I was wrong. George was wrong. We need the chance to make things right."

The night of the rainstorm, when Jimmy and I had shed our clothing and our walls, he'd admitted how hurt he still was. How deeply his family's actions had cut. That wasn't just a man needing to heal. That was a little boy who missed his mother and father and wanted to reverse time. And Sophia *had* had her hooks in my man—conniving woman that she was. It's possible George's interference had saved his son a lifetime of heartache, but underhanded deception would get them nowhere.

"It's not for me to judge what happened in your family. I wasn't there. I don't know the details. But this? Sneaking into our lives? It's not okay."

She nodded slowly. "You're right. It's not. But when I saw Jimmy with you, and the way my boy smiled? I realized you were making him happy. He wasn't going to let us in, and I was running out of options. It was wrong to send George here, but my husband had to work things out for himself. See you and understand his son was building a life, one we wouldn't be a part of. I'd also hoped he'd get a window into the damage he'd done. Without that, any meeting with the two of them would have turned ugly. I'd have lost Jimmy, once and for all. I'm not willing to let that happen."

It felt as though I'd swallowed a brick, my body unbearably heavy. Before this epic disaster, I'd grown to like George. He was straightforward—or so I'd thought—and filled a void in my life, and George's fondness for his son wasn't contrived. Our last conversation, after I'd confessed Jimmy was scarred by his family's actions, George's emotions had run high. That was also the day I'd realized how much I loved my bad boy.

And I did. A sweeping love. The kind where you'd overlook being wronged if it meant seeing your lover happy. Although I wouldn't forgive his parents' deception easily, they weren't trying to hurt us. They were fighting to save their family, something Jimmy needed as badly as them. More, even. How could I deny him that?

I rubbed my chest, as though the movement would soothe my erratic heart. "It will take a while to get my head around this, but if I can help your family, I will. For Jimmy. But I can't guarantee he'll listen to me."

She exhaled and stopped fidgeting. "George was right when he said you were special. No matter what happens, I'm glad Jimmy found you."

Now I wanted to cry and…hug her? Which was strange. This whole mess was odd and unfathomable, my emotions pulling me in a thousand directions.

George joined us, but I wouldn't let him sit until he apologized for lying to me. He hemmed and hawed, but I shot him my best scowl, and he conceded. A first step forward. They then explained their plan, minimal though it was. They wanted Jimmy to join his brother and run the winery, give him everything they'd taken away. It would begin with a meeting, with George admitting the errors of his ways. I was to pave the road and convince Jimmy to hear him out.

Total piece of cake. *Right.*

That coma/head trauma scenario was sounding better and better.

After goodbyes and promises to be in touch, I made my way to Jimmy's place. This visit was supposed to be about telling him I loved him and sharing my school news. Now I was contemplating dropping this parental atomic bomb, but heaping him with stress when he needed to be on his A-game for the contest didn't feel right. It would have to wait until after.

But I couldn't delay seeing him now. I had to remind myself of what we had and staunch my panic that this would turn into another picnic disaster, with him blowing up at me.

My heart wouldn't survive the fallout.

Full of trepidation, I hurried to his apartment. I started opening his door, when I noticed a tall man inside. Probably Owen. We'd yet to meet, but Jimmy had mentioned seeing him today, at a soccer game or something. He was happy to have his old friend in town and said it was because of me, that I'd made him realize all he'd been missing. Maybe I'd affected his life as much as he'd changed mine. Maybe he'd understand why I wanted him to give his parents another chance, despite their underhanded meddling. Or maybe he wouldn't.

My stomach lurched.

The two of them were in the kitchen and hadn't noticed me. Owen was in shorts and a tank top, a soccer ball under his foot. The back of his neck was sweaty. I placed my hand on the door to open it fully, when Owen said, "I still think fucking with your family winery is trouble. Once you do it, there's no going back."

I snatched my hand away, unease prickling up my spine. Instead of going in, I squished out of sight, like a creeper. Like some girl who eavesdropped on her boyfriend. This day was spiraling from bad to worse.

Jimmy's voice drifted out, his words adding to my dread. "If I don't do it, I'm just as bad as them. And every time one of them gets involved in my life, something goes to shit. Rachel accidentally answered a call from my mother, and I turned into an asshole. We also fought over other stuff, but I nearly lost her, and it's not okay. Once this is done, they'll leave us alone. It's not like they thought twice when they ripped the winery from me."

"You told Rachel yet?"

My ears burned. I was humiliated at how desperate I was to hear Jimmy's answer, that I was still eavesdropping.

"No. But I will. Tonight. I've been scared she'd freak out, but she needs to know."

My mind spun, attempting to piece together the meaning behind his words, but standing in the shadows felt as wrong as what George had done—lurking around, hoping for information.

I wiped my damp palms on my shorts, then shoved the door fully open. "What do I need to know?" I forced brightness into my voice.

Jimmy was downing a Gatorade and stopped mid-swallow. He and Owen shared a look, probably wondering what I'd over-heard. *Too much and not enough.*

Even though I harbored a secret big enough to fill the Pentagon, and he clearly had one of his own, I couldn't help but look. *And look.* Jimmy's brow was slick with sweat. He'd tossed his shirt on the couch, and his workout shorts hung low on his hips. His chest and abs rippled with his deep breaths. If Owen weren't here, if our lives hadn't gotten irrevocably complicated, I'd lick a path over Jimmy's pierced nipples and down his happy trail, not stopping until he was hard and in my mouth.

But Owen was here, and there was something Jimmy hadn't shared with me. Something important enough that he was scared.

One foot on his soccer ball, Owen spun to offer his hand, but he pulled it back. "I'm Owen, but I doubt you want to touch my sweaty hand."

Mine was damp, too, from nerves, not exertion. "We can save that for next time, but it's great to finally meet you. How's the move been?"

"Can't complain. Things are more laid back than D.C., which is nice, and I'm volunteering on a Habitat for Humanity project." He was handsome—tall and lean and fit, the type of man I would have imagined for myself, before Jimmy. My gaze fell back to my bad boy, the only guy for me. His strong jaw pulsed, wariness in his wide stance. Unusual for him. Everything about this situation was off, setting alarm bells ringing in my head. My stomach didn't just lurch. It dropped to my feet.

Jimmy clapped Owen's shoulder. "Thanks for the game. Next time I'll kick your ass."

Taking the cue, Owen picked up his ball. "Not in this lifetime." He said a final farewell, leaving Jimmy and me alone, facing off.

I waited on his confession, while he was unaware I was hiding the tiny, unimportant, *miniscule* fact that I'd been hanging out with his father for weeks and had just had a conversation with his mother. *Kill me now.* Yesterday I'd been on cloud nine, everything in my life falling into place. Now I was just falling.

Still, I couldn't ignore the tightness on Jimmy's face, or the fact that he was scared I'd freak out. Words didn't get more ominous than that.

Practically holding my breath, I asked, "What haven't you told me?"

CHAPTER 22

JIMMY

WHAT HAVEN'T you told me? It should have been a simple question, one I'd pored over for weeks. But this was Rachel, the woman who valued family above all else, and I was about to prove I was an asshole. I'd tried to rethink my plan, reassess if walking away was better than spilling the truth. Better than destroying the winery I loved. Then anger would cloud my mind. My father's nasty words would loop, his choice to cheat our customers unforgivable. This was the only way, and it was time Rachel knew.

"When I told you I joined the contest because I thought it would be fun, I lied."

"Okay…" She waited, arms folded around her waist, wariness in her stiff stance.

I jammed my hand through my hair and focused on the floor between us. "Offshoot Winery's head winemaker has been messing with our Cabernet Sauvignon, blending in more than the twenty-five percent of other varietals allowed."

I looked up, and her eyes widened. "Shit."

I forced an awkward laugh. "More like huge fucking disaster. I tried talking my brother and father into doing something about it, but they were happy to plod along. It had been happening awhile, without anyone clueing in. They figured if it ain't broke, don't fix it."

"But if people knew, they could be sued, couldn't they? The wine world would be horrified."

In Italy, a man had been charged for passing off cheap wine as a premium Brunello. In New York, Rudy Kurniawan had been sentenced to prison for falsely labeling wines and swindling people out of millions. My family's transgressions weren't so notorious, but the winery wouldn't escape unscathed.

I confessed it all to Rachel, spilled the whole sordid story: seeing the contest flyer the night we'd met, needing to expose the lies by leaking them through the final round. My hope to finally let go of my past. As I went on, Rachel's face transformed from flushed to ashen, one hand clutched over her chest. My heart nearly busted through my ribs.

I expected relief, my secret finally in the open. Instead my neck prickled, the air in the room suddenly suffocating. The sweat on my skin turned clammy.

"You'll destroy them." Her anguished whisper nearly cut me down.

I worked my jaw, everything feeling hazy. Wrong. Bad. "Breaking the rules isn't cool, Ray. It's gone on too long, and if it bites me in the ass later, my name will be ruined. If I do it now, I can claim I just found out. I'm aware of the fallout, that my family won't forgive me. It also means they'll finally leave me alone—*us* alone. I can move on. Don't you want that?"

"Yes, I want that. But not like this."

"It's the only way."

She made a frustrated grunt, arms tense, like she wanted to shake me. "In your stubborn head, maybe. But sabotaging your family winery, the winery that's in your blood, will make it worse, not better."

I fisted my hands, wishing I was at the gym, punching bag swinging, all my frustrations pummeled into leather. She didn't understand. Even when she'd worried her mother wouldn't support her choice of men, Lydia had proven her wrong. Rachel had only ever known love. "I've tried. For two years, I've tried to put this crap behind me. But my parents aren't like yours. They are vindictive and selfish. I need to sever my ties with them."

Panic flitted across her face. "Your parents don't deserve this."

"You don't know them or what they deserve." There was that tone of mine again, biting and nasty. The asshole lurking below the surface. When I'd sipped my first glass of Offshoot wine in two years, I'd been rude to Rachel and had cut her off. I'd barked at her when she answered my mother's call. Now I was lashing out...and it gutted me. I could barely control the sting of my voice. I didn't understand why the hell my family still affected me so much. Ashamed, I dipped my head and rubbed my neck.

No. I wasn't over what my parents had done. Not by a long shot. And Rachel was getting dragged along for the bumpy ride.

I was about to apologize, when she said, "Actually, I do know them."

My head shot up. "My parents?"

Slowly, she nodded. Slowly, apprehension fisted my gut. When she didn't elaborate, I said, "I don't follow." I didn't *want* to follow. There was a feral look about her, like she was cornered, no escape in sight.

I stood bare chested and queasy, her khaki shorts and white T-shirt a preppy contrast to my ink. I should have been all over her, teasing her inner thighs with my fingers, getting her ready for me. Instead tension hung between us. And doom. I could sense it. Whatever she was about to say would be the final blow.

It was a sucker punch.

"Your father has been exercising at my gym. For a while. I

didn't know who he was," she added quickly, talking over herself. "I swear, I didn't know. Then he was there today with your mother, and they admitted who they are. They are so torn up and sorry and want to make amends. Which means you can't do this thing. You can't destroy them and the winery. They want you to run it again, with your brother."

The room swayed. Rachel knew my *fucking* parents and wanted me to work with them like nothing had happened? Like they hadn't committed fraud and booted me from their lives? A sharp pang slammed into my ribs, worse than sparring at the gym. How could she be on their side after everything I'd told her? Unless she'd been lying this whole time, toying with me.

My mind stilled. Eerily, almost. Something shifted, a sinking feeling that had me reliving the shittiest day of my life. The day Sophia had turned down my proposal.

I stepped back from Rachel, bile building. "You're telling me you've spent time with my parents and didn't tell me? That you didn't realize who they were?" *Lies. Lies. Lies.*

She sniffled. "No. I mean, *yes*…just your father at first, but he didn't—"

"You know the people who ruined my life, and you never mentioned it? Until what? Until you knew my actions would ruin their winery?" *Until she realized what she'd lose.* I barely recognized my voice—flat and detached, listing my thoughts as they formed. The pieces of her story slotted into place, taunting me with the truth.

I'd misjudged a woman again.

Calmness weighted my bones, a sudden quiet. Like my heart had simply stopped. "How long have you been planning this?"

She squinted at me. "Planning what?"

She was good, I'd give her that. I gestured wildly, one hand slashing through the air. "*This.* I mean, I swear to God, Rachel, you certainly had me fooled. Because that's what I do, I guess. Too damn trusting, like my grandfather. I just never fucking learn."

She reached out, but something in my glare had her yanking her hand back. "You're not making sense, but whatever you think I did, you're wrong. I'd never hurt you. I…" Her brow crumpled. "I love you."

I winced, her words another harsh blow. God, how I'd wanted to tell her the same. Before her deception. Before my life came crashing down. "Bullshit," I said.

Her skin paled. "Excuse me?"

"*Bullshit.* Our relationship has been nothing but lies."

"What the hell are you talking about? Did that soccer ball hit you in the head?"

Her vehemence was a dagger in my heart, her deception suddenly clear. My body still craved her, needed her in a visceral way, one touch able to dull my turmoil, one kiss obliterating everything but us. It was all poison now.

There was nothing left to do but end this madness.

"You can stop pretending, because I get it—your glorious deceit." The timbre of my voice dropped, roughened with resentment. "You've been after a winery gig since before I met you. You somehow realized who I was at that first bar and thought you maybe had an in. Even asked me to give you a winery if you won our blind tasting. The idiot I am, I didn't clue in. Thought you were joking around. Looks like the joke's on me."

The scenes flipped through my mind, faster and faster. A wildfire surging. My accusations rose with the flames. "You worked me over, had me falling over myself to be with you, while you got to know my parents. You convinced them to let me back in the family business, so you'd end up sitting pretty, working the job you'd always wanted, the prestige of Offshoot Winery putting dollar signs in your eyes. I get it, Rachel. I fucking get it now. It's pretty smart, actually. Con the broken man with promises of love and affection. It's all so fucking clear."

I hadn't just misjudged her; I didn't know her at all. And I'd fallen hard. Harder than for Sophia, by a landslide, leaving me lied to and used again, treated like I was a means to an end.

I was an idiot.

Her eyes sparked, the innocence I loved darkened with malice. She poked a furious finger at my chest. "How dare you."

I snorted, done with her lies. "Pretty sure I'm not the one in the wrong here."

"Unbelievable." She shook her head, like *I* was the traitor. "Did Sophia mess you up this badly? Are you so oblivious you think I've been hatching some secret plan to take over your winery? That's beyond ridiculous."

"What's ridiculous is that I let myself be fooled again."

She flung her arms in the air. "You're a fool, all right. And an asshole. I made that winery crack at The Blue Door because Cameron mentioned something about it to Gwen. I didn't know your name then, didn't have a clue who you were. I can't even believe what I'm hearing."

"*Enough,*" I bellowed, the sound like a hammer on a bell.

Rachel's shoulders shot toward her ears.

Mine caved forward. "Isn't it enough?" My energy leached out, my arms loose at my sides. "Just admit what you did and we can both move on."

A tear slipped down her cheek, the salty slide of it burning through my chest.

"I didn't lie to you, Jimmy. I love you. I didn't know who your father was until today, but I've grown to like him, and your mother is genuinely crushed. You're just so stuck in your head, you can't see it."

God, she seemed sincere. And devastated, a quiet fury heating her blotchy cheeks. And love? I'd been consumed by my love for her the past weeks, keeping it in, letting it grow. Hearing her say the words was crushing. I couldn't make sense of anything: her actions, my parents. The wrecking ball Sophia had swung boomeranging back for a final blow. *Me* possibly duped again. It was worse this time, a swell of betrayal knocking me off my feet. Because Rachel was everything. My head pounded—faster, harder—until the screaming pain nearly blinded me.

Even if she wasn't lying, Rachel knew how Sophia had manipulated me. I'd shared with her the details of my parents' betrayal—the tainted wines, my birthright yanked away, my father's swinging backhand and cruel words. She knew, yet she didn't care.

I blinked through the pain. "If you really didn't know who my parents were until today, then tell me who's side you're on, because it sounds like you're more upset about them, about me exposing *their* lies, than about the hell they put me through."

Her chin trembled. More moisture shone in her eyes. "Yours," she said hoarsely. "I'm always on your side, which is why I want you to give them a second chance. So you can heal."

I could barely look at the woman I thought I loved. "It's like you don't even know me. Like you haven't listened to a word I've said the past months."

"But that's the thing—I *have* heard you. I heard your voice when you talked about the winery, the longing and the heartache in it. That place is a part of you. Tearing it down will destroy any chance of returning there, of ever fixing things with your family. And I know your father is a stubborn grump...but he's also sweet. Once, at the gym, I was telling him about my boyfriend—*about you*. And he—"

"*Jesus.* I don't want to hear about the time you bonded with the asshole who told me I was a mistake. I'm not the mistake here, but you and I..." The air thickened in my throat. "You and I apparently are. I'm done with my family. Done with falling for the wrong women. This is just... I can't keep..." Breathing hard, I jabbed the toe of my sneaker into the floor. "You'd better go."

Her tears streamed then, and I wanted to reach for her. Apologize and rewind. Tell her I loved her so much it hurt. It all felt so real, her anguish.

But if she truly loved me, she would stand by me when it counted. She wouldn't be here, begging me to forgive my parents and turn a blind eye to the wines they'd defiled. Her devastation was either an act to keep me and the winery she craved, or her version of love needed an overhaul. Whatever her motivation, I was done being used. I was done always finishing last.

Never again would I let a woman close to my heart.

She walked toward the door, but stopped with her hand on the knob. She looked over her shoulder, eyes wet with tears and…something else. Something forlorn twisted her features, as though she were lost. "I never expected to meet a man like you. You made me better, made me feel so much. And this pain right now? It's because of you, too. I love you more than I thought I could ever love another person. I've also never felt so betrayed. I'm not Sophia. You're the one I care about, not your family or your money. But you've got the chance to fix things before it's too late, and that's a chance I never had. I know how much more *that* hurts than anything your parents said in anger. Don't ruin it the way you just ruined us."

With that she left. She didn't slam the door. She walked out, stoic, but my fortitude slipped. It downright shattered. The finality of her words and the desolation on her face sent ice through my veins. The walls spun. They fucking tilted.

I dropped forward, hands to my knees. My temples pulsed with a strobe light of shame. I still couldn't see the truth, couldn't recognize a tree in the forest pressing closer. I had no clue if I was right or wrong or just plain stupid. I was sure I was over Sophia's actions, past all that bullshit. Had I been deluding myself?

Everything was tangled—her, my parents, however the hell Rachel had met my father. I tried to picture him at the gym, but couldn't imagine the man in sweats. He was always in slacks, thinning hair slicked back, dress shirts crisply ironed. If I didn't feel like I was about to puke, the image would have been comical.

The contest was in three hours. That left one hundred and

eighty minutes to figure out what to do. I grabbed my workout bag and boxing gloves, shooting out the door and peeling off on my bike to the gym.

When my first punch landed on the leather bag, the vibration rattled up my neck. I hit harder. And harder.

Whack. Sophia tearing out my heart.

Whack. My parents capsizing my life.

Whack. Rachel crying.

Whack. Rachel hurting.

Whack. Rachel walking out the door.

Whack. Whack. Whack.

I punched until my knuckles throbbed, pummeled the bag until I could barely hold up my arms. It took an hour before my mind began to clear. Thoughts I'd avoided for years got knocked loose, each memory more painful than the last. I'd buried them, thinking it was the only way to move on. All I'd done was let them fester, poison me. Air sliced through my lungs as I slumped on a bench, towel around my neck. Sweat dripped off my forehead.

Rachel must have been telling the truth. Too much had happened between us for it to all have been lies. She hadn't been taking their side, she'd been trying to do what she thought was best for me, so I didn't live with devastating regrets. I'd been too messed up to listen, to see.

I saw now.

A right hook to the jaw would hurt less.

There was only one way to make things right. I had to get her back; that wasn't optional. But I had to sort my life first. Stop running and deal with my family and my past.

CHAPTER 23

JIMMY

The sun lit my table, the outdoor café busy with friends sharing stories over espresso and biscotti. Two women beside me laughed, a nearby man and young girl chatted warmly. My impending get-together wouldn't be so blithe.

Especially not with how dead I felt inside.

However I'd suffered after Sophia, it didn't hold a candle to the past week. Eating had been a challenge, sleeping a write-off.

After that intense boxing session, I'd pushed into Crush and told Alonzo I was stepping down. The relief that crashed over me had flooded my chest. I hadn't realized how tense I'd been, that I'd been dreading following through with my plan. April took my spot and wound up beating the Schnozinator. Quite the win for her. Still, whatever release I'd achieved was short lived.

Since then, I'd powered through my shifts at Rudy's Tavern, my remaining hours spent on my bike or boxing, none of it easing the sting of hurting the woman I loved. Now I was meeting the person partly responsible for my bad decisions.

I noticed her heels first—four inches and bright red. Her legs were as shapely as I remembered, womanly curves showcased in a tight dress. Nowhere near as sexy as Rachel. Nowhere near as classy. A familiar ache took root in my chest at the thought of her.

I looked up. "Thanks for coming."

Sophia's answering smile didn't reach her eyes. "I don't have much time."

"This won't take long." Just long enough to work through the baggage I'd stored the past two years.

She sat, folding her hands on the table, making sure her rock of an engagement ring was front and center. The thing could sink a battleship.

A waiter asked for her order and she waved him off. No need to pretend we were old friends catching up.

I cleared my throat. "When you turned down my proposal, it sent me for a spin. I've fallen in love with someone else, but what went down between you and me has caused me to hurt her. There are some things I need to know."

"The woman at the grocery store?" She studied my inked arms, the cuff on my wrist, my rings. Disbelief still shone.

"Yeah. Her." My ray of sunshine. The woman who owned my heart.

The woman I'd devastated.

I sipped my espresso, the bitterness lingering on my tongue. Time to cannonball into the deep end. "Did you ever love me?"

I'd spent so long *not* thinking about Sophia and my relationship, I wasn't sure what had been real, especially when my feelings for Rachel were a million times stronger than anything I'd felt for Sophia.

She met my eyes, a note of sadness in her blue gaze. "Initially. It was fun and exciting for a while, but the sneaking around got old."

"It did." We'd waited a while before telling our parents,

knowing they wouldn't approve. The illicitness had its appeal. "And after?"

She wiped stray crumbs from the table. "After, less so."

Less so. Two damn words. I had never accused her of using me. She'd broken up with me, tossed my proposal in my face, and I hadn't had the balls to ask her why. Back then, the timing told me all I needed to know. Her family had been struggling, more money going out than coming in, and she'd been looking to hitch a ride. Hearing her admit she'd used me would have made the fallout that much worse.

But I needed to hear the words now. Needed to learn if I'd assumed wrong or right, and she wasn't making it easy.

"Thing is, Sophia, I've spent the last two years pretending I'm over what happened between us. Don't get me wrong"—I raised a hand in defense—"this isn't me looking for an in. We were wrong together, on a number of levels. Ending it was the right thing. This is about me having closure."

A man walked by, taking an eyeful of her cleavage. She replied with a flirtatious smile, enjoying the attention. Sophia always loved to be admired. She shifted on her seat, discomfort appearing in her pinched brow. "At one point, I did love you, but later I realized you maybe didn't love me. We both wanted something from each other."

That had me leaning closer. "You wanted everything I came with, right? The winery? The security?"

She snorted. "Don't say it like it's evil. Yes, I wanted security and a comfortable life. It's not a crime. People have married for a lot less."

"Doesn't make it right."

"If I'm here so you can give me crap for what I did two years ago, I'm leaving. It sucks you're still messed up, but I don't have to sit through this."

No, she didn't. I didn't want to extend this conversation any longer than needed, either. "What did you mean we *both* wanted something from each other?"

She cocked her head, the look on her face incredulous. "You really are clueless about yourself. As stubborn and as blind as your father ever was."

"Tell me what you really think."

She rolled her eyes at my sarcasm. "You used me as much as I used you, Jimmy. All you ever wanted was attention from your father, and if he wouldn't give you affection, the next best thing was his anger. You wanted to marry me to get back at him. If you'd had the winery, I may have dealt with it. But why would I tie myself to a man with no prospects when it was clear I was a means to an end?"

I slumped in my chair, the wind sucked clean out of my lungs. *A means to an end.* I'd thought as much when recalling her treatment of me, and I couldn't even deny her accusation. The night of the rainstorm, when Rachel and I had almost split up, she'd asked if I'd proposed to Sophia to aggravate my father. I wasn't willing to listen then, cutting our conversation short.

I was all ears today.

I replayed my glee when telling my father about Sophia. How his face had purpled. How he'd made the time to talk—*yell*—at me weekly, trying to convince me to break things off. I'd reveled in it.

Marrying Sophia would have been the biggest mistake of my life, and if I'd still had the winery, that's exactly what would have happened.

Losing it had saved me from that fate. My *father* had saved me from it.

I scrubbed my face, then shook my head. "I really fucked up."

Sophia didn't ask if I was referring to her or Rachel or my father. I was guilty, in some part, of sabotaging each relationship. With Rachel, the blame was mine alone.

"Anyway," Sophia said, "is there anything else? I need to get going."

Nothing, unless you included the mountain of apologies I

owed Rachel, and the uncomfortable conversation I'd be having with my parents. "That's it. And I'm sorry for my part in things. For not being honest with myself or you. I hope you're happy." Any enmity I'd harbored vanished. We were two people with a tangled past, good memories and bad. Good choices and bad. Chances were, if we hadn't gone through the wringer, I might never have met Rachel.

Sophia held up her hand and wiggled her ring finger shamelessly. "Life is great."

I chuckled. At least she owned who she was.

Next up were my parents.

———

Their apartment building was clean and bright, the lobby filled with Turkish carpets, beveled mirrors, and Renaissance paintings. I gave my name to the concierge, who waved me along. By the time I got to their door, my resolve faltered. Two years was a long time to break contact, the chip on my shoulder practically cemented in place. Still, I had to start somewhere, find a way to open a discussion. Considering the contest fiasco, probably best if I began there.

My mother answered after the first knock. "Jimmy." Her dark eyes watered, and guilt suffocated me. Exactly why I'd avoided her all this time. One look was all it took.

But I was far from alone in what had gone down between us.

I'd texted her yesterday, asking for a meeting, and she'd replied in seconds. Now neither of us spoke. She didn't comment on my T-shirt or ratty jeans or ink, and I didn't tell her she still looked beautiful. Her hands lifted, like she wanted to hug me, then she stepped back.

I'd never have imagined my parents in a city apartment, but there was a wall of windows and high ceilings. Plants filled a space next to a desk. I'd figured they'd spend their retirement on the vineyard—my father's dream. But my mother had grown up in the city and missed the action and people. Looked like he put someone else first, for once.

My gaze shifted to the painting to my right. It hung alone, a light shining from above, highlighting rows of vines stretching into the distance. It wasn't particularly good. Crude, really, the perspective slightly off, muddy colors in the foreground. I'd painted it in high school and now it hung in their hall.

The urge to offer my mother that hug pulled at me. Instead I walked past her. Each *thunk* of my boots on their white floor echoed, the only other sound the swish and crinkle of a newspaper being read. My father. He'd lost more hair and looked thinner, his button-down creasing over protruding shoulders. Probably those hours at the gym.

"George." My mother passed me and sat in the chair beside his, helping fold his paper. "Jimmy's here."

I didn't imagine my visit was a surprise, but my father looked at me like I was a guest, someone interrupting his reading time. Already, I wanted to scream. Rail at him for never giving me attention. Never loving me like a father should love a son.

Tamping down my anger, I sunk into the white couch opposite them, legs apart, arms crossed. We stared at one another.

And I couldn't take it. They didn't get to sit here in their perfect apartment, with my painting on their wall, smothering me in silent guilt when they were as much to blame for our fallout as me. If one of us had to be the adult in this situation, looked like it was on me to buck up.

"I joined a contest a couple months back, that sommelier thing the Adriano brothers organized. Rachel and I got to know each other through it, but the real reason I was there was to leak the Cabernet issue. To tell critics you've been mislabeling wines."

My mother didn't flinch. She crossed her legs and smoothed her black pants, but she snuck a look at my father. His bushy eyebrows didn't budge. His mustache didn't twitch.

"We know," he said.

Rachel. It must have been Rachel. To warn them? To sabotage me? But the truth rang clear this time. She would have told them *for* me. To save the winery, hoping I'd find my way back there. My ribs nearly suffocated my heart.

"I didn't do it," I said. "I wanted to, but I couldn't follow through. Mainly because of Rachel. I bowed out of the contest and have done a lot of thinking the past week. Realized I played a part in what happened with our family. I'm still furious with you both, not sure we can move past it, but I'm tired of running."

Neither of my parents spoke. My father sat like a king on his throne.

My mother's lips thinned by the second. Then she hissed, "*George.*"

His eventual comment: "You are a coward."

I shot to my feet, one second from barreling out of there. "A coward mislabels wine to save his ass. A coward goes to hit his son because he lost *land*. A coward never apologizes for being an absentee parent." I jammed my fisted hands into my front pockets.

He sucked his teeth. "This is how it is? A son yelling at his father? It is disrespectful."

"This isn't 1950, and maybe you deserve to be yelled at. Shaken, in fact. Anything to open your eyes and see *me*. I am my own man. A damn good one, at that. No thanks to you."

He matched me glare for glare. "Your mother did not teach you to talk like this."

My mother was clutching the arms of her chair, gaze flitting between us, forever letting her boys fight their own battles.

My father was right, though. She'd taught me to sit straight and respect women and defer to my elders. *My pappous.* She'd handed me the building blocks of life and trusted I'd make something of myself. I'd done that, at least. Rachel wouldn't have fallen in love with a disrespectful failure.

"You're right." I extricated my hands to cross my arms. "I had a wonderful mother and grandfather, and a lot of what I am today is because of them. The stubborn side of me, the part that almost married the wrong woman to prove a point, is all you."

I was on my feet, towering over him, but his glower made me feel two feet tall. Like nothing had changed. Like he'd continue to dominate my life. Force me back into my rut, the place where I'd work a dead-end job and ride my bike to forget the world. The place where Rachel and I couldn't be together, because she deserved more than a man just existing.

Then my father did the unthinkable. He said, "I am sorry," and I rocked on my heels.

He pushed out the words, his stubbornness unabated, and it should have been enough. I'd waited two years for his apology, but it barely made a dent.

"You are my son," he went on. "I have always been hard on you. Pushed you. You are smarter than your brother, and I knew you could do more. But you were stubborn, too."

"The apple doesn't fall far from the tree," I replied, but my frustration dissipated. He'd never told me I was smart before. Never praised my intelligence or shown pride in my accomplishments.

When I'd earned my Master Sommelier title, he'd nodded and said, "Good." I'd spent a year building a pile of flash cards a mile high, living and breathing wine, licking wet stone and eating under-ripe melon to develop my palate. He'd given me one fucking word.

Hearing a compliment now nearly knocked me over.

Still, the air between us was far from clear. "You told me I was a mistake and cut me out of the winery, and all you can say is it was because I was smart? Because you needed to push me? You'll have to do better than that, or I'm walking back out that door." Which wasn't how I wanted this meeting to end. I was tired. This constant strife was a drain.

My energy waned until I sat on the couch, the cushion

collapsing under my weight. We needed to resolve things, one way or another.

He grumbled under his breath, and Alena Giannopoulos kept her vigil, leaving us men to duke it out. That simple act had me grinding my molars.

Until my father coughed. The phlegmy sound lasted a good ten seconds. I frowned at my mother, who left and came back with water. That call a while back, she'd mentioned to Rachel he was unwell. He'd been attending the gym, that much I knew. But the rest? He could have cancer and I wouldn't be any wiser.

Suddenly, I wanted to know. Find out if he was ill and do something to help. He wasn't getting any younger.

Once he recovered, he faced me. "What I said was wrong. You are my pride. My heart. What I did, I did because I love you. That Sophia girl was trouble. If it meant stopping that wedding, I would do the same again."

Still bullheaded as always, but the anger I'd nursed for years bled out. With Sophia today, the why of his actions had become clearer, but hearing him say it hit home. As did hearing the word *love*. Not a term my father used loosely. He loved me enough to hurt me. Fucked up, maybe, but I was worried I'd end up like him, cold and unfeeling. In truth, he felt a lot more than he let on. He wouldn't win Father of the Year, but I was emotionally exhausted. If forgiving him meant coming up for air and finding my way back to Rachel, I'd take his olive branch.

"I'm sorry, too—for my part. Dating Sophia was me lashing out at you, which wasn't okay. If I'd married her, it would have been for the wrong reasons and I would have regretted it. I actually saw her today."

Another flash of anger clouded his face. "You should not see her. Rachel is the sort of woman a man marries, not that Sophia girl."

I was the last person he needed to convince. Unfortunately, I let that ship sail and broke my compass. "You don't have to worry about me reconnecting with Sophia. I just needed to sort some things out. And yes, Rachel is amazing. I love her and plan on fighting for her, but it'll take a miracle to get her back."

He grunted his approval, quite the honor from him.

My mother's eyes shone. "She's wonderful, Jimmy. Such a sweet woman. I have to believe she'll forgive you, in time. I owe you an apology as well. I should have jumped in when things got heated, at least forced this conversation earlier. It was poor judgment on my part, but your father and I have talked a lot, and we'd love nothing more than for you to come back to the winery. Dimitri wants that, too. He actually wanted to be here today, but we asked him to allow us this time. Is that something you want? To rejoin the family business?"

In some ways it was too little too late, but I'd opened up to Rachel, talking about the land and the grapes, unaware how much I'd missed it. Not just any vineyard. *My* vineyard. The one where my grandfather had taught me to test the fruit and smell the air. The one where I'd sipped my first Cabernet Sauvignon.

Yes, I wanted to work that land, but only under one condition. "Not with the current winemaker. Not by breaking the rules. If I came back, things would have to change."

My mother smiled, rueful. "Dimitri forced the issue a year ago. We kept Alex on staff, but your brother insisted we fix his recipe. Dimitri has met a lovely woman, Natalia, and they're getting married next summer, at the winery. She's been wonderful for him."

I planted my elbows on my knees and shook my head, unsure when my little brother had become a man. He'd stopped cutting corners, had fallen in love, and I'd missed it all. I'd also almost destroyed our business when they'd already righted their wrongs. More apologies to give. More fences to mend.

I was ready for it. "Then it looks like we'll have a lot to discuss. I have other plans, too—events I want to host in Napa, including being part of the Healing Hearts luncheon. Rachel's mother is a volunteer and I've been helping her. I'll come to the valley in a few weeks and talk to Dimitri. We'll go from there."

My mother pressed her lips together, tears welling, and I couldn't keep my distance. I pushed to my feet and pulled her into a hug, letting her cry against my chest. My own emotions burned behind my eyes. She still smelled like lilac, the soft scent returning me to days helping her in the garden and cleaning up after a meal. I missed her. It was as simple as that. We still had talking to do, but holding a grudge hadn't exactly worked in my favor.

"Is Dad okay?" I whispered in her ear. He wouldn't like me asking after his health. Headstrong until his last breath.

She patted my back. "Fine. High blood pressure, but the exercise is helping."

I released her, and she wiped the corners of her eyes. My father stood, and we shared a handshake. He'd never been a hugger.

As I headed for the door, he called my name. I turned to catch another scowl. "No more tattoos, yes?"

"I was planning on getting one on my face," I replied, leaving before he could throw a fit.

Probably not the best joke for his blood pressure.

I should have felt a thousand pounds lighter, but I was still heavy with thoughts of Rachel. Winning back the love of my life wouldn't be easy. I'd treated her like shit. Insulted her. If I were Gwen or Ainsley, I'd warn her to keep her distance. Tell her dating me would only end in heartache.

But Rachel and me—we were legendary. We were meant to be together, and I'd do whatever I needed to prove my worth. Matter of fact, there was one thing in particular that would blow her mind. Something that would prove how serious I was, whether she chose to forgive me or not.

CHAPTER 24

RACHEL

"I'm a bad person," Ainsley said. Her back was, *thankfully*, to me as she dried her hair, the gym locker room empty except for her, Gwen, and me. Ainsley liked to dry her hair topless, nothing but a towel around her waist. Talking to her boobs always made me uncomfortable.

I knotted my towel around my chest. Snugly. "You're one of my best friends, so technically, you *can't* be bad."

"Did you kick a puppy today?" Gwen asked. "Trip an old lady on purpose?"

"No. Seriously." Ainsley ran a brush over her last section of hair, her honeyed strands billowing like a shampoo ad. She shut off the drier and faced us. "If karma is a real thing, I'm going to end up so screwed."

Boobs. All I could think was: Boobs.

Gwen wasn't fazed. "Is this about Emmett? Because he turned you down?" She dropped her towel and pulled on her thong. *Only* her thong.

"No," Ainsley said, but she smirked. "You were right, though. The guy is a one-man pride parade. I never had a chance." Her smile slipped. "It's just, I love being a personal shopper. I really do. But I'm contributing to the downfall of society."

Gwen tousled her hair, a quick flick of her fingers that had every wave landing just right. I ran my fingers through my straight strands, but it reminded me of Jimmy's hand in my hair, his nails dragging along my scalp.

Everything reminded me of him, including the piercing I'd gotten last week. The event had involved me jumping out of the chair five times, while Gwen rolled her eyes and I panicked and the piercing guy laughed, but I did it. Every time I looked at the hoop through my belly button, a thrill rushed through me. I'd signed up for motorcycle classes, too. I was finally owning my inner bad girl.

Without the man who'd helped me find her.

"You may not be contributing to world peace," Gwen said, "but I don't see how your job is setting back humanity."

We brought our makeup bags to the counter, mascara and blush studiously applied. Me between my half-naked friends. Images of Jimmy spun like a broken record through my mind, so I kept quiet, their conversation rolling without me.

"I buy gifts for mistresses," Ainsley said. "I'm helping men cheat on their wives."

Gwen cringed, pausing mid-mascara application. "It is pretty shady."

"Exactly! If I don't redeem myself, I'll get visited by the Ghost of Christmas Past, and I do *not* want to relive my high school days."

"So change jobs. Take a page from Rachel's book and start fresh."

"Aside from the fact that I need the money, I like what I do… just not that aspect of it. And are you ignoring me, Rachel? Because this silent treatment isn't cool."

Before I could answer, Gwen snickered. "She's just uncomfortable. She hates talking to us when we're topless."

"Yep," I said, but their nakedness wasn't the only thing stealing my speech. These days, if I opened my mouth, I'd lament about how confused I was. And sad. Really sad. I was tired of my voice. "Just can't focus when 'the girls' are out. They are that distracting."

Ainsley stepped into her jean skirt and made a show of shaking her shoulders (and breasts) before getting dressed. "I consider it a compliment. But back to my disreputable life. I need to make a change. Not become some born-again do-gooder who gives her savings to charity and lives off smiles and happiness, but...I don't know. Contribute more, maybe?"

Her tone was light, but her face was pensive, like the day we'd had our smoothies and she'd asked if I thought the post-wish blackout was odd. I was no longer sure the event had been a magical twist of fate. I'd be returning to school in August. My tuition hadn't been paid yet, but I'd been accepted, which meant my resolution was nearly complete. I expected the enchanted power outage to somehow polish the rest of my life. Outside of school, my life didn't feel particularly shiny.

"What about volunteering?" I asked, forcing my focus back to Ainsley. Whether this was about her wish or not, her frustration was palpable. "Something to make you feel like you're helping."

She pushed at her cuticles. "Could be smart, but animal shelters spike my allergies, and working in a soup kitchen isn't my thing. You know how I get around meat."

Her vegan-loving self would toss her cookies at the sight of a chicken bone. "Would you consider construction? There are always Habitat for Humanity projects. I know of one going on."

Because Owen had mentioned one such project the day Jimmy and I had broken up.

My mind often traveled to that time, and many before it, snagging on details like a fisherman desperate for a catch. I couldn't see a motorcycle without my belly tumbling, couldn't glimpse a tattoo or dark hair or ripped jeans or belt buckles or leather jackets without fantasizing, wishing Jimmy were waiting for me, at home, with nothing on but a wicked smile.

The cavity in my chest widened. It had been four weeks, and the man was nothing if not persistent—calling constantly, sending emails and texts.

I'm sorry, Ray. So damn sorry.

You're my sunshine, baby. Let me make things right.

You deserve the world. I will prove how wrong I was.

More of the same flooded my phone, but I never replied. Ainsley, however, did. Her text read: *Message her again, and a Candiru fish will appear in your toilet bowl.*

He didn't relent, and I read his words greedily.

"That Habitat thing isn't the worst idea," Ainsley said, wrenching me from my depressing thoughts. "Construction guys are hot."

Owen certainly was. Devastatingly handsome, really. But not as sexy as my bad boy. I clacked my molars together, reminding myself he was no longer mine. "If I were still with Jimmy, I could have helped—his friend volunteers at a site. But I bet it's easy to research online."

The notion forced a much-needed grin to my face. I'd once witnessed Ainsley swear like a truck driver after smearing dirt on her white stilettos. Stick her high-fashion self on a construction site, and she'd be liable to break a nail and breathe fire. Video footage would be necessary.

Gwen zipped her gym bag. "Don't let them give you power tools. I'm not picking you up from the hospital." Then to me, "Any news on the Jimmy front?"

We gathered our stuff and headed for the door, me trailing behind. "He's as persistent as ever, but I haven't replied yet. It's not that I hate him for what he said or can't find a way to forgive him. I'm just...I don't know. I feel stuck."

Before his onslaught of texts, he'd sent me a note, long and eloquent. He'd explained how messed up he'd been, stuck in the past, stubborn to the last. He even told me about an eye-opening conversation with Sophia (*Banana-fana fo-phia*). It all made sense.

When with Jimmy, I couldn't mention Sophia without being met by a brick wall, and the reason he'd joined the contest proved he hadn't dealt with his issues. He'd twisted the situation with me and his parents, and had transposed all that negative energy on yours truly. It sucked. Like *eat a bag of gummy bears and inhale a pint of rum raisin* sucked. The girls had even taken me to a bar and pinned his picture on a dart board. Excellent therapy.

He'd since apologized to the moon and back, and I wasn't one to hold a grudge. Still, I couldn't reply. Not to yell at him. Not to ask him to stop. Not to forgive him or tell him I dreamed about him nightly, and that I'd gotten into my Viticulture program and was excited and couldn't wait to pick courses and learn all things wine and finally have a career I loved. I couldn't break my silence, and I didn't know why.

He hadn't given up, *yet*. If that time came, I wasn't sure what I'd do.

"Anyway," I said, "there's too much going on to focus on him. I'm picking courses soon, and the luncheon is this weekend."

Gwen stopped, and I nearly slammed into her. "Are you wearing that hot outfit I bought you?"

I shoved her forward. "I am. My mother might have a cow, but I don't care. I feel sexy in it."

"You are sexy, in that and in your sweats."

We made our way to the street, and I scanned the road for a motorcycle, as usual. When I didn't see Jimmy, disappointment rolled over me. I'd have to sort through my feelings soon.

———

For the next few days, I continued on in my indecisive haze. A dimmer had been set to my world, removing the bounce from my step, the cackle from my laugh. My mother's luncheon was a welcome distraction.

The Healing Hearts function was in full swing, the outdoor tent swathed in pink, gray, and white flowers. Original paintings were showcased against the sides, each in memoriam of someone lost to heart disease, all up for silent auction. My mother had commissioned one for my father—a sailboat cresting a wave, conquering the seas. He'd have loved it.

I smiled for what felt like the first time this decade. As I took in the space, my mood brightened further, and when I noticed the drink stations, my heartrate rocketed, each beat pounding to the jazz band's drumline.

Just as Jimmy had suggested, five displays had been set up, each hosting a different wine. No labels were visible, only blind pours offered. Guests swirled and sipped and squinted, trying to guess the grapes, even the years and wineries. I doubted many would come close, but their enjoyment was obvious. The activity was the perfect way to loosen up the crowd, and their wallets. The concept was brilliant.

Jimmy must have been helping my mother with the event, even after we'd broken up. If he'd been struggling as much as his texts suggested, *as much as I had been,* working with my mother, who'd never breathed a word of their communication, would have been challenging. But he hadn't backed out, because he was a good man. A man whose emotions had gotten the better of him, but that meant he was passionate. And fiery. And sensitive.

And worth fighting for.

Which is exactly what I suddenly wanted to do: fight for him. Because a life without that kind of electricity was no life at all.

Thanks to my mother, I'd paid my tuition this morning, but the act had lacked a certain thrill. Not calling Jimmy to share the news had been excruciating, his daily absence diluting my enjoyment of everything. He was sunshine, not me. I was a grape thirsting to ripen, his energy my life's blood, and I was done putting him off.

My mother, unfortunately, chose that moment to nearly careen into my side. "Laura Ketlar has done nothing but take credit for my work. Ordering the rentals doesn't mean she singlehandedly"—she waved an impatient hand through the air —"organized the event. She didn't lift a finger to help with the grunt work."

As hard as I tried to listen, my heart had migrated to my throat, my need to escape and call my bad boy all consuming, but the fundraiser was a big deal. My mother needed my support. "Well, I'm impressed. You've outdone yourself this year."

She scanned the space, one eyebrow expertly raised. "The caterers are a server short. They thought they'd slip it past us. The whole thing is shameful, really."

That and the unrest in the Middle East. "No one has noticed, and look how many people have bid on Dad's painting. The whole thing is a success."

She squeezed my elbow. "You're right, as usual. It's just taken so much time and—" She stopped midsentence and scrutinized my wrist. "Is that a rash, Rachel? Is your purse on you? Use some cortisone right away and again tonight. If it's not better in a day or two, make an appointment with Dr. Rancor."

"On it," I said. No need to share that it was a mosquito bite. Why rob her of her daily dose of overreacting?

A trait that had her examining my choice of wardrobe. "And that outfit is way too revealing. This isn't a costume party."

"That's a shame. I was counting on winning the Most Likely to Get Arrested for Prostitution costume award." I could only imagine how she'd react to my piercing.

"Honestly, Rachel. You and your brother will be the death of me. And did you hear Piper Lewis named her daughter Feather? Of all the things."

She ran with her new topic, and I didn't bother keeping up. I glanced at my legs, admiring their length in my heels and short skirt. No, my outfit didn't blend with the pantsuits and cocktail dresses adorning the crowd. The notion only heightened my confidence. If anything, I felt sexier. Jimmy would have stood out, too, if he were here. All rough and inked, drawing curious looks from the guests. He would have had *me* hypnotized.

"Ma," I said, interrupting her rant. "If Jimmy and I were still together, would you have given him a hard time, too? You know, asked that he dress a certain way, have him cover his ink?"

She placed her hands on both of my cheeks, sending her shoulders pads near her ears. "You're my girl, and I'm sorry for what I said. You look beautiful today. I'm just stressed and nitpicking." She patted my cheek and released me.

The compliment was lovely, but she'd avoided my question. "What about Jimmy, Ma? When I was with Gabe, you banned us from your parties. Would having Jimmy here have made you uncomfortable?" Her answer didn't matter. It wouldn't sway me from my decision to accept Jimmy's apology, but it would be nice to know she'd have welcomed him here.

Her reply came slowly. "When you were with Gabe, I'd been going through a tough time. Most of my friends were friends of convenience, and I never really felt like I fit in. I took some of that out on you. Things are different now. I've met wonderful women through this organization, and Jimmy is nothing like that Gabe boy."

I held my breath, nosy and nervous. "So you like Jimmy? I mean, it looks like you've been working with him on this event, so I'm guessing you've spent time with him."

Her eyes sparkled, like when she'd passed me my tuition check, pride in her glowing smile. "When I first saw Jimmy, I only saw his rough exterior, and those...tattoos. Afterward, I saw a strong man who was led by his emotions. A potentially dangerous combination, but Jimmy has a heart of gold. Your father would have liked him, too. I'd be proud to have him here."

"Really?" I couldn't fight the scratchiness in my throat. I'd stopped listening to my father's voicemail as of late, waiting on advice that would never come, but her admission meant the world. I'd have been proud, too, and honored and thrilled to have him at my side.

I wanted him here with me now.

"Yes, really," my mother replied as she waved to a friend. "Jimmy is smart and creative, and his knowledge of wine is astounding." One foot forward to mingle, she added, "You should enjoy yourself today. I hear the souvlaki is something special."

She winked, leaving me speechless and slightly creeped out. (Reminder to self: never discuss sex with my mother.) Her inappropriate comment also had my heart thundering. My eyes flitted around, sure Jimmy and his "souvlaki" were here. My neck tingled, just below my ear, a place he'd often worshipped, with his tongue and teeth and lips. I touched the spot, shaking slightly.

Was he watching me now?

As if on cue, a deep voice curled from behind me. "That outfit should be illegal."

So should his rumbling baritone. I stood, faced forward, my body alive with desire. "Just something I picked up."

I wanted to see myself through his eyes. My calves lifted by my high heels. The curve of my spine revealed through the dipping fabric. I wanted to see *him*. See if his eyelids had lowered like they did when he was aroused. Check if his jaw had slackened.

"I'd like to strip it off you." His hot breath hit my ear. Goose bumps cascaded down my neck.

Holy hell. Four weeks. It had been four weeks of confusion and longing, and now he was here, just behind me. I imagined us in a game of trust, those team building exercises where I'd have to fall and believe he'd catch me. And I did. If I gave up my balance and let go, I had no doubt he'd latch his arms around me and hold tight.

Unable to resist a glance, I peeked over my shoulder and whimpered. He was in dark jeans and boots, his gray button-down shirt tucked in, a purple vest stretched over his chest, thin black tie disappearing below. Wild hair. Dark scruff. Cuffs rolled to his elbows, all that glorious ink on display. The clincher was his eyes—hope and love and regret swirled in ribbons of blue.

I was done for.

"You're not exactly dressed to blend in," I said. "Are you trying to distract me?"

"Is it working?"

"Maybe." *Definitely.*

"All is fair in love and lust, then."

"Isn't it 'love and war'?"

"This isn't war, Sunshine. It's many things, but it isn't war."

Except he'd laid siege to my heart, the delicate tissue surrounded and blockaded, nothing moving in or out but memories of us. Some days it was hard to function.

Instead of stepping beside me, he pressed closer to my back and laid his large hands on my hips. "You really do look stunning." His breath grazed my ear again, and I nearly melted.

"So do you," I replied, and, God, I wanted to touch him. I couldn't take not facing him.

Belly aflutter, I went to swivel, but he held me firm. I'd been frozen since our fight, unable to make a move, but now I knew what I wanted. Namely, *him.* My arms around his waist, my head against his chest, his heartbeat pounding in my ears. He was having none of it.

He pulled me tighter to him. "How about a wager?"

"I could be tempted." As long as the bet revolved around which of us got naked first.

"I'm sure you could, and I'll even let you set the stakes."

"Without knowing the game?"

He pressed his lips to my temple. "I won't lead you astray, Ray. I love you."

A shiver ran down my spine, his beseeching voice guiding the sensation. "You love me?"

"For so long. I should have said it sooner, but I fucking love you. So much it hurts. You own my heart."

Aside from his ten thousand texts, we hadn't talked through our problems, but his confession had my limbs tingling, heat radiating through my body. My life had turned around in the past months. I had a future filled with wine and learning, and I couldn't wait to be an aunt. My mother was still overbearing and difficult, but she supported my choice of career and men.

It was time to keep moving forward and give Jimmy a second chance. "I love you," I whispered. "So much it hurts."

He spun me, so quickly I gripped his shoulders to keep from toppling. Tenderness softened the steel in his blue-gray eyes. "I'm sorry. The things I said to you were horrible. I'd take them back if I could. I know you, Ray. I know you'd never use me or side against me. Even thinking how I lit into you makes me sick. I'm not sure I deserve your forgiveness, but I'm done burying my past. It's part of me. The good and the bad. I want nothing more than for you to be my future."

God, his sincerity. It coated every word and soothed my bruised heart. A balm I was ready to accept. "It's okay. I understand. But you ever accuse me of stuff like that again, assume the worst without a discussion, and an apology won't cut it. This is a one-time deal."

He straightened, fierceness in the sharp lines of his face. "As it should be."

We stood like that a moment, and I could sense his need, both of us fighting the pull to grab each other and kiss until we'd erased our pain. My gaze fell to his tie, the silky fabric, wondering how it would feel around my wrists. Maybe a little pain wouldn't be so bad.

He dug his thumbs into my hipbones, possessive and hot as hell. "Don't worry, I'll string your arms up with it later."

"Presumptuous much?" But the man could read me. And sweet Jesus, the visual. My skin nearly lit on fire.

"Just calling it like I see it. And you, Sunshine, have it bad for me."

Suddenly parched, I scanned the area for a glass of water. A sprinkler to run through? Then I was picturing a dripping wet Jimmy, and I could barely swallow. "Let's get back to this contest of yours."

People milled around, curious glances coasting over us. Jimmy and his ink garnered much interest, as did my revealing skirt and halter top. They could look all they wanted.

He winked. "A blind tasting, of course."

"Back to where we started?" *Our second chance.* He nodded, but staying among these people when he could be apologizing in private lacked appeal. "Can this game wait until later? I believe your tongue has more atoning to do. Certain places on my body haven't decided if you're forgiven. It could take weeks."

He chuckled and nestled his hand into the small of my back. "I've missed you like crazy, and not kissing you right now, everywhere, is killing me, but I want to do this right. It won't take long."

Grudgingly, I yielded. He led me to one of the stations, where I promptly downed a glass of water. That's when I recognized April in her black slacks and top, pouring wines.

"You won!" My shout had glances flying my way, but I hadn't seen her since I'd been booted from the contest. We weren't exactly close, but she'd always been nice, and beating the Schnozinator was no easy feat.

She beamed. "I did. Thanks to Jimmy. If he hadn't stepped down, I wouldn't have had the chance."

"Well, it's nice of you to help today."

"Like I said, I owe him. He even got a bunch of my friends work. Vesper closing down left a lot of people in the lurch."

The club where I'd met Jimmy. Disappointment weighted me. I would have loved to revisit Vesper with him, explain how a mysterious power outage had propelled me to fulfill my wish. I may have questioned the wisp of magic I'd felt that night, but I couldn't deny it now. I mean, here I was, the day I'd paid my tuition, finally ready to forgive Jimmy and move forward.

Ready for love.

This was the domino of happiness I'd hoped for.

"I can't believe it closed."

April rolled her eyes. "The place was a death trap. Blackouts every couple weeks. Electrical problems. They couldn't afford to fix it."

She excused herself to serve patrons, and I stared dumbly ahead.

Jimmy slid his hand across my waist. "You okay?"

I wasn't sure. I'd waffled about the "magical" blackout on and off since my birthday, but the possibility of its legitimacy had led to that horrible butt shot. It had pushed me to enter the sommelier contest. It was why I'd enrolled in school. Believing the wish would knock the rest of my life in order had spurred me on, when all I ever really needed was to *believe in myself.*

Talk about being clueless. "I'm fine. Just surprised about the club. So…" I looked around, feeling lighter than I had in weeks. Magic hadn't led me here. I'd led me here. "Where's this mysterious blind tasting?"

He moved behind the table and placed one glass on the white tablecloth. With the same grace he'd displayed in the contest, he poured a mysterious white wine into the crystal—elegant movements for such a rough man. The alcohol swished and clung to the sides, its legs dripping downward. When my father had told me the alcohol bleed left on a glass was known as "legs," I'd rolled my eyes, sure he was lying. Today their sexy drag left me breathless.

Mischief in his smirk, Jimmy pushed the glass toward me, along with a pen and piece of paper. "One wine. One taste. If you guess the name of the wine and the vineyard, you win. If you don't, you lose. First you have to set the stakes. Write them down. I won't look until it's over."

"Any limitations?"

"No." Then his hand shot up. "Actually, one. It can't involve Ainsley and her vicious forms of torture."

I snickered. "Condition accepted."

I swirled the glass, the light transforming the liquid from straw to gold. Offering forgiveness was easy, simple words spoken, acceptance to ease Jimmy's mind. But actions spoke louder than words. Jimmy had explained what he'd done and why, offering so many apologies he was in danger of losing his Man Card. If I entered our second chance unsure, waiting for him to mess up again, neither of us would win. He'd acted like an asshole, he'd hurt me, and we still had much to discuss. A discussion that should come from a place of security, for both of us, which meant taking a risk.

A totally massive risk, but destiny, apparently, was mine to make.

Before I could reconsider, I wrote my stakes and folded the paper, edges matching up. I placed it aside, perpendicular to the table. I lined up the pen, too.

The second I let go, Jimmy nudged the pen askew.

I returned it. He nudged it again. I glared at him, and he winked.

"I'd like to change the wager," I said.

He snatched the paper and pocketed it. "Not a chance."

God, he was difficult. And cute, smiling like he was. Time to taste some wine.

CHAPTER 25

JIMMY

RACHEL LIFTED the glass to her nose, and I could almost smell each teasing note. I wanted to get drunk on *her* heady scent. Standing this far was torture, every inch of my body craving a taste of her, a touch, an inch to savor. Anything. But I had more say.

She swished the wine around her mouth and swallowed, the length of her neck opening up as she tipped her head back. I stared, unabashed, taking in the necklace that dipped between her cleavage. Her leopard-print skirt was criminal, her mile-long legs smooth and perfect. Legs I'd rather have wrapped around my head.

Heat flooded my groin.

Another swirl of her glass. Another sip. Then a sly grin tipped up one corner of her mouth. "You didn't think I'd recognize your family's Windswept Chardonnay? What kind of novice do you take me for?"

"Maybe I was looking to lose." Except I had no idea what I'd be losing. This was about handing Rachel control. I could apologize all I wanted, beg for another chance, claim I'd never hurt her again, but if she didn't believe me, we'd never work. Trust was paramount. So this was both of us tasting blind, feeling the other out. But if she ignored my Ainsley condition, I'd have to book a one-way ticket to Siberia. Fucking terrifying, that one.

Before I removed the paper from my pocket, I pulled the bottle in question from below the table and hid the label with my hand. "You guessed right, but we've rebranded it. We're tweaking the recipe, too. That will develop in time, but the plan is to make it our flagship wine, grow the business around it."

"Do I get to see this flashy new label?" She rubbed her hands together, eager. Clueless to what I'd done.

If I'd gone too far, if she wasn't ready, there was a chance I'd scare her off, but I still had to man up, put my heart on my sleeve. No bluffing about who I was or how I felt.

Swallowing hard, I revealed my masterpiece, and she sucked in her breath. We were at a charity function, people milling everywhere, but it was like the edges had faded into darkness, a spotlight separating us from the crowd.

"Is that what I think it is?" she asked.

I offered a tentative nod. "It's you."

She yanked the bottle from me and had that look about her, like she wanted to press it against her breasts and stare at it for weeks and assign it a permanent location in her alphabetized wine fridge. I rubbed the back of my neck, tension ebbing.

She ran her fingertips over the wine's new name, *Sunshine Chardonnay*. A crude drawing of the pond we'd picnicked at filled the label. She blinked, and a tear slid down her cheek. Last time she cried, it was because I'd said unforgivable things. These tears made my heart squeeze in a different way.

"I can't believe you did this," she whispered.

I wanted to round the table and kiss her tears away, but it wasn't time yet. "I plan to do much more for you." I jutted my chin toward the bottle. "Read the description."

Lip tucked between her teeth, she flipped it over. Her chin trembled as she scanned the words. I didn't need to read them. I'd written each one.

Sunshine is a ripe wine full of life. It may change, depending on the year and seasonal conditions, but it will always brighten your day. Nurtured with love, its hints of spice set it apart, its creamy mouthfeel decadent, every nuance a taste to savor. And Sunshine's legs are a thing of beauty. Our flagship Chardonnay is an expression of who we want to be.

Shaking her head, she wiped at her eyes. "You made my mascara run."

"Sorry?"

"Don't apologize."

"Not sorry?"

Exasperated, she crushed the bottle against her chest, going for the boob rub after all. "This is the nicest thing anyone's ever done for me. I have my own wine."

"Yeah. Okay. But maybe save the full-body contact for later." My dirty princess was drawing a crowd.

"Need I remind you that *you're* supposed to be the wild one? Stop smothering me."

I planted my hands on the table and leaned toward her. "I plan to smother you plenty. Later. For now, we have a wager to complete."

Huffing out a playful breath, she clutched the bottle and crooked her finger, beckoning me to follow. I did, magnetically. I'd have trailed her to the ends of the Earth, if she asked. She led us to a quiet corner of the tent, behind a divider. The noise dulled, jazz tunes fading to swirling notes. She turned and pulled me against her.

"This is too much." She clutched my tie, face pleading...*for what?*

"It's not enough, Ray. One apology, a thousand, would never be enough, because you're it for me. I need you to know I'm willing to build my world around you. You make me want to do better, be better. You're my sunshine."

I lifted the bottle from her hands and placed it on the ground. She didn't release my tie, so the whole thing was awkward, my upper body twisting while I reached down. I chuckled, but my laugh faded once I had her in my arms. "I'm a passionate guy, which means I might make some bad choices from time to time. It also means I'll love you fiercely. I'll also grovel. Whatever it takes to make amends. I won't bury things again. Consider it a hard lesson learned." I lowered my lips until they ghosted over hers. "Will you forgive me?"

"I already did."

"Say it again. Then I'll apologize again. I'll do it until I've erased all your doubts."

Instead of answering, she tugged my tie, and our lips connected in our corner of the world. The back of her top dipped low. So low, I slipped my fingers inside. Skin as smooth as velvet greeted me.

Her mouth was eager against mine, and *fuck*, she tasted like apples and sunshine and lemonade. She tasted like Chardonnay and a future we'd build together. We moved against each other, mouths wet, tongues tangoing with sensual groans. I was hard already, my fancy jeans about to split a seam, but I pulled back, aching. I had to. Any longer and Rachel's mother would never show her face in this crowd again.

Rachel flattened her hands on my chest. "Did I win?"

I blinked a few times until her meaning registered. "That's up to you." When she frowned, I went on, "Technically, you won. You knew it was an Offshoot Chardonnay, but since the name of the wine is different, you can claim a loophole."

I didn't know what wager she'd written, had no idea if winning or losing would bode well for us. This was me handing her control again. I was hers to keep or discard. I'd live with the fallout.

"Win," she said, releasing my tie and smoothing it down. "I win. But you might not like my prize. So I offer you the same loophole. If it's too much, you can shoot me down."

Well, then. Curiosity nipping at me, I reached into my pocket and pulled out her neatly folded paper. She knotted her fingers in an anxious twirl.

Ready or not…

Her letters were straight and neat—typical Rachel—words that blockaded my throat and compressed my ribs. Words I hadn't dared hope for.

"You mean it?" I asked.

"I do. I love you, Jimmy."

I reread her chosen prizes:

If I win, we move in together. If you win, we move in together.

My heart damn near exploded. I wasn't sure I deserved a woman like Rachel, but I'd spend a lifetime trying. I refolded the note and tucked it away. "I'm keeping this under lock and key. There's no backing out now."

"No loophole, then?"

"Are you kidding? It took me ages to get a sleepover. You're stuck with me, Sunshine."

"With Superglue," came her reply. Then she said, "I got a piercing."

Come a-fucking-gain? "Where?" I grabbed her hips, my grip a little too strong. *A fucking piercing.*

Her shy smile nearly split me in two. "I'll show you later."

Wound up and horny as hell, I kissed her hard, trying to figure out where I'd find that little piece of metal. Her nipple? Belly button? Lower? I growled into her mouth when two women walked by, horrified whispers shared. I could barely see straight.

I tugged Rachel toward the main room, her lips swollen and well-kissed, mine hungry for more. We could have taken off and finished what we started, but I wanted to see the look on her face when my bid won her mother's commissioned painting. It would be the first piece of art hung in *our* place.

Under the framed quote I'd recently purchased:

"If you obey all the rules, you miss all the fun." ~ Katharine Hepburn

EPILOGUE

THREE MONTHS LATER

RACHEL

"We should do this weekly." My head was on Jimmy's lap, our pond in front of us, birds singing above.

"Sorry, Sunshine. No dice." He stretched like a cat. The sexiest feline I'd ever known. "This is a celebration, which means you'd have to enroll in a new program. Start a different career. Actually…that wouldn't be a challenge for you."

"Still a comedian."

Shifting, he pulled me between his legs, my back to his chest. "I could even help you come up with new ventures."

I nuzzled closer. "Like what?"

"Since you have a Big Bird fetish, you could host those furry conventions. The ones where people dress up as fluffy toys and get it on."

I rammed my elbow into his side. "Hilarious."

Locking me tighter between his legs, he pushed his nose through my hair. His wet lips landed on my neck. "How about we stick to viticulture, then?"

"Sounds like a plan." Especially if every aced test became a celebration with wine, cheese, and us fucking like rabbits under a blue sky. It had been quite a day.

He pressed a kiss to my jaw. "I'm proud of you."

I was proud of me, too. Since my first class two months ago, I'd attacked my course load head-on—sitting front row, scribbling furious notes. I was ahead on readings and had upped mine and Jimmy's tastings at home. I was going to rock my degree.

In this moment, though, all I wanted was Jimmy tangled around me like a grapevine, our special picnic spot quiet but for the frogs and insects and birds.

He stroked my legs leisurely. I leaned my head into his neck as the day slipped by, quiet conversation coming in waves. October sunshine danced on my skin.

"I forgot to tell you about your dad," I said, grinning at the memory. Jimmy hummed in my ear. I went on, "When I saw my mom in San Fran last week, I met him at the gym. He was trying new equipment, and it was beyond hilarious." The image of him standing in front of the chest press (*not* seated, as was normal), while trying to squeeze the pads together with his hands was classic.

"Put it up on YouTube next time."

God, that would be mean…but hysterical. "He'd never trust me again."

"He doesn't know what YouTube is, so he'd be clueless. And that man worships you."

"He grunts at me."

"That's high praise from George Giannopoulos. I'd have killed for a grunt in high school."

A butterfly, yellow and black, flitted past us, nearly touching my knee. It hopped around, flying from place to place, as though it didn't know where to land. How I used to feel. Untethered. Unsure where to anchor myself. Until Jimmy. I'd forgiven George and Alena their deception, earning another father from the deal, though he was challenging at times. More roots grounding me.

But my favorite root snaked his arms tighter around me. "I love you, Ray."

Those words never ceased to turn me boneless. "I love you more."

"It's not a contest."

"Isn't everything with us?"

"Okay, Sunshine. You love me more. But my dick wants to enter into the running. He's got it bad for you."

The candidate in question poked my back. "Maybe I'll tie *you* up this weekend. Ravish your body. Use a blindfold."

"Such a tease."

"*The Tease of Monte Cristo*," I said, instigating my name game.

His body shook with a light laugh. "*Raging Tease*."

"*The Lord of the Tease*."

"*Raiders of the Lost Tease*."

"That one sounds like a porno," I said. "Actually, they all do. Which gives me another idea for our weekend…"

He nipped my shoulder, my body cocooned in his. We both sighed.

Eventually, he shifted backward and flipped me around, facing him. "My parents want to meet your mother, asked what weekend was good."

Wow. A daunting prospect, but not surprising. We'd been living together three months, which made the progression natural. Still, the monumental event felt big, and sad. Every milestone in my brother and my lives would be celebrated without our father. Dad wouldn't witness the birth of his first grandchild, wouldn't be there for my graduation day. He wouldn't meet Jimmy or his parents. Not in the flesh, at least.

He was watching us, somehow. Of that I was sure. "If it's at my mother's place, she'll serve her onion dip and Stanley will accost your father."

Jimmy chuckled. "Then it has to be there. But don't warn my

folks about the dip. Watching them choke it down will be priceless."

"You're awful, but thank you."

"For what?"

"For showing up in that bar and asking to buy me a drink."

"Thanks for screaming pussy. Which is something you should do more often. Actually, we haven't been out drinking in a while. Might be time to get you liquored up. I'll pop some popcorn and watch you embarrass yourself."

"You really are the sweetest boyfriend."

He smiled at my sarcasm, and I kissed his nose.

"I wasn't going for sweet, Sunshine. I'm the wild one, remember?" He lay down and pulled me with him, pressing my head to his chest.

Th-thump, th-thump went his heart. Mine trotted in time.

Our parents meeting might mean a ring was on its way. Scary and exciting—my life moving forward at a steady pace. A life I barely recognized. We were living in Napa Valley, and I was finally following my dreams. I returned to the city often to see Cora and her growing belly, my brother waiting on her hand and foot. Even my mother had an admirer.

And my life in the valley was a breath of fresh air. Jimmy had taken his rightful place at his family's winery, working alongside his brother, while still following *his* dreams and spearheading a new Napa festival. He woke up driven, ready for each day, taking pride in his accomplishments.

I couldn't have asked for anything more.

I wasn't sure where Gwen and Ainsley were with their birthday wishes. They knew Vesper had closed down. Unlike me, they weren't under the misguided impression that magic had touched our resolutions. But I was thankful for the silly assumption. Without that push, my life wouldn't be opening like a fine wine, depth and character building. All it had taken was a little courage, belief in the impossible, and one very bad boy.

———

THANK YOU FOR READING RACHEL AND JIMMY'S STORY!

To learn how Ainsley makes a perfect fool of herself while she unwittingly thinks her studly crush is gay, one-click *Off-Limits Crush* now! And…guess what?

I HAVE A TREAT FOR YOU!

Want to read Rachel and Jimmy's steamy one-night stand that she didn't remember?
Receive the instant FREE exclusive chapter by snapping it up **HERE**.

———

Keep reading for an excerpt from *Off-Limits Crush*.

OFF-LIMITS CRUSH EXCERPT

Ainsley

A four-letter word meaning a horny covering.

I went to type *Bull* into my crossword app, but that didn't make sense, horns notwithstanding. Neither did *Knob* or *Flap* or *Fang*.

Beak

Peak

Deck

Wing

No. No. No. No.

Frustrated, I tapped my toe while the decadent aroma of melted chocolate curled around me. Another minute and I'd be a floating Minnie Mouse, my nose led by the divine scents. If heaven had a chocolate shop, it would be Aazam's Sweet Treats. Towering truffles, smooth peanut butter cups, and mouth-watering bark lined the shelves, nut clusters drenched in chocolate teasing me. Aazam was a genius with the cocoa bean, *and* all his products were vegan. A man after my own heart.

The virtuoso held up a finger to tell me my order would be out shortly. I allowed myself a deep sigh. He really was gorgeous. As delicious looking as every morsel in the place. Dark hair and skin, a beard that was sure to tickle, not scratch. Eyes so soulful they practically sang the blues. His lips should be downright illegal, plump and smooth as they were. They had me thinking up other four-letter words for horny things.

Kiss

Suck

Hump

Lick

I nearly wrote *Muff* into my phone, but erased each letter. My G-rated crossword app might explode. I'd become addicted to the word game recently, a way to pass the time while waiting for the doors to open at a Tiffany's sale or a secret pop-up store. As I was about to admit defeat on the horny covering—*Bark? Bibb? Clip?*—Aazam assaulted me with his killer smile. *Wow.* Heart, meet belly.

He lifted a brown box tied with bright green ribbons. "Ready for you."

Not only was he ready for me (God, how I wished), but he slid over a piece of my favorite seventy-percent chocolate with candied violet. High from his smile and the rich smells, I took a bite before thanking him. Double wow.

When I stopped moaning and opened my eyes, I said, "Are you sure you're gay?"

If I didn't know better, I'd say my chocolatier was blushing under all that dark scruff. "Last I checked."

"Like really sure?"

"Yep."

"Not even bi? I promise I'm great in bed."

That had him chuckling. I added a bottle of his chocolate-spiked perfume to my order. A couple dabs on my neck always put the sexy in my step. He ran my credit card, then locked his John Lee Hooker eyes on me. "If I were straight, I'd be all over your offer. Especially with that outfit of yours. Make sure you flaunt it today. Any heterosexual male in a thirty mile radius will trip over himself to get your number."

My gingham wrap dress *did* give me cleavage for days, but the only two men who'd dialed up my lust-o-meter recently had proven poor choices. Emmett, the Adonis at the gym—*gay*. My heavenly chocolatier, Aazam—sadly, *gay*.

Gwen and Rachel had pegged Emmett's sexuality right away, my best friends razzing me endlessly. My denial lingered until I'd witnessed him locking lips with a man. Aazam had blatantly turned down my dinner date offer. He'd sent me home with chocolate, a hug, and a mildly bruised ego.

My gaydar was clearly broken, the instrument fogged up by raging hormones.

I needed to find release.

Finishing off my piece of *almost*-better-than-sex chocolate, I turned with a wave, but swiveled back. "What's a four-letter word for a horny covering?"

Aazam scratched his bearded cheek, then clapped. "Nail!"

"Nail? Like"—I fluttered my manicured hand—"*nail*, nail?"

"I think so."

I'd never been a language geek, unless *Prada* and *Gucci* were involved. But my new hobby had fired up my synapses, transforming me into a well-dressed linguist, who often cheated to finish puzzles. Aazam, however, was a total word savant. I'd once asked him for a five-letter word for a coastal feature, and he'd said, "Bight," in two seconds flat.

Apparently a horny covering didn't involve licking muffs (dammit). Horny coverings were *nails*.

"You're a genius," I called as I hurried out the door.

I hit the road, two more stops left before I called it a day. Neither errand pleasant. I tapped my horny coverings against my steering wheel, the edges of my nails clipped and buffed to perfection. Ms. Mae's hand massage this morning had rendered my skin soft-as-silk, my mind nearly comatose. And her polish job? My tiger-striped French tips, with their flamingo-pink high-lights, deserved to be hung in the Museum of Modern Art.

Picasso had nothing on my nails.

He also had nothing on the azure blue Versace draped over my back seat. I'd strip my nails bare for a night in that dress. It was perfection personified, and the slit up the front would high-light Mrs. Arlington's legs—her greatest asset. She would be thrilled, which meant her husband would be thrilled, which meant I'd deserve the hefty bonus coming my way.

I should be sale-at-Sephora giddy.

Except for the box of chocolates hijacking my passenger seat. Another gift purchased on my client's behalf, Mr. Infidelity himself, Thomas Arlington the *third*.

His most recent mistress had a soft spot for sweets. In particular, Aazam's eighty-percent dark chocolate bars sprin-kled with cayenne pepper and pistachios. I noticed the pack-aging in her trash the first day we'd met, along with a broken pocket mirror. A replacement mirror, with similar gold detail-ing, had arrived on her doorstep that week, the chocolates following regularly, all punctuated with love notes from her doting philanderer.

Clamping my jaw, I drove faster and turned up the music. Nothing like a little Pat Benatar to lift my mood. Love was a battlefield, all right. A battle I had no interest in joining. Not when it was littered with duped women and lying husbands. Count me in for the pillaging afterward, though. If it came with a straight Aazam, or hunky men in kilts whose Scottish accents could slip into my Victoria Secret Cheekinis, then giddy-up. Unfortunately, these days, all my *oh-my-God-yes-yes-yeses* applied to stellar purchases, not savage plundering.

I parked near the Arlingtons' house. Thomas's Porsche wasn't on the street. He could be working or golfing, or invading enemy fields…

I pulled the Versace from the car, cradling the plastic-wrapped fabric like a Fabergé egg.

A doorbell ring later, Sloane swung the door wide. "Just the lady I wanted to see."

She ushered me past a pair of dirty work boots, the clanging from above hinting at construction work. Remodeling their bathroom, if I remembered correctly. She disappeared into their modern townhome, and I laid her dress over her leather couch. I checked and rechecked my watch, urging the second hand to tick faster.

Spending time with Sloane was always uncomfortable. She'd chat about her morning playing tennis, and I'd smile and answer while thinking, *your husband is a lying sack of shit*. A sack of shit who helped pay my bills, which allowed me to wire cash to my parents.

My golden handcuffs were cemented in place.

Sloane returned with an envelope and presented it to me. "Thank you."

I took it by the edge and looked up at her. Even in my pink Manolo Blahniks, I was a head shorter than the statuesque brunette. "Thank you for what?"

"For that dress, for one. Your eye for clothing is remarkable." She ran her fingers over the clear plastic. "And for always going out of your way for me. I know you work for Thomas, but your help with the shoe emergency was above and beyond. Plus, you've become a friend. So, thank you."

Running over a pair of heels because hers had snapped in the middle of a fundraiser wasn't part of my job description, but the friend part had me wanting to slither out of the room. Friends told friends when bad things were happening. Friends saved friends from future heartache. Having been on the receiving end of a cheating manwhore once, I wouldn't wish it on anyone.

Without opening the envelope, I pushed it back at her. "Thank you, but I can't. I'm happy to help."

Please, get me out of here.

A loud bang blasted from above us, and we both winced. "Bathroom reno is turning into a bit of a nightmare. And"—she raised a sculpted eyebrow at the envelope I was attempting to refuse—"I'm not taking that back. It's a gift." She picked up her dress and hugged it to her skinny frame, a body she kept painfully thin (green vegetable diet), likely for her scumbag husband. "It's spectacular, Ainsley. Thomas will love it."

That part I didn't doubt. Give me ten minutes in someone's home, and I could list their favorite beverage and coffee addiction, where they purchased their linens, judge their waist, hip, and bust measurements (Sloane was a size celery), and the jewelry they coveted, all with a nod and a walkthrough. Which is why Thomas had passed my cards to his friends, and why I mainly shopped for overpaid lawyers who "worked late" and had unscheduled "business meetings."

I was to personal shopping what Walter White was to methamphetamine. I was *great* at my job. I loved scouring stores for that *oh-my-God-yes-yes-yes* item. I also contributed to the downfall of society and needed cash. (Instead of *Breaking Bad*, my HBO series would be called *Killing Love*.)

Insert heavy sigh here.

"The dress will look stunning on you," I said. "Have a fun night, and you shouldn't have gotten me anything, but thank you." I saluted her with the envelope, like an awkward army recruit, and hurried toward the door, speed walking so quickly I nearly tripped on a nail. *Not* a horny covering. I picked up the offending piece of metal and hightailed it to my car as fast as my heels would allow.

Now I had to gift chocolate to the Mistress.

Once that joyful deed was done, I sat in my Mini Cooper and opened Sloane's envelope. Two tickets to the San Francisco Ballet's *Cinderella*. Not only was she sweet enough to buy me a gift, she also ran a small bookkeeping business, she could walk a red carpet with enough confidence to draw paparazzi...and her husband was cheating on her.

I slumped into my seat, unsure how much longer I could keep this up. I loved aspects of my job—piecing together clues to discern the perfect gift or outfit, helping someone look their finest—but the rest of it was a giant pile of suck that paid well.

I picked up the metal nail from my passenger seat and flipped it through my fingers. If I had to write a crossword clue for this sucker, it would be:

Four-letter word for a pointed spike I'd like to jam into my eye.

I couldn't quit my job just yet, but I could at least do something to lessen this sticky feeling. Like I'd been sprayed by a rogue perfume sampler. Needing assistance, I picked up my phone and dialed Rachel.

Three rings later, she answered. "I just had an orgasm."

"Manual or with a certain tattooed hunk?"

"Tongue climax *without* the hunk or batteries. This Chardonnay is sinful."

Aazam's chocolate did the same for me. "I could use a drink about now. Probably a box of wine."

She coughed through the line. "Don't even joke about that. And why do you need this *box* of wine you will not be drinking?" I could practically see her give a heebie-jeebie shake. Total wine snob.

I crossed my legs and let one shoe dangle from my toes. "Is your life perfect?"

She snorted. "No one's life is perfect."

I waved an impatient hand, as though she could see me. "I'm talking generalities. The big stuff."

"I don't know. I mean, I love living in Napa. Viticulture school is tough but rewarding. I'm an aunt to the cutest girl birthed this millennium and, well...*Jimmy*." She sighed on his name, no explanation needed.

Those two couldn't look at each other without every person in the room swooning or puking. What they had was intense. It was sweet and heart melting and slightly sickening to witness. It also wasn't why I'd called her. "You fulfilled your birthday wish, didn't you?"

Silence answered me. Then, "I felt weird talking to you guys about it, not knowing if you'd worked on yours, but I did. Why? What's up?"

"I just see everything in your life falling into place, and I wondered if that was part of the reason."

She didn't answer right away, and my mind tripped back to that night, as it often did. The night of our shared twenty-seventh birthday. Being born on April 12th was as lucky as happening upon my first *Vogue* magazine. My two best friends had also come into the world on April 12th. Even luckier was finding the three of us coincidentally wasted and celebrating the start of our twenty-first year in the same bar.

We'd spent every birthday together since, but it was *last* April 12th that had plagued my mind the past six months: the wish each of us had made that night. No. Not a wish. *A life-changing resolution.* The type of plan that would shake things up and trigger a domino effect of awesome. We'd linked our pinkies and promised to fulfill them by our next birthday.

But I hadn't done a thing to realize mine.

Rachel broke her silence. "I believe fulfilling my wish played a part. Being a tad superstitious, I still don't want to hear yours before it's fulfilled, but mine was to find a rewarding career, which I'm working toward. So it's like carrying out that one big change affected everything else."

Exactly what I'd hoped for…yet I'd stalled. To fulfill my resolution, I had to become a better person, which meant making amends for my glorified-pimping job. "If you're right, I need to get my ass in gear. I only have six months left."

"Miracles happen all the time."

"True. There *was* that time my brother got laid."

She snickered. "No way. That chick took pity on him. It was for sure your housewarming gift."

"I'm an excellent sister." Who'd framed a condom with the tagline "In case of emergency break glass."

"You can do this, Ainsley." Rachel's soothing tone slid over my tense shoulders. "Regardless what you wished for, I'm guessing work stress is getting you down. A friend of Jimmy's volunteered at Habitat for Humanity. I know I've mentioned it before, and I'm not sure if he's still there, but he liked it. Doing something focused on helping others might make you feel better. Whatever you decide, I believe in you."

That made one of us. "I'll consider it."

"That's the spirit. Oh—and Jimmy went to the city last night to meet some restaurant people. I'm joining him tomorrow. I have to see my family and spoil my niece, but we'll squeeze in some girl time."

"Roger that."

I hit End and stared at my dashboard. The fact that Rachel sensed my wish without me breathing a word of it was a testament to our friendship. I was also a step ahead of her. I'd made a list of Ainsley-tailored volunteering:

Doing makeovers.

Helping fashion victims.

Saving discarded haute-couture items, one Dior at a time.

Soup kitchens involved touching meat. Animal shelters made me sneeze. Working with the elderly reminded me of my grandparents; I'd probably spend my time bawling on some granny's flower-print lap.

That left the Habitat build. Last time Rachel had mentioned it, I'd been too anxious to sign up, but if Rachel—who'd held more jobs than a multiple-personality Millennial—could fulfill her resolution and stick with a career, I could wear sneakers and dirty my hands. Plus I didn't need experience to work on a Habitat project, and I'd be helping put a roof over a family's head. Something I was already familiar with, but paying *my* parents' mortgage wasn't bettering society. It was taking care of my own. Just like the framed condom.

Confidence growing, I turned my ignition and pointed my car away from Nob Hill's Victorian homes. I headed for the address I'd driven past too often this month. Each drive-by had involved me slowing down, my heart revving up, and I'd peel past the construction site. It was ridiculous. I was an adult. Doing something new, by myself, shouldn't have reduced me to a Stage Five stalker. Still, each time I'd contemplate stopping, I'd be transported back to high school and the last time I'd stepped outside my element.

That shit show had involved a Chucky's Chicken paper hat, enough grease to drown a small country, and me praying to the porcelain gods before my shifts. Each yack fest was followed by a thousand screw-ups, then co-workers would lob insults my way, like they were spectators watching me die a glorious Roman Gladiator death, cheering for blood.

But I was done creeping the building site. I wouldn't drive by out of fear again, or put off volunteering by claiming I'd sign up online. No. This time I would force myself out of the car. I would put the "con" in contractor and fake it until I made it. I would study my dictionary app and learn every construction term there was. I wouldn't make a fool of myself, circa 2006. (The Chucky's Chicken Maggot Incident was responsible for my vegan ways.)

By the time I parked at the curb, it was late afternoon and the Habitat build was winding down. When construction had begun a month or two ago, people were always scurrying about. Today there were only a few volunteers around, most looking ready to leave, but I wouldn't let that stop me.

According to their website, twelve two-bedroom townhomes and eighteen three-bedrooms were being built. Affordable houses for the less fortunate. Serious karmic opportunity. The orange hardhats were a concern—not my greatest color—but wearing one would be my first sacrifice.

I looked down at my cleavage and frowned. Walking up in my Michael Kors dress would have me labeled Pampered Princess next to the dirty T-shirts and ripped jeans worn on site. The museum-worthy fingernails and Blahniks wouldn't help, either. They'd assume I dished out thousands on my wardrobe and appearance, when in reality I could sniff out sample sales better than a Chanel-trained bloodhound, a handy superpower when bartering for manicures and haircuts.

If I didn't look volunteer-ready, I would at least sound it. I scrolled through my dictionary app and studied up on construction terms.

Boom. Brace. Framing. Fuse. *Infiltration.*

The latter sounded more special ops than volunteer work.

Hammer. Circular Saw. Drill. Screw. *Nail.*

I laughed at the last one, horny-coverings quite the focus of my day today. English hadn't been my best class in high school, but the language had become a fascination since playing my crossword games. One word could have so many definitions. I even watched spelling bees and loved the part where they'd have to use the word in a sentence.

My manicured nails *deserved a two-page* Marie Claire *spread.*

I would hammer nails *like a regular Bob the Builder.*

As I gripped my door handle and prepared to earn my Girl Scouts' Good Samaritan badge, I looked up and saw an unfamiliar man on the site. Or, more precisely, an apparition in the form of a dirty, sweaty, panty-melting hunk. If this were a music video, mist would be floating up from the ground, the sun setting, this man wiping his brow as Faith Hill sang about bare feet, country nights, and skinny dipping in a rambling river.

In worn jeans and work boots, he looked part cowboy and all rugged. His ratty white T-shirt clung to his broad chest, biceps bunching as he lifted wood planks. He didn't talk to anyone. Just went about his work. The pinched lines of his face hinted at a broody nature, and I liked me some tormented heroes.

My hormones sparked to life, Aazam's recent rejection and my dry spell fanning the flames. A new definition popped into my mind, sending a smile skipping across my face.

I wanted to nail *that man.*

One-click *Off-Limits Crush* today!

ALSO BY KELLY SISKIND

One Wild Wish Series:

He's Going Down

Off-Limits Crush

36 Hour Date

Over the Top Series:

The Snowflake Effect

One Degree of Perfect

Slammed into Focus

Showmen Series:

New Orleans Rush

Don't Go Stealing My Heart

The Beat Match

The Knockout Rule

The Bower Boys series:

Fall in love with the Bower brothers! A decade after being forced into Witness Protection, they're finally allowed to return home and fight for the women they lost.

Visit Kelly's website and join her newsletter for great giveaways and never miss an update!

www.kellysiskind.com

ACKNOWLEDGMENTS

First and foremost, I'd like to thank Chardonnay. I took my research for this book very seriously, dedicating many hours to learning the intricacies of wine. No bottles were harmed during the writing of this novel, but many were consumed. And enjoyed.

Aside from copious amounts of "research," writing this novel allowed me to work with amazing fellow writers I'm also honored to call my friends. Brighton Walsh, your continued guidance and expertise has been a lifeline. Your insights are invaluable, and your cover-designing skills are the bomb. Esher Hogan, your eyes were the first on this piece. Your enthusiasm kept me writing, even on those blood-from-a-stone days. J.R. Yates, my partner in crime, your time and friendship mean the world, and your ability to catch pesky errors has saved my ass more times than I can count.

Jamie Howard, if it weren't for your spot-on notes, Rachel wouldn't have learned how to ride a motorcycle or have gotten that sexy piercing. Jimmy and I both thank you. Kristin B. Wright, aside from your always insightful feedback, you convinced me to rewrite the start of this book. It's miles better for it. Heather Van Fleet, beta reader extraordinaire and awesome person—our chats get me through tough days, and your wisdom smooths out the rough patches in my work.

Jennifer Vipond, expert sommelier and all-around awesome person, I love you more than Chardonnay, which is saying a lot. Thank you for reading this book and imparting your knowledge.

You helped take the authenticity of the novel the last mile. Tammy Cole—from day one, you have been such a supporter of my work. I can't thank you enough for cheering in my corner and reading my early drafts. Your honest feedback is indispensable.

Tamara Mataya, your top-notch editing skills brought this puppy together. Liz Lincoln Steiner, having your eyes on the final pages eased my mind. And a big thank you to Shelly Hastings Suhr for helping me out in a pinch.

To Kelly's Gang on Facebook: you ladies make every day fun and never cease to put a grin on my face. There isn't a better Facebook group around. To my fellow troublemakers in The Den: you give me a piece of sanity in this crazy business and make navigating the ups and downs bearable. I'd also like to send hugs to the Life Raft ladies, the Golden Heart Dragonflies, and my Pitch Wars family. I never expected to meet so many amazing people on this writing journey.

I owe my love of wine to my father, whose excitement over every opened bottle still infects me. My parents' unending support floors me to this day. I love you both. To my husband, thank you for keeping our wine fridge stocked, and for putting up with my crazy. I couldn't do any of this without you.

To the bloggers who promote my work: you humble me daily. You are all such an important part of this process. Thank you a million times over. Last, but never least, to my wonderful readers: thank you for taking the time to live in my world. You are the reason I write. You are the reason Jimmy and Rachel exist. If you ever wonder if you should leave an online review, the answer is YES. Those are the little things that keep us writers going. Reading your thoughts means more than you realize.

ABOUT THE AUTHOR

Kelly Siskind lives in the wilds of Western Canada. When she's not out hiking or skiing, you can find her, notepad in hand, scribbling down one of the many plot bunnies bouncing around in her head. She loves singing while driving, looks awful in yellow, and is known for spilling wine at parties.

Sign up for Kelly's newsletter and never miss a giveaway, a free bonus scene, or the latest news on her books.

If you like to laugh and chat about books, join Kelly in her Facebook group, KELLY'S GANG.

Connect with Kelly on social media:
facebook.com/authorKellySiskind/
instagram.com/kellysiskind/
https://www.tiktok.com/@authorkellysiskind

www.ingramcontent.com/pod-product-compliance
Lightning Source LLC
Chambersburg PA
CBHW061615190726
48288CB00007B/2331